When Terror Strikes

Anthony Milligan

ISBN-13: 978-1500980597

DEDICATION

This book is dedicated to all those brave men and women everywhere who fight to protect the world from terror and violence and for the peace and freedom of us all.

A special mention for my friends Andrea and Berny Marsden, for their unstinting help and encouragement during the writing of this book.

Author's note:

This story is entirely a work of fiction any resemblance to any person living or dead or past incident is purely co-incidental.

Jack Belthorn

Jack Belthorn was, by his own admission, not a nice man. Nice men had short lives in his business.

Belfast 1976

The day that changed Jack Belthorn's life forever started normally enough. He was manning an observation post on the top floor of a derelict mill, watching a terraced house opposite waiting for Sean Foyle, a Loyalist errand boy. Foyle brought guns from the caches to where they were required then took them back again afterwards.

If he could follow Foyle or pick him up for questioning who knows what they might discover. People thought the British army were soft on the Loyalist terrorists. Not so. Illegal weapons on both sides of the sectarian divide meant big trouble.

Under the creaking leaking roof, the office was a sparsely furnished single room. A steel desk, a non-functioning telephone and a couple of uncomfortable straight backed chairs were scattered about like junk shop rejects. Peeling wallpaper and the sound of pigeons rustling in the roof space completed the air of dereliction.

Jack sat in the window being careful not to move the blind as he stared hour after hour at the empty rain swept street. Christ, he thought, this was a dire piss hole of a place. He'd been perched on an uncomfortable office chair so long he swore he was suffering from terminal arse cramp.

He glanced at his watch, Emerson was late. He'd have to bollock him.

This was the second consecutive day the OP had been used. It was too bloody long for safety in a local area where everybody knew everyone else, strangers stood out like a bull dog's bollocks. In this neighbourhood, however, there were few choices for concealment whilst watching the target so the risk had to be taken.

At night, the ground floor was used by rough sleepers and wino's. Some of those street people were as sharp as shit house rats and would soon detect intruders.

He heard the creaking of the old service lift as it climbed laboriously to the floor below. The gates groaned open and Jack heard someone stumping up the stairs. This could not be Emerson, surely? He drew his pistol and lay on the floor behind the filing cabinet aiming at the door. Footsteps clumped along the corridor and the door was flung open. 'What the fuck?' said a startled Emerson as he stared at Jack's pistol.

Jack was furious 'Why don't you blow a fuckin' bugle to make sure every bastard in Belfast knows we're up here?'

'Sorry Jack, there was a wino hanging about on the front stairs so I went around the back. I found the master switch for the service lift and picked the lock' he looked crestfallen 'I didn't think it would make such a bloody racket.'

'And now every fucker in town knows we're up here. Come on lad, time we were gone.'

Fresh from training in England the Lance Corporal looked bemused. 'Do you think he wasn't just a wino then?' He sure looked the real deal.'

'Who knows? Do you want to stay here and find out the hard way?' he asked as he rapidly gathered up his kit.

Emerson's face paled but he pulled out his pistol, checked it and took off the safety. 'Oh Christ, sorry boss.'

It was too late to be sorry and Jack didn't have time to explain that this was Northern Ireland not a mainland training exercise. Here, carelessness got you killed.

Peeking out into the corridor it seemed all was quiet. If anyone was climbing the stairs it would be a couple of minutes until they arrived. They had to be quick and quiet. At the end of the corridor was a fire escape but if the wino was an IRA spy they'd have it covered. It had to be the stairs.

Jack squeezed the tit on the handheld radio twice. It was supposed to be an emergency signal that would summon help. The answering mush, mush sound didn't happen. Fuckin' typical shit kit he thought, about as reliable as a political promise. He pressed the tit again and whispered, 'hello zero this is one, one alpha, radio check over.' Nothing. Bugger it, it was time to bug out.

They tiptoed along the corridor weapons half extended, keeping to the walls. Creeping down the darkened stair well quietly was almost impossible. The stone steps were worn and wet, the banisters broken in many places. The steps were coated in pigeon shit and assorted detritus making every step treacherous.

Two floors down and two to go, Jack was about to pass a doorway when he thought he heard a faint sound. Was is a shoe scrape or a rat scurrying? The hairs his neck prickled; he had learned to rely on his instincts and now was no time to ignore them. He flattened himself against the wall and signalled Emerson to do the same.

A full three minutes passed but Jack couldn't afford to be in a hurry. Then it came again, the same sound. As he watched a pistol barrel emerged from the room along the door jamb followed by a wrist barely a foot away.

Jack brought his own pistol butt down on the wrist hard. The gun clattered on the floor. He jumped around the doorway. The guy was staggering off holding his wrist. Catching him was easy, shooting him would have been easier still but the dead don't answer questions. 'Stand still' he ordered. The guy stopped, put his hands up and slowly turned around.

'You're Brits?' he asked surprised 'I'm Amos Jackson, Sergeant, Royal Ulster Constabulary.'

And so it turned out, Jackson had been posing as a wino on the lookout for the same guy as them. He had discovered their presence due to Emerson using the lift. He thought they were a Provo (Provisional IRA) hit team said to be operating in the area.

'Bloody Keystone Cops, why don't you ever communicate with us? I could have killed you.'

'What, and have our ops ballsed up by Fred Karno's barmy army?' came the snotty reply.

Cock-ups like this were not uncommon as army intelligence didn't trust the RUC and the RUC didn't trust the army so information was not always shared, even though they shared the same police station.

Jack was a member of the Army Intelligence Corps, known as "The Grenn Slime" to other Army units. More specifically, he was attached to the 14th Independent Company known as "The Det" short for The Detachment. "The Det" were responsible for intelligence gathering, and briefing the special forces, plus all the shady, deniable stuff.

Jack and Emerson left then with no further need for stealth. Jack sent Emerson to collect his car and return to base. He felt angry, another cluster fuck assignment was blown. He collected his car from the used car lot where I had arranged to park it with a contact.

He was late now, tired, hungry and thoroughly pissed off. After establishing the ID of the RUC Sergeant and trading more insults with him, all Jack wanted was to return to base. He needed to complete his report, eat something and get to his room. There was a bottle of Bushmills Irish whisky that needed attending to.

The downtown traffic would have built up by now so the trip would take ages. Bollocks, he thought, using the short cut he'd taken yesterday was a risk worth taking. It would save a good half hour in crawling traffic.

The rain had finally stopped as he drove the big Granada 2.8 Ghia down the long, rough cobbled street through a staunchly Republican area. Not even the well sprung car could stop the uncomfortable jolting and he slowed down.

Half way down the street Jack's short hairs started prickling. Something was not right. Then he saw it.

He was approaching a two hundred metre stretch were there were no parked cars on either side of the road. The children that had been playing on the pavements yesterday were also missing. He quickly slipped his gun out, thumbed off the safety and stuffed it between his thighs as he accelerated hard. He was a couple of seconds too late.

A car flew out of an alley just in front of him blocking the road. 'Shit' he cursed as he spun the wheel, his aim was to ram the ambusher's front wheel and spin him out of the way. He was far too close and smashed into the driver's door instead.

Glancing in the mirror Jack saw another car enter the top of the street and start accelerating towards him. He had to get out or his car would become his coffin.

He threw the door open and dived to the cobbles as the passenger of the blocking car emerged. He looked shaken, Jack was supposed to have slammed the breaks on when they blocked him not ram them.

He rolled away as the guy fired; the bullet passed Jack's left ear too close for comfort. Then he was up in the kneeling position and put a round into the gunman's chest as the guy steadied himself for another shot. As the man was still falling Jack swung on the driver. He could hear the follow up car screeching to a halt behind him. The doors would be opening and god alone knew how many armed men would be tumbling out.

On autopilot now, his training had kicked in, thought was not necessary. The driver was stuck in the car, the Granada still rammed into his door. He was desperately winding down his window, sticking his arm out to line Jack up with his big Colt .45. Before the man could extend his arm fully, Jack snapped off a shot that took the guy him through the bridge of his nose. He was slammed back into the headrest, blood spurting down his front.

Instinctively Jack dived to his right, rolling away as a Provo behind him with an M16 rifle scoured the street where he'd been half a second before. The man kept his finger on the trigger whilst trying to adjust his aim. Big mistake. The weapon ran up and off to his right. Jack's next shot went through his chest.

The man who had emerged last was a cocky bastard. So sure had he been of an easy kill he was only just clearing his gun from his coat. He managed one hasty shot in Jack's direction. Jack gave him a mirthless smile and watched his horrified face before he double tapped him chest and head

Jack wasn't out of danger yet and quickly swept the street looking at windows and doorways searching for snipers. There were none.

The people who had been watching from behind net curtains would be stunned by what they had just witnessed. That gave Jack time to collect the weapons before they could be spirited away to be used again. Cocky bastard's pistol was an old Smith and Wesson .38 revolver, it was lying next to his head in a small puddle of blood.

As he collected the M16, Jack couldn't resist asking the corpse of its former owner 'did no one ever tell you about short controlled bursts, mate?'

Jack threw the weapons onto the back seat of his car and quickly made his way to the front car.

People would be getting over their initial shock now. Phones would be ringing, he hadn't got long.

A young lad of about fourteen suddenly burst out of a nearby house and made a dive for the first man's gun.

'Don't touch it' Jack yelled. The kid froze in the act of bending down, staring petrified into the unwavering Browning barrel.

'You're a brave lad' Jack told the youngster 'but if you touch that gun I'll have to kill you.' He flicked his head and lowered his weapon slightly. The kid took the hint and scrambled away just as a camera flashed in a nearby window. Oh, fuckin' great, he thought, now they have my photo. Bollocks!

He quickly retrieved the last of the weapons as doors started to open and people began to emerge. Some of them still looked bemused but a good many of them were angry and shouting.

They were armed with an assortment of hammers, baseball bats and kitchen knives. Another minute and he'd be hacked to death; his pistol wouldn't stop all of them. An axe hurled from the rear of the crowd landed at his feet kicking up sparks as it flew away. He pointed the weapon at the front of the crowd 'who wants it first then?' he asked quietly. This was not the time to show fear.

The mob slowed but still advanced some of them edging around to come at him from the side and rear. Jack pointed his weapon at a fat man he took to be a ring leader 'One more step and you're dead.' The guy looked into Jack's cold grey eyes and halted, knowing this was no bluff, unsure what to do next.

Seeing him halt the rest of the mob stopped, looking towards the fat man for guidance. This gave Jack the time he needed, he leapt into the car and threw it into reverse. He rammed the rear blocking car pushing it up the street, its tyres juddering on the cobbles. The crowd to his rear scattered in panic to avoid being run down. A huge stone smashed in his rear windscreen as the mob closed in once more howling for blood. A youth dived at the smashed window trying to pull himself into the back seat.

Slamming the Ghia into first Jack floored it, spinning the wheel hard right. The youth flew off onto the cobbles screaming as the broken glass granules slashed his hands. Jack clipped the front of the blocking car sending it slewing sideways over the body of the first gunman and roared off, the tyres smoking and screaming.

He punched the steering wheel furious with himself 'You twat, you stupid twat' he told himself aloud 'what the fuck were you thinking of driving through an area like this?'

Next day the Red Tops were full of the usual rah, rah headlines. One led with FOUR, FIVE, SIX! The article was full of bull about how a lone Special Air Service soldier, ambushed in hostile territory, had killed four gunmen with five shots in six seconds. Where the hell they'd got their info from Jack didn't know, nor did he care. The SAS could have the glory, and why not? It was they who had taught him to shoot.

Jack's boss was incandescent with rage and hauled him and Emerson up for a much deserved bollocking. She was minded to send Emerson back home for extra training but Jack managed to talk her out of it. The man had learned his lesson. Emerson swore he'd up his game, he'd never do anything like that again. 'And besides, boss' he pleaded 'where better to gain experience than on the job?'

It transpired that Jack's car, a pool vehicle, had been used in an SAS operation the week before. Unknown to the security services, it had become compromised. The number had been circulated around the Provo's and their supporters. They had had time to set up the ambush and warn the street's residents. The ambush was to be a show execution for propaganda purposes, hence the camera.

Left alone with his boss Jack could see she was sad but firm. Now the enemy had his photo he, and anyone working with him, was in grave danger. 'The Provo's can't let this go Jack, they'll lose too much face. They'll be hunting you with everything they have.' He was returned to the UK next day by helicopter.

After a couple of weeks leave Jack was posted to SAS HQ near Hereford as an assistant liaison officer. The work was interesting but not exciting.

A month later Emerson was gunned down and killed. The Provo's announced they had got the man who had killed their comrades. It only dawned on Jack then that, apart from age, Emerson had been the same build, eye and hair colour to himself. What no one knew at the time was that the photo, taken in haste, was out of focus.

The army denied the claim of course but then leaked to a known informer, a reporter, that it was indeed the man. This piece of misinformation would not harm Emerson but would further protect Jack.

Jack felt enormous guilt. He blamed himself for his colleague's death. It hurt him deeply when he found out that Emerson's fiancée was six months pregnant. He couldn't even go to the funeral because the media would be there. Someone might recognise him as the true killer.

Although he did his best, Jack was beset with guilt and his work began to suffer. Rather than go into decline he left the army. They gave him a new identity as a belt and braces safeguard against possible future security leaks. He declined the offer of relocation to Australia. He was now Jack Ellis and his file was classified Ministerial eyes only. After a couple of dead end jobs, he started his own security company.

Turkey 2015

In the top floor penthouse suite of the Istanbul Pasha hotel, John Westaway carried a drone out onto the broad roof terrace. It was a substantial ultra-lightweight machine full four feet in diameter with a large propeller on each arm coupled to its own powerful electric motor. It had the look of an expensive toy, like something an amateur film maker would use, except its purpose was lethal.

This'll take you bastards out he thought, smiling happily. You've had it too good for too long, assholes. It's time you paid your dues.

Westaway rang his control 'Hi, it checks out, everything is A-OK and ready to go.'

There was a grunt on the other end 'we'll be in touch.' The line went dead.

'And have a nice day yourself, you miserable bastard' he muttered into the dead phone before dropping into his pocket.

At forty nine years of age Westaway knew this was likely to be his last active operation as a senior CIA field officer. He needed this one to go right not only for himself but for countless innocent people affected by ISIS. If it went as expected then a plum posting to London as a liaison officer would be his. Westaway took his laptop with its attached joystick and tested the machine in safe mode yet again. He concentrated on each check feeling relieved that everything still worked despite the rough transport and the torrid heat.

He glanced at his watch it wouldn't be long now, surely. He checked his watch again a few seconds later betraying his nervousness. Then a twinge of excitement ran through him as he experienced the old, familiar tingling buzz as the time for action drew near. It ran from his hairline to finger tips to his balls and down to his toes.

That the machine would be carefully reassembled and forensically examined afterwards he had no doubt. Nothing could be traced back to America or the CIA there were no fingerprints or DNA on anything. All of the machine's components were easily bought on the Internet. There were no manufacturers' marks or serial numbers on anything. The strike had to be effective yet appear slightly amateurish, like the work of any one of the many warring factions in the region. The job could have been done more easily with a modern drone and a Hellfire missile flown from thousands of miles away. However, America could not afford to be seen striking at the citizens of a friendly power, especially when some of the said citizens were high ranking military officers.

He examined the rocket slung under the drone with pride. It had been built to his specifications not that he was a rocket expert the explosive warhead was his field of expertise. He required only a short rocket motor because range was not a factor so a larger warhead could be carried. Around the two kilograms of military grade plastic explosive, was a jacket of aluminium slugs, light but they would shred any human flesh within a hundred feet. In a confined space it was simply non-survivable.

Westaway turned his attention to the short range transmitter that he would operate coupled to a laptop computer. He twisted the top of the joystick and watched as the drone's camera swivel, precisely responding to his light touch.

His phone rang. 'Yes?'

'You ready?'

'Yes.'

'The General arrived two minutes ago. He's inspecting the guard. Stand by.'

He cut the call first, feeling a childish thrill for beating his controller to the punch. This was it. Game on.

Now the success or failure of the entire mission rested squarely upon his shoulders. Westaway allowed this thought to nag him for only a second then he pushed it out of his mind. 'Focus John' he muttered, 'total focus.'

Taking the laptop back inside he poured himself a small scotch, tumbled in a couple of ice cubes and sat down in a leather armchair. He knew he wasn't supposed to drink this near the start of an operation but hell, this was his bit of rebellion and, once again, he felt a thrill of pleasure. Slowly sipping his drink he let the smooth liquid roll around his mouth savouring its fiery flavour before swallowing; god he felt alive.

This had been a long intricate operation with hundreds of intercepted e-mails and phone calls. The Pentagon and GCHQ in Britain had spent months of painstaking analysis, of plotting and planning. Bribes had been paid, bugs planted and even a homosexual honey trap used in this cat and mouse game. Now all the pieces of the puzzle were in place; this was the culmination.

Ten long minutes dragged by before his phone buzzed again. The text simply read "Pegasus Executive Travel. Thank you, your flight is confirmed." It was the final clearance code though why his controllers found the need for coded massages when the phone was encrypted he could only wonder. He supposed it was that old habits die hard.

'Thank God' he muttered and went over the procedure one more time running through the details in his mind. After swallowing the rest of his drink Westaway went outside onto the patio. It was time.

*****

On the fourth floor of a shabby administrative building in a heavily guarded military compound on the outskirts of Istanbul was an incongruously clean and luxuriously appointed suite of offices. They belonged to Lily Pad Oil Brokerage Services though no sign advertised its presence. Around the boardroom table sat the seven directors holding their Annual General Meeting. General Abdulla Abdullah sat at the head of the table feeling bored, his fingers slowly revolving a string of worry beads.

When the monotonous voice of his colleague finally stopped Abdullah spoke impatiently. 'I think we can accept the minutes of the last meeting as a true record, now to business.' He paused and fussily brushed a speck of cigarette ash from his crisp linen uniform. 'Last year was good as we know but this year is even better.' A self-satisfied smile spread across his swarthy face. 'The dividend for this the final quarter will be twelve million dollars each plus an extra six million for me as chairman's annual bonus.' He glared a challenge around the room feeling contempt for his four civilian directors. He needed their contacts and capital to finance the project and they needed his influence and protection from official interference. He raised his right hand 'All in favour?' six hands shot upwards. 'Carried unanimously.'

'The purchase of oil from Daesh at a third the market price continues to make us great profits' the general continued 'whilst the stupid Americans and their foolish friends dither and dally dropping a few bombs here and there we shall continue to prosper. Now that the Russians have involved themselves there will be further confusion, endless bickering and yet more dithering.' The general rubbed his hands together rolling his beads 'our customers at home, in Iran and Jordan are keen to buy as much oil as we can supply so we shall prosper even more gentlemen.' He glanced down at his notes as the board members thumped the table in enthusiastic approval.

'Expenses' Abdullah announced, making it sound like a swear word. The room immediately fell silent 'I have taken certain measures to cut these to a bare minimum. All ears pricked, anxious to hear his next revelation.

'The fact that we have to pay $1200 per truck to pass through the Peshmerga checkpoints is, I know, a bone of contention among some of you. He scowled, sensing that the civilian board members were critical of his failure to negotiate a better deal. He lit a cigarette blowing a cloud of smoke towards the ceiling before continuing. 'If among our members there is someone who believes he can succeed with the Peshmerga, he has my permission to try.' As he scanned them several pairs of eyes looked down towards the table.

'The level of bribes among our countrymen still poses a significant drain on profits as some people, who believe themselves to be indispensable, keep demanding more and more.' his eyes narrowed to slits 'I can report that arrangements have been made for certain people to be removed and replaced by much more co-operative officials.'

'But surely the Minister cannot be...' one civilian director began to object.

Abdullah silenced the man with a glare. He felt a surge of cold satisfaction and his glare turned into a sarcastic smile 'Oh, of course not Mustapha my friend' he spread his arms in a gesture of magnanimity 'your dear cousin the Minister is far too important to be swept aside like some petty official.' he paused savouring the moment 'he has, however, recently been videoed in the er... 'in the throes of ecstasy' shall we say, with a very attractive young man.' Satisfied smirks and nods of approval went around the table. The Minister's ever increasing demands would, from now on, be curtailed.

*****

Westaway pulled the arming pin from behind the rocket's warhead and a second from the rocket propulsion pack. He went indoors again closing the blinds against the bright afternoon sun. He sat down at the laptop and started the drone. Flying it up above the terrace rail the faint hum of its motors was barely audible from where he sat. He panned the camera downwards. The street was as busy as ever but no one was looking up.

The penthouse had been chosen because the hotel was the tallest building in the district and was not overlooked. He swung the drone outwards then flew it up to five hundred feet. The co-ordinates were already set so he pressed the 'auto fly' button and the machine took itself the four kilometres to its target. Over the heavily guarded compound it flew unseen. Identifying the administration block Westaway made the drone descend rapidly then expertly slowed it to hover outside the window of the boardroom of Lily Pad Oil Brokerage Services.

Below, the guard on the door of the building heard a faint humming and stepped out of the doorway where he'd been sheltering from the hot sun unseen by Westaway. The guard looked up and for a second he stood staring, mouth agape, unable to believe his eyes. Giving a startled shout of alarm he clawed the Kalashnikov from his shoulder letting fly with a wild burst in the general direction of the drone. Westaway zoomed in the camera swinging it left and right checking all targets were present. He had no inkling that his project was in imminent danger of being shot down.

All seven men were positively identified from the pictures he'd studied. 'Great' he muttered, feeling a calm satisfaction at the certainty of success. 'Gotcha assholes!' On a whim, he suddenly flew the drone in to six feet from the window. He wanted to see these men look horrified in the second before they died. 'Look what you've got coming you bastards' he muttered.

As he moved the joystick forward the guard fired a second better aimed burst. Most of the bullets passed harmlessly through the space vacated by the drone but one bullet clipped a rotor. The machine immediately fell away to its starboard side the front dipping earthwards as Westaway fought desperately to control it. The camera swung crazily up and down for a moment and he caught a glimpse of the sentry grabbing at his webbing pouch for a fresh magazine. The drone had dropped five feet below the window level. He corrected a yaw to port and eased back the joystick. The machine responded sluggishly to his coaxing rising slowly and stabilising.

Westaway knew he had just a couple of seconds to get this right. He gave thanks that he had spent hours of practice on the simulator putting in a lot of time in on emergency drills.

In the board room three civilian directors ran to the window alarmed at the shooting, staring down puzzled at the drone failing, momentarily, to grasp its significance. Abdullah drew his pistol and cocked it as he ran for the door several yards to his right.

Westaway saw the boardroom window now and three feet above the drone three faces suddenly reflecting the full horror of realisation. The ceiling of the office steadied as he canted the front of the machine upwards. There was no time to align the perfect shot. He pressed the firing button and the rocket flew through the window bursting on the ceiling with all its lethal fury. The laptop screen flashed and went blank as the drone was destroyed by the rocket's detonation.

Westaway's hand was shaking, his mind reeling. That had been a damn close call, too close. What the hell had he been thinking about? He cursed himself for a damned fool, why had he not fired the instant he got the chance?

Throughout the reconnaissance period the guards' routine had been carefully noted. Four men patrolled the perimeter fence and two guarded the entrance barriers. there were twelve more in the guardroom on standby. There had never been an individual guard on the admin building but then, Abdullah had never been present until today. He should have realised the possibility. He felt deep relief that the rocket had found its mark but had it been a total success?

Had the delay given any one of them time to reach the door and maybe survive? One thing for sure was that almost all were too far from the door to have reached it in time. The only one who maybe had a chance was the most important target of all General Abdullah himself.

In the boardroom six of the most prolific Turkish oil smugglers and a multi-million-dollar source of ISIS funds were reduced to heaps of torn smoking flesh. In the corridor outside the boardroom a badly injured General Abdullah lay underneath the heavy door he'd so recently slammed behind him. He moaned semi-conscious the blood oozing from his shattered body.

Outside on the ground one of the sentry's lifeless legs protruded from under a mass of fallen rubble.

Westaway connected to a secure server and sent an encrypted message after which he dismantled the transmitter placing it in a large hold-all along with the laptop, joystick, phone and the two arming pins. The specialist cleansing team would deal with that very shortly. Picking up an Irish passport in the name of Seamus O'Hare he took his unhurried departure.

Twenty four hours later, at RAF Akrotiri air base on the island of Cyprus, twelve British Typhoons and six Tornado GR4's took off heavily laden with 500 pound Paveway laser guided bombs. From Incirlik air base in Turkey American bombers were climbing skywards and all around the Mediterranean French and Russian bombers were becoming airborne. The Russians had cooperated at last and now a co-ordinated airstrike of huge power made its way towards the oilfields of ISIS their mission to destroy the wealth producing wells that funded the jihadists. At Ajeel north of Tikrit in Iraq and at Qayara, Himrin and other key targets the oilfield workers had no inkling of the devastation about to be wrought upon them. At sea, American, British and French war ships arrested a number of oil tankers carrying their illicit cargoes to refineries in Jordan and elsewhere. Only one tanker refused to heave too when ordered. The Ali Wahid, captained by a fanatical IS supporter, defied the 'weak West' to arrest him firing on the would-be boarding party with AK 47's. The captain of the arresting American Destroyer saw no reason to endanger his mens' lives and ordered the boarding party's immediate recall.

Seeing the boarding party turn away, the men aboard the Ali Wahid were jubilant, dancing, waving their weapons in the air and shouting Alluha Akbar. Minutes later the American captain gave another order and the Ali Wahid was sent to the bottom with all hands by an anti ship missile. A clear message had now been sent to those who grew rich on the black markets buying and selling ISIS oil that they had no hiding place. In destroying the ISIS oil wells the head of the snake had been struck but the creature was far from being dead.

Imam Fahad Bhakti

'Asalaamu Alaikum' Imam Fahad Bhakti greeted his brother-in-law. 'Wa Alaikum asalaam' replied Uthman Hassid 'what news my brother?'

Bhakti sat and slowly poured tea from an ornate silver teapot into delicate china cups placing a cup before Hassid before answering. He chose his words carefully, how much should he tell his brother-in-law and most importantly how to present the information? Secrecy was of utmost importance to him. When he finally spoke, it was in Arabic and his words came quickly. 'The London target has been selected and now is subject to my detailed research. 'It is big. The biggest.' He felt a rush of excitement but forced a calm exterior.

The Imam, unusually, always wore Western clothes except when conducting religious services. Sitting on piled cushions on the expensively carpeted floor of his large house overlooking Hampstead Heath in a lounge suit he cut an incongruous figure. He was forty two years old but with his sunken eyes and Grey beard he could easily have passed for fifty.

Hassid trembled inwardly in Bhakti's presence. He hero worshipped the Imam, regarding him as a great man of power, a prophet even. 'The men you are recruiting from the madrassah are fine devout young men but please remember to continue to check every one of them most thoroughly.' Bhakti said 'none are to have any previous involvement with ISIS. None to have a criminal record apart from minor traffic offences. No converts to be selected. All chosen must have been born in this country of good family.'

'I remember your orders well Fahad and have adhered to them.' said Hassid feeling more than a little bewildered at the Imam's need to repeat his instructions 'the recruitment goes slowly but well. I can turn most devout young men who are idealistic into true active believers without too much trouble' he said casually, making it sound like radicalisation was a simple, every day process.

Bhakti pondered on this statement for a few seconds. Hassid's attitude seemed almost nonchalant and it irritated him. 'Make no mistake Uthman, it is a task of crucial importance. No one that you have the slightest doubt about must even be approached. This is far too important.'

Bhakti was feeling frustrated by Hassid and he thought he'd detected a note of irritation in the man's voice, too. He felt the need to impress upon his brother-in-law more forcefully the great importance he attached to this strike.

He sipped his tea gathering his thoughts again, finally he spoke 'Uthman, you have seen the strikes here and around the world, the brothers hitting an Indian hotel, a shopping mall in Kenya etc, no?'

'All good work by brave martyrs' Hassid declared at last showing a degree of enthusiasm 'I once met the leader of the Kenyan assault. A great man.'

Bhakti looked grave 'it is for that very reason that contact between us must be strictly limited' he said sombrely 'your links with the movement may be very tenuous but they are still links. In today's climate of suspicion you can ill afford to do anything to bring yourself to notice.'

'I understand brother, I am most careful, always.'

Since coming to England Bhakti had painstakingly nurtured his image as a moderate community leader. He'd gone on television to preach peace and tolerance. He wore what he considered dreadful Western clothes to demonstrate how well integrated and Westernised he was. He consorted with and cultivated politicians and cabinet ministers to ensure acceptance. The Flame of Truth madrasah set up in his name must remain above suspicion. The Imam felt a deep need to ensure his second-in-command also demonstrated his great passion and commitment.

Hassid picked up the Imam's mood and responded 'I understand brother and I am deeply grateful for the honour of being chosen to play such a leading role.'

Bhakti's ignored Hassid's sycophantic reply, his face took on a dark look 'the bombs that fell on Baghdad and killed my father, brother, mother and cousins will be avenged, Uthman.'

Bhakti's fists now clenched and unclenched, his face contorted into a mask of pure hatred. 'I have played the forgiving, tolerant cleric too long. All these years I have waited for this opportunity to strike at the heart of the Great Satan of the West' spittle was foaming at the corners of his mouth and his eyes bulged. His voice rose harsh and rasping as he felt the bitterness of the past flood every fibre of his being.

'It is not for me to be satisfied with the deaths of a few shop keepers and their customers Uthman but to strike such fear and dread into the corrupt heart of their Establishment that they will never be the same again. This country will be changed forever and I will change it.'

Hassid watched, his eyes glowing in adoration, soaking up Bhakti's passion. He waited, unspeaking, until the Imam had calmed down. He knew his brother-in-law well, these rare outbursts never lasted long. Bhakti sat back reaching for his cigarettes with a trembling hand. After a few deep inhalations, his face and manner returned to normal.

'Inshalla brother, I will soon be an instrument of your vengeance' Hassid whispered in awe.

After sipping more tea Bhakti spoke again, this time calmly with no trace of his former rage. 'There is however a major problem that I have had to overcome, Uthman.'

'Really brother?'

'It was one of funding.'

Hassid cocked his head to one side, lifting an eyebrow, his eyes narrowed in curiosity. His thin face expressed a questioning look but he said nothing.

'Since our oilfields were destroyed and other problems heaped upon us, such as bank accounts being traced and frozen, funds are no longer as plentiful as they once were' he said 'I was tasked to source funds for the operation myself. To that end I have recruited a man called Khan, ostensibly a prominent businessman. He made a large donation to the building of the madrassah as you may remember?'

'Of course, a philanthropist of great wealth and generosity.'

Bhakti sneered as a feeling of revulsion swept through him. 'That is the image Khan likes to portray' he said 'the reality is much different. He runs a chain of successful restaurants and takeaways up and down the country, yes, but he is a major drug dealer with a taste for whiskey, murder and girls as young as eight.'

Hassid felt shock and surprise hit him like a double fisted blow 'If he is not to be trusted why are we using him Fahad?'

'Because greed can always be relied upon Uthman and a fear of beheading often helps, too.' Bhakti smiled grimly at his macabre remark. 'I have contacts in Afghanistan who produce high quality drugs. Setting up this deal took many months of careful negotiation but I succeeded in making special arrangements to supply him at a price he could not hope obtain anywhere else.'

'How does this help us, brother?'

'He receives a huge discount in return for which he gives us thirty three percent of his profits.'

Hassid fell silent absorbing this news, a feeling of unease creeping into his heart. His brother-in-law was so secretive it made him feel distrusted. 'How much does he know?'

The Imam squirmed on his cushions, embarrassment flushing his face. He adjusted his position before answering. 'He is no fool as you can imagine' he said cautiously 'he knows I am demanding funds far in excess of those needed to run the Flame of Truth madrassah. Funds we need to buy arms, vehicles and highly specialized communications equipment.' His voice dropped to almost a whisper as he admitted 'he also knows there is to be a strike in London but, of course, he doesn't know where or when.'

Hassid gasped 'How could he possibly know that?' he said his face betraying utter shock and astonishment.

'A henchman of his has a favourite nephew who was one of our very first recruits. You remember that in our early enthusiasm the first recruits were told of a great strike in London. As I said, Khan's no fool. He gathers intelligence like a sponge in case it may be useful at a later date.'

Although Bhakti despised Khan he respected the man's ruthless approach to running his businesses. 'He has eyes and ears everywhere, in the Borough Council, in the police, everywhere. He uses murder, blackmail, bribery and extortion as everyday tools of his trade. Competitors that oppose him simply disappear without trace. He told me what he knew in order to inform me he could use the information against me if it ever proved necessary.'

Hassid's eyebrows shot upwards his voice incredulous 'he has threatened you?'

'Of course not, he had no need to; we both understood exactly what was meant.'

'Give me the name of the nephew and I will execute him myself.'

Bhakti smiled, he admired Hassid's loyalty but he counselled caution. 'No Uthman, that would be counterproductive.'

When Hassid frowned he explained 'the young man concerned has vital I.T. skills that we need. He has already been cautioned that he is putting his family in danger, but it is a warning that we should heed.' Bhakti smiled coldly 'you, my brother, will be responsible for liaising with this Khan creature whenever necessary, I suggest you use a go-between. The Westerners have a very apt saying: "If one sups with the devil, one should use a very long spoon." When we have achieved our purpose, Khan will be disposed of.'

Hassid smiled bleakly his eyes flashing in unholy anticipation 'That would be my pleasure' then his face changed and he asked 'just what is our target Brother?'

Bhakti poured more tea and offered Hassid a biscuit before replying. 'Any psychologist will tell you Uthman that the thing with secrets is the holder of the secret finds himself compelled to tell someone as demonstrated by our young IT friend. It's human nature.' He smiled 'That, my brother, is one of the reasons why only I know the target and the time. And that is also why you must keep our followers in ignorance as much as possible.'

Hassid felt a surge of anger, how dare the Imam doubt his loyalty? 'You insult me brother' he said his voice trembling 'you know I would never say a word. I would rather kill myself.'

Bhakti smiled benignly he had not meant to insult Hassid. 'Peace Uthman, peace' he said holding up one hand 'it is not that I doubt you but, should you be picked up by the authorities, you cannot give away that which you don't know.'

Hassid went to protest but Bhakti again held up his hand. 'Uthman, the people in MI5 have resources not only for physical and mental torture, which you could no doubt withstand' he said appeaseingly 'but they also have drugs, very refined and sophisticated drugs that make a man say things he later regrets.'

'But evidence taken this way would never be allowed in a court' Hassid said.

Bhakti's laugh was one of genuine mirth. Such naivety he thought. 'Many a man has died Uthman regretting that he had underestimated the British. Behind their facade of gentility, impeccable manners and their endless spouting about the rule of law they are the most ruthless thugs on earth. How do you think they built an empire?' He adopted a gentle tone now feeling genuine affection for Hassid 'You my brother, husband of my dear sister, father of my beloved nephews and nieces are the man

I trust above all others but please understand the London strike and its security comes above all else.'

Hassid felt chastened and a tear appeared in the corner of his eye. In the years they'd known each other not once had the Imam shown him anything but trust. 'My humble apologies Fahad it is I who insult you, please forgive my outburst.'

Bhakti clasped Hassid's hands in his looking into his eyes with a feeling of deep affection. 'There is nothing to forgive beloved Uthman, you simply demonstrated yet again your total commitment.' Smiling, the Imam said 'What I can tell you is that this strike will outshine even the great victory of the Twin Towers. It will be celebrated forever among righteous believers everywhere. The blood of the kuffar will run deep in the gutters of London.'

The Fall of the Ferret

Looking around the overcrowded carriage for a mark Freddy (The Ferret) Fenton spotted an easy target standing near the doors. She was a frail looking elderly woman with a careworn face swaying with the motion of the London Underground train. She was facing the doors side on to him, an old fashioned but good quality handbag over her arm. She looked lost in her own thoughts. He gave a sigh of satisfaction, a tingle of anticipation ran though him.

As the train decelerated to the next stop Freddy, feeling the confidence of the long practiced professional, pulled the brim of his baseball cap as far over his face as it would go and squeezed his way between passengers using his elbows and the odd 's'cuse me' to close in for the take.

Timing was crucial, do the job as the train decelerated but before she was forced to move by alighting passengers. Then away off the train head down to avoid the cameras catching his face.

Covering the target from view with his body and voluminous jacket Freddy's hand expertly slipped the bag's catch. He quickly located and liberated her purse pushing it into the special pocket inside his coat so that it dropped all the way down to the bottom of the lining. He then deftly closed the bag again to delay discovery of his theft. The whole operation had taken just five slick seconds.

A growl of anger came from Fenton's left, he felt shocked when he saw an older man in the end seat glaring at him with cold fury.

'Come here you thieving little shit' the man spat and started to rise but was impeded by passengers pushing towards the doors of the now halted train.

The older guy looked about sixty with washed out Grey-blue eyes and a large hooked nose that gave him a hawk-like appearance.

The man got up and lunged for him. Freddy felt panic rising in him. 'Come here you.'

The doors hissed open and Freddy leapt off, ducking the outstretched hand, He hit the platform running, the man in pursuit

'Stop that man' Jack roared.

A few passengers cast a brief, curious glance at him and continued towards the escalators, none seemed aware of what had happened.

Jack gave chase but the thief outpaced him. He returned to look for the pickpocket's victim but the train doors closed and it moved off. He cursed himself inwardly. He'd been a fool to try and catch the much younger guy. 'What the hell were you thinking of' he muttered to himself.

Jack had, however, caught the strong smell of tobacco on the thief and noticed his fingers were stained dark with nicotine. He won't be running far he thought.

Leaping off the escalator Freddy looked around through his narrow brown eyes. It was just as he expected, the older guy was nowhere to be seen. He dodged, breathing heavily from his exertions, into the public lavatory and into a cubicle.

'Jesus, I hope this one's worth it' he muttered to himself. Opening the purse he quickly pulled out the contents. There was two hundred and twenty pounds in notes and some loose change, a bus pass, cash card and a bingo club membership card. There were also some old black and white photos of a couple with a young girl at the seaside and another of the same couple, the man in old fashioned Army uniform posing with his new bride.

'Ah nice one' Freddy gloated under his breath. He tore up the photos and other paper stuff and flushed the debris down the toilet. Shoving the cash into his pocket he then wiped the purse vigorously with dampened toilet paper before stuffing it behind the porcelain. Emerging from the toilets Freddy looked cautiously around. Seeing nothing suspicious a wave of relief swept over him. He swaggered out of the station a smug smile on his face. He donned a pair of sunglasses, lit a cigarette and drew in a relieving lungful of smoke. They'd need to be a bit quicker than that old fart to catch The Ferret he thought; I've earned a coffee.

Across the street, an old experienced pair of eyes were watching him through a newsagent's window.

Taking his coffee the Ferret slid into a bench seat at the back of the shop. He felt happier now things had returned to normal. He chose a seat at the back of the cafe with his back to the wall because he liked to see who was coming and going. It was an old habit of self preservation to always sit with his back protected and where he could observe.

Freddy casually watched a young woman at a nearby table dressed in cheap skin-tight jeans with slashed knees and a sleeveless top which revealed several gaudy tattoos. She had a baby boy of about a year in an old push chair and was neglecting both her coffee and the sleeping child to busily text on her phone.

Benefits bimbo he thought, curling his lip, purse is in the shopping bag, phone's a load of crap, she's not worth a flying fart. He looked down to his own coffee stirring it slowly.

A shadow passed over The Ferret and he looked up, startled. The train man slid along the bench seat trapping him in the corner against the wall.

Jack glowered at Freddy. 'I saw you just now robbing that old woman' he said his voice betraying no emotion.

Looking into the cold grey eyes Freddy felt fear rising 'Sorry mate, yer must 'ave mistook me fer summon else innit' he said in his East London twang. He forced a smile 'I dunno whotcha on about.'

Freddy was good at spotting people who might be following him yet he'd seen nothing of this man since the train. He hadn't even seen him come into the café. Now the man's killer stare and icy calm manner were freaking him out.

'Why don't you cut the bullshit eh?' the man said.

Freddy slipped his right hand into his pocket closing it round the knife that was his last resort in a crisis though he'd never actually used it before. Undecided on his next move he asked nervously 'wot d'ya want mister?'

The man stared, watching the flicker of fear in Freddy's eyes and the slight twitch on his thin lips. 'I want you to stop picking pockets' he said almost casually 'retire or you'll be retired, that plain enough?'

Freddy's jaw sagged. He couldn't have been more surprised if the man had asked him to drop his trousers and dance on the table. He stared at the man as if he had not heard him correctly, feeling bewildered. Is he having a laugh or what he thought? At the same time he was curious to know just who he was dealing with. 'What are yer then mate, ex Filth?' he asked belligerently.

Jack replied calmly 'I'm much worse than any policeman mate, much, much worse.' There was no hint of boasting in the man's voice, just plain statement of fact.

Freddy gave a nervous laugh, he looked around the almost empty cafe as if seeking an escape route. There wasn't one. There was no one in the place capable of helping him if he kicked off with a fuss that he was being sexually harassed. He killed that that idea almost as a soon as it was born. Should he flash the knife? No, not yet.

He decided bluff was his best bet. Curling his lip he leaned as near as he dare into the man's face, sneering 'you got no proof an' no powers of arrest arse 'ole an' yer an old git, too, so why don't yer piss off before yer gets 'urt, yeah?' He stared at Jack, hoping he looked hard enough to act.

Jack's face remained placid. He didn't move an inch away from Freddy. Staring obliquely into the thief's eyes unblinkingly he placed both his hands on the table, his fingers tapping lightly. 'That knife in your pocket won't do you any good and if you try it on I'll break your arm.'

These last words shook Freddy to the core; there was no anger in the man's voice, no threat in his body language. Again, his calm words sounded like a plain statement of fact. How the hell could this bloke know I have a knife let alone that I'm holding it he thought? He let the weapon slip from his nervous grasp and brought his hand out onto the table.

'What d'ya want mate? Fer Chris' sake, what d' fuck do yer want?' He was feeling seriously rattled now and his voice betrayed the panic that was rising within him.

'What's your name?' the man asked.

'The name's Freddy, surname don't matter' then he added defiantly, 'Who der fuck are ya man?'

'The name's Jack, surname don't matter' Jack mimicked and then instantly regretted he had done so.

Well listen Jack, if yer don't fuck off sharpish I'm gonna make a phone call, right?' Freddy bluffed, in the desperate hope of scaring off this worryingly confident older bloke. Narrowing he eyes in what he thought of as his best 'hard look' he hissed 'I can 'ave half a dozen well hard blokes down here in minutes, get me?'

Jack ignored Freddy, looking for all the world like he hadn't heard him 'I told you just now Freddy, you're retired mate and I meant it' he paused staring hard into Freddy's eyes his frozen smile conveying the utter contempt he felt.

A surge of anger swept through him; who did this cocky little shit think he was? Jack suddenly whipped the edge of his right hand hard into Freddy's solar plexus with deadly accuracy. The air whooshed out of the pickpocket in coughing gouts as he sagged in his seat struggling for air, his senses reeling.

Jack leaned into Freddy's face and spat venomously 'that's the trouble with hard men Freddy, the bastards are never around when you need 'em. Now, retire or else!'

With that Jack was gone leaving Freddy to slowly recover. The girl at the nearby table never even looked up from her phone. Freddy was so shaken that he took the rest of the week off.

*****

Mrs. Hart got to the bus stop and reached in her bag for her purse. It was gone. She searched the bag frantically for a couple of minutes, her bus came and went. She sat down in the bus shelter feeling utterly bemused, tears streaming down her face. It wasn't the pension money, though God alone knew how she'd manage without it, it was the shock of losing the precious black and white photos of her dead daughter taken on holiday in Clacton fifty years previously. It was as irreplaceable as her wedding photo with her late husband Stan looking so debonair in his Army uniform fresh back from the Korean War.'

My pictures, my pictures' she muttered holding out a helpless hand to a lady passer-by 'they took my pictures.' The shock was too much for the eighty-six year old, tears flooded the wrinkles of her crumpled face and spilled onto her coat. She lost control of her bladder as she keeled over.

*****

Jack was sitting in his armchair reading his local paper when he came across an article on page six that caught his attention. A Mrs Hart had collapsed with a heart attack shortly after being robbed on the underground. She had been rushed to hospital where she briefly recovered consciousness and made a statement. She had a relapse the next day and died. The accompanying photo of her was an old one but Jack recognised her immediately as Freddy's victim.

'That slithering bloody reptile, that nasty little shit' he said aloud as he brought his fist down hard on the chair arm. He was not an emotional man by normal standards but he hated thieves with a passion. Growing up in the orphanage it had been difficult to prevent money or precious possessions from disappearing. Being forced to hand over things of value to bigger bully boys had filled him with burning shame and humiliation. As he grew older he joined a boys' club and learned to box. The incidents of bullying ceased after he pounded a few faces, but he still had to be wary of sneak thieves.

A picture of the cocky pickpocket came into his mind. 'It's time you got yours you bastard' he muttered aloud.

Now sixty eight years old, Jack Ellis had been retired for the last three years since his wife Joan had died. He had sold his security consultancy for a good price and spent a lot of time at the gym, swimming or with friends at his archery club.

It crossed his mind to simply report Freddy to the police. Maybe I should, too, he thought. Then cold anger rose again within him. He looked at the big green eyes of Mischief as she sat regarding him curiously 'what the hell, puss, the slimy bastard would only get a slap on the wrist even if I proved his guilt.' The cat merely yawned and stared licking herself.

'No way would they charge him with causing her death, Missy. At eighty six Mrs Hart could have popped off at any time. That little bastard killed her, though, as surely as if he'd knifed her.'

Like a lot of people who lived alone, Jack often spoke his thoughts to his pet. It never once struck him as odd.

His trouble would be finding Freddy in London. It would be like looking for a single fish in the North Sea Jack thought.

He considered that thought for only a moment before deciding that the thief wouldn't go just anywhere. He would most likely target tourists as they were usually carrying money and valuables.

They were also off guard in a strange city and they were temporary visitors so once they went home and claimed on their insurance they ceased to make a fuss.

Jack could not rest that night he tossed and turned then when sleep finally came he dreamt of Freddy sneering at him, challenging to find him. When he awoke in the dawn light he had a plan in his head. He smiled to himself, threw a purring Mischief off his bed, and went and made coffee. Yes, he would give it a shot. He knew Freddy wouldn't retire and, after all, he'd made him a promise, and a promise was a promise.

Jack looked young for his years his thick brown hair was only now starting to go grey. His active exercise regime, meditation and a good diet kept him trim and as fit mentally and physically as a man of his age could expect to be. He and Joan had an active sex life until she was diagnosed with breast cancer a year before she died. He missed her terribly that first year feeling hollow, empty and useless then gradually the pain in his heart started to ease.

Jack's anger was still cold and controlled within him. He felt his rage like ice in his veins; it was a hard, self sustaining thing. He thought Freddy, you need to suffer some of the grief you so casually inflict on others, you bastard.

He ruled out killing Freddy. There were worse things than dying Jack believed and, if he was successful in his mission, Freddy would soon be the recipient of some severe and lasting misery.

The early spring sunshine was warming the beginning of the tourist season and Jack had an idea which venues Freddy would be working. Jack asked around the people who haunted the tourist areas. The beggars and street people looked on him with suspicion and simply shook their heads. After three days of fruitless searching he spotted a skinny young guy selling drugs near King's Cross railway station.

'You know a dip called Freddy, mate?'

'Maybe, maybe not' the youth said weighing him up with a sly glance. 'what's it worth to you.'

Jack produced a twenty pound note and held it before the man's face. 'I need to talk to him.' The guy made a grab for the money but Jack pulled it out of reach. 'Info first, sonshine.'

The kid looked peevish 'Dunno where he lives guv'nor but I know where he hangs out most Saturdays, if it's the same bloke.'

Jack added another twenty 'do tell.'

The man's sly eyes looked at the money greedily then he glanced sideways up and down the street. Jack read his mind. His hand shot out and gripped him by the Adam's apple, thrusting him up against the wall. 'If you're thinking of snatching the money and running lad, that would be unhealthy.'

The dealer's eye stared, wide with fear as he made choking noises unable to speak, his hands grabbing ineffectually at Jack's arm. Looking into this older man's pale grey eyes he saw a killer and his guts turned to jelly. Jack released him suddenly and he sagged against the wall

The dealer was bent double clutching his throat gagging and gasping. After a minute, he recovered enough to speak. 'He's football mad guv'nor, a big Spurs fan, never misses a home game. Uses the East stand. Gets there early.'

Jack gave a cold smile 'There now, that wasn't hard, was it?' He added another ten to the forty. Putting his hand in the man's inside pocket he removed his wallet. Glancing at his driving licence as he stuffed the money in. 'Well now, Mr Silas Grant of 124 Faraday Towers, if Freddy finds out I'm looking for him I'll know who told him' he leaned into Grant's face 'then we'll have another chat one dark night, one you won't enjoy.'

Grant nodded, unable to speak. This mad old man terrified him, he knew he'd keep his promise about the chat.

Jack bought a Spurs scarf and woollen bobble hat which he crammed on his head pulling it down over his ears. A long wig and a cushion under his clothes fattened and altered his body shape. A pair of horn rim spectacles and an old raincoat completed his change of appearance.

He was early and spent an hour wandering about, mingling with the growing number of supporters. He was leaning on the side of a mobile burger stand slowly chewing a tasteless hotdog watching the growing crowd when he finally spotted him.

Even though he was trained to spot people, he almost missed him as Freddy the ferret slid along the wall to the turnstile entrance. He was wearing a huge oversized coat and his scarf was almost covering his entire face. What confirmed the ID for Jack was his man's body language. Out of long habit Freddie halted just before going in and scanned the crowd left and right. No innocent fan would do that.

God, he's a slippery bugger and no mistake Jack thought. Dropping the hotdog into a bin he quickly followed him. He found a seat three rows behind him.

After the game Jack kept Freddie in sight but stayed well back. Using all his skills, Jack still found it damned hard work following Freddy to his home unseen. God, he thought, this guy is slicker than snot on a glass handrail. He watched as Freddy finally slid home to a rundown block of flats in Lewisham. He had doubled back three times in the process. Now he knew where he lived his chance had come to put his plan into action.

Next day Jack took a heavy brass Zippo lighter from a drawer; it was one he'd bought as a leaving present for his friend Paul during his service days. His thoughts returned now to Paul and the ambush that he'd died in.

He felt a deep pang of sadness envelope him for a moment remembering their close friendship. Paul had been a great mate and a staunch colleague who would always go out of his way to help him. Jack hadn't had an opportunity to get the lighter engraved at the time because of his unforeseen posting back to

England. He had just put the lighter in a drawer as a keepsake to remind him of Paul. Now he'd found a use for it and he considered the sacrifice worth its loss. He knew that Paul would have approved.

'I'd like this engraved please' Jack told the market stallholder exactly what he required.

'No problem, it'll be about an hour Guv, that all right?' the stallholder said.

'Sure, I'll see you then.' An hour later he collected he lighter, paid cash and went home. In his cellar, he worked on the thing for about an hour until he was satisfied then polished it until it gleamed. He spent a moment admiring the deep diamond pattern the engraver had cut in the front and sides of the case and the inscription on the back. 'Yup' he muttered to Mischief 'that should do us nicely puss.' She simply purred and rubbed herself affectionately against him.

Next morning Jack dressed carefully before leaving home. Arriving near Freddy's place he watched and waited feeling a sense of excited anticipation growing within him. He believed that Freddy was a creature of habit and would leave home soon.

The Ferret looked about the carriage with his usual care but saw nothing of immediate interest. Then at the next station, as he changed trains a bent old man leaning heavily on a thick bamboo cane got on just before him. The man was wearing a wide brimmed black hat and had long grey hair and beard. He climbed slowly aboard and shuffled to a seat leaning heavily on the stick. After two stops the man got up and made his way slowly, head bowed, past the thief to the door.

One glance told Freddy he had found a mark for protruding slightly from the old man's coat pocket was a registered envelope. Freddy's heart leapt with joy. This was too good an opportunity to miss and he closed in.

Stepping off the train with the man Freddy bumped into the old fellow. 'Sorry mate' he mumbled and quickly made off. The registered envelope could only mean something of high value, it felt heavy and he wondered what it could be. He had only seen the old guy from the back but he had the impression that he looked Jewish so gold perhaps? Diamonds even?

Freddy dived eagerly into his 'private office' as he called public lavatories and entered a cubicle; tearing open the envelope he slid out the contents. He found a small heavy gift-wrapped object, unwrapping it he saw it was a high quality brass Zippo lighter.

What the fuck? he thought, feeling disappointed as he turned the lighter in his hand. He read the inscription: 'To Freddy happy retirement.' Freddy felt a stab of fear rush through him, what the hell was this? He was still haunted by visions of a vengeful older man who'd hurt him and severely rattled his confidence.

He calmed himself immediately, taking deep breaths and exhaling slowly. Christ, he thought, thousands of people are called Freddy.

You're letting some daft old fart that you'll never see again scare your mate.

He flicked the Zippo lid open it looked a perfectly normal lighter, brand new, too. He sniffed the wick it smelled of lighter fuel. He stuck a cigarette in his mouth leaned in and flicked the wheel to see if it worked and the sparks flew bright. They were the last things Freddy ever saw.

With a brief, vicious hiss the Zippo exploded blowing the fingers off his right hand. The diamond pattern shrapnel ripped into his face tearing his flesh and reducing his eyes to a bloody jelly.

At the urinal, a bent old man finished his business and, ignoring the screams coming from the smoking cubicle, walked quickly out, a grim smile of satisfaction playing about his lips.

The incident made the front page of the local paper. It had also been on the local T V news. Jack was interested in the spin. The victim's girlfriend claimed he'd picked up a cigarette lighter in the street and it had blown half his hand off and blinded him. She portrayed him as the hapless victim rather well Jack thought.

Jack Ellis

Growing up in the orphanage from the age of ten the happy warm security of life with his parents was just a blurred memory. To Jack, the only happy family he remembered from his youth was in the military and that had been cut short by circumstances beyond his control. In his military career Jack had done some dark deeds for Queen and Country until the line between right and wrong had become barely discernible.

The fact that he had assassinated people didn't bother Jack one bit. It was part of his make up to look at things in black and white. His targets had all been guilty of heinous crimes causing many innocent deaths but they were beyond the reach of the law. Four of these people had been targeting him directly. They had each richly deserved their fate and he had simply delivered what they'd earned.

Jack rose and took the wedding photograph of his parents from its place of honour on his sideboard. His hands caressed it with reverence. The young man smiling out at him in Royal Air Force uniform wearing a Sergeant's stripes and pilots' wings was his late father. The beautiful bride with the radiant face, his mother. He was saddened because could barely remember their voices now.

He tried to imagine for the thousandth time what it must have felt like to be squeezed into the tiny Hurricane cockpit taking off with no guarantee you'd be returning in one piece or spiralling down in flames burning in this machine which had suddenly become a coffin. He felt a surge of admiration for his father who started the war as a Sergeant pilot flying Hurricanes and ending it as a squadron leader.

Nine confirmed kills, shot down twice and the hundreds of sorties flown, the Distinguished Flying Cross he'd been awarded. After the war Jack's father, also called Jack, had converted to piloting freight planes in the Berlin air lift until his untimely death.

Jack still had a clear memory of the awful moment his aunt Beryl, his dad's sister, broke the news that their little Auster, his parents' pride and joy, had crashed and they'd gone to heaven. He remembered living with his aunt Beryl, a dear sweet natured soul, until she died two years later.

He was sent to the orphanage where he felt strange and alone. He recalled silently sobbing into his pillow until sleep claimed him. Everyone he knew and loved was gone. Mr. Orme, the House Father, a kindly practical man, told him gently there was little chance of him being adopted. Adoptive parents wanted little babies not boisterous ten year olds.

Just before his sixteenth birthday fire had swept the orphanage and he's had to evacuate quickly, the smoke already swirling about the dorm. He'd gone to his locker to rescue his few valued possessions but Mr. Orme had pushed him towards the door yelling at him and the others to get out. He manages to grab the picture of his father and mother but lost all the others as Orme grabbed him again, forcing him outside.

Years later he read the account in old newspapers in the library how his parents had died. His father Jack and Miranda, his mother had decided to fly to Ostend for the weekend leaving him with aunt Beryl. Their engine had cut out on take-off due to contaminated fuel and they'd plunged six hundred feet into a wood.

Jack talked little of his upbringing even to his late wife Joan. He'd always answer her questions about his orphan days honestly but as briefly as possible. His standard put-off phrase was 'It was long ago and far away and better told on another day.'

Joan had grown used to this couplet and resigned herself to not asking after their first year of marriage.

Waldo Williams

Waldo Williams lay back on his sofa smoking a large joint, drinking his ninth strong beer of the evening and listening to the overloud rap music as he watched the party. Arseholes, he thought, a pack of pricks and wasters. He felt nothing but contempt for them.

These people were his dealers, his runners, his errand boys and minders. The women were mainly their girlfriends, partners or just junkie whores looking for a free fix. Waldo liked to keep his people tight in his pocket because that way they spent almost all of what he paid them on the drugs he sold. Some of them didn't want his cash, they preferred to be paid in drugs. He despised them all.

A pretty black girl wandered over, thighs brushing seductively together as she progressed across the room. She squeezed her shapely arse onto the little of the sofa not occupied by Waldo's six foot two frame. She leaned over him thrusting her ample breasts into his face 'Hi honey, how you feelin' tonight?' she cooed stroking his crotch.

Waldo's eyes flashed dangerously as he pushed her away with such violence she slid onto the floor her with a thud. Her short skirt rode up showing anyone who cared to look she was going commando that night. 'Piss off' Waldo spat. 'That shit don't wash with me slut, you want your fix you pay cash like every other fucker.'

'Fuck you arsehole' she yelled and got up pulling her skirt down. 'Here was me just trying to be nice, you cunt.' She leaned too close to him whilst she said this letting her anger overcome her caution. She was rewarded with a vicious slap across the face that sent her spinning backwards crashing over a coffee table. She went sprawling once more flashing her womanhood to the room.

'Who's with this bitch?' Waldo roared at the staring crowd, his mind in a drug induced turmoil of hatred. No one answered. It didn't pay to annoy Waldo Williams. After a few seconds, he called his chief henchman 'Jonny, get this bitch out of here will ya?' Then at the crowd in general he yelled 'You other bitches want drugs? I take cash not cunt, OK? Jesus, you should all know that by now.'

The hapless girl was bundled out into the street nursing a thick lip and the party resumed as though nothing had happened. Waldo Williams was in a foul mood. He'd heard earlier that day that some dealer who had been beaten and robbed had put it about that he thought Waldo's men were responsible. His soldiers were disciplined and didn't do shit like that, it caused too much hassle. One thing Khan wouldn't tolerate was needless hassle. It shifted focus away from business.

A couple of hours later another girl walked into the party. She was tall, slender and clean-cut. She was primly dressed in a knee length denim skirt and a close-fitting pink tee shirt which enhanced her perky breasts. Her abundant, normally flowing golden hair was pinned back into a severe bun. Her huge deep blue eyes stung as she searched though the cannabis smoke.

Waldo was in a dark corner chatting to a very attractive young girl. It was obvious the youngster didn't belong there; she'd be around fourteen or fifteen at most. The kid held a beer in one hand and a cigarette in the other, doing her best to look older than her years She looked in awe of Waldo.

'Hi Waldo, remember me?' she said to his back. 'Still chasing little girls I see.'

Recognizing her voice Waldo whipped around 'what the hell do you want Marcia? Didn't I tell you to piss off and never come back?' 'You did Waldo, and I wouldn't be here now unless it was urgent.'

'Urgent for who bitch?' he curled his lip.

'Urgent for our son Waldo, he needs stuff, you know, clothes, food and a decent place to live.'

Waldo felt his anger flare instantly and his eyes blazed.

'Well fuck you Marcia.' His shoulders hunched as he leaned into her face threateningly. 'That little bastard ain't mine you cow so fuck off while fucking off's a chance you've still got.'

Marcia didn't lack courage and she was desperate. Thrown out by her ultra-religious parent as soon as it became apparent she was pregnant, she now relied on state benefits. 'You know damn well he's yours Waldo. I don't want to involve Social Services but....'

At the mention of Social Services Waldo exploded. He slapped her hard across the mouth, sending her reeling to the floor. He grabbed her hair and dragged her to her knees.

'Listen you two-timing bitch' he screamed 'that bastard kid ain't mine, see? I reckon you've been screwing around behind my back you stinking whore.'

Marcia stared up at him, the pain swirling through her head in waves. She wondered now how she had ever seen anything in this brutal thug.

Gathering all her courage she glared into his contorted face defiantly. Through swollen bleeding lips she managed to speak, her voice barely audible. 'I was a virgin when we met, remember? A clean living, church going girl who thought she could help you make something of yourself' she paused briefly 'why won't you have a DNA test to prove it if you're so sure the boy's not yours?'

Marcia's show of open defiance sent Waldo berserk. He punched her hard in the head and Marcia's eyebrow split wide sending blood cascading down her face. She moaned and slumped to the floor feeling herself slipping out of consciousness. Waldo immediately started kicking her body, screaming his hatred.

The only person in the room who dared to do anything to stop Waldo was his Segundo Jonny Burke. He grabbed him in a bear hug and threw him aside. Waldo spun around his eyes flashing fire, he took a drunken swing at Burke who sidestepped with ease and grabbed him in a bear hug again. 'Waldo, for Christ's sake man, you'll kill the bitch' he shouted 'we can do without that much heat man, there's too many witnesses.'

'Get the fuck off me you bastard' Waldo bellowed throwing himself from side to side but he couldn't break Burke'sgrip. He was dragged away from Marcia who lay moaning on the floor in the foetal position, barely conscious.

'Listen you crazy bastard, if you go on kicking the bitch like that she'll die, yeah?' Waldo was beginning to relax just a little as his red mist started clearing.

'Look at me mate,' said Burke, spinning him round holding both his arms, trying to get eye contact 'look at all these tossers, do you think there's no one here who wouldn't grass you up for the price of a fix?'

'Nobody here would grass to The Filth.' Williams said stubbornly.

'I'm not talking about the cops, Waldo, I'm talking about Khan. If he knew you'd topped this bird in front of witnesses he'd be pissed off man, fuckin' well pissed off.' Burke paused, trying to gauge if what he was telling Williams was getting through. 'How do you know Marcia didn't tell some cunt she was coming here tonight, eh? Khan don't need you involved in unnecessary murder shit man, it would boil his piss big time.'

The mention of Khan's name finally did the trick. Khan didn't object to murder but he had to sanction it and it needed to be done discreetly. The last thing he needed was stupid punks killing each other over some petty grudge. It drew unwanted attention from the media and the authorities and that was bad for business. No one played it wrong with Khan without paying a heavy price. People who displeased the man tended to disappear.

'OK, OK' he growled 'let go of me man, I'm cool, OK?'

Burke finally released his grip on Waldo's arms. He'd hated the man since he'd made a play for his fourteen year old sister a month ago. He'd stepped in immediately and told him to back off. Williams had had enough sense to do so. He needed Jonny Burke.

If anything were to happen to Waldo he, Jonny Burke, would be next in line to run this part of Khan's operation. Tonight, however, had not been the right opportunity. If he'd let Waldo kill Marcia so publicly Khan would want to know why he hadn't stopped him. In his paranoia Khan was likely to blame him as well as Waldo and deal accordingly. It would have been far too risky.

Waldo walked back to where Marcia lay. He picked up a bottle of vodka from a side table and knelt beside her lifting her head and resting it on his knee. He forced her full lips apart, pouring the raw spirit down her throat. It caused her to cough and splutter, choking for air. He paused to allow her a few gasping breaths then poured some more. When the bottle was almost empty he let her flop to the floor. 'Call a taxi and get her to fuck out of here Jonny.' he said coldly, then he then looked around the room. Some people were watching openly most were huddled in small groups pretending to be deep in conversation, noticing nothing.

'Kill the music' Williams bawled. He then addressed the room 'If any shit comes from this the story goes that she was drunk and fell outside on the pavement, OK?' He glared at each of them in turn defying anyone to argue. No one did. Most cast their eyes down and shuffled their feet.

'This two-timing bitch deserved what she got for trying to rip me off for someone else's bastard' he paused but no one spoke, everyone knew who'd got the girl pregnant. 'Any of you bastards thinking of grassing me up better think about what it will be like to live without your bollocks or your nipples, *ladies*.' He paused again, staring then raising his right hand in the air he said 'music maestro, the party goes on.'

But the party died after that and people started to drift away. Waldo didn't care, they'd be back tomorrow, they needed him more that he needed them. He looked across the room to where the young girl he'd been lusting over cowered in the corner, terrified by his violence. Walking over he grabbed her arm leading her to his room. 'Come on sweetheart' he said in a voice that brooked no argument 'it's bedtime.'

Marcia staggered from the taxi and dragged herself up three flights of stairs to her grim bed sit. She had left her one year old son Jackson with a friend that night. Thank God he had been spared seeing me like this she thought. Lurching to the bathroom feeling drunk and dazed she knelt before the toilet bowl. Pushing her fingers down her throat she forced herself to vomit.

After what seemed an age her head stopped spinning enough for her to stand and reach the washbasin where she splashed her face with cold water. She then drank two large glasses of water.

God, what a mess she thought, staring horrified at her battered image in the mirror. She took a sponge from the shower and rubbed off as much of the congealed blood as she could manage. Her left eye was closed and the cut above it needed stitches; she was in agony from two cracked ribs and other injuries. She took twice the recommended dose of painkillers and crawled into bed, too exhausted even to undress. There, as abject misery swamped her, she eventually cried herself to sleep.

Victims

'Hi-ya Jack it's me, I'm coming round to see you, OK?'

Jack smiled broadly, he was always pleased to hear from his goddaughter, it brightened his day immensely when she visited. 'Sure thing Sally, I'll put the kettle on love. You alone, or have you captured some poor hapless lad?' He enjoyed teasing her and she enjoyed his teasing.

'Nah Jack, the lad managed to escape' she laughed. 'I'll see you in five, OK?

Sally didn't come too often now she was seventeen. Her social life among her peers was busy and lively and college was time consuming as it should be for a teenager. He grinned happily to himself as he filled the kettle, eager to hear her news and gossip. 'Sally's coming Missy, best behavior, OK?' he told his cat cheerfully.

And then she was with him laughing, telling silly jokes, relating her parents doings and what dad thought of this and what mum had said about that. Granddad was a bit grumpy and granny had been down with a cold. She mockingly chastised him for not having her favourite biscuits in and asked cheeky questions about his love life. Mischief climbed on her knee head butting her for attention. She laughed delighted tickling her furry ears 'this animal knows a mug when she sees one, Jack.'

And then she was gone in her whirligig way, kissing him lovingly on the cheek and waving enthusiastically as she hurried off to meet some friends. Her visit had lasted almost an hour but to Jack it seemed like five minutes. He'd see her parents and grandparents that weekend at the Archery club, maybe she'd be there, too. She had told him she wasn't certain, it depended on what her friends were doing. Jack was looking forward to a great weekend.

Joan had always doted on Sally, treating her like the daughter she'd never had. They had baby sat her, watched her take her first steps and Joan had willingly collected her from school when her mother couldn't for one reason or another.

Jack loved Sally deeply; he had coached her in archery from the time she had been big enough to hold a bow. Sally had always taken instruction from him far more easily than from either of her parents. She was an intelligent girl and picked up skills quickly.

A loving child, she'd called him Uncle Jack until she was fifteen. After that it was simply Jack.. He felt his heart soar as he closed the door behind her. It gave him great pride and satisfaction to see her growing into such a bright, beautiful, confident young woman. He and Joan had tried hard enough for a child of their own but it had just not happened.

*****

Sitting on the upper deck of the bus heading into the Saturday night townscape the two teenagers were looking forward to the evening. 'I've got some stuff Sally' Tracy said, closely watching her friend's reaction 'you know, to make sure we get a real buzz tonight.' She opened her purse and showed Sally four pink pills.

Sally's face switched from a frown to a pained smile and back again, her full mobile mouth not sure what to express. 'Oh.. er I promised my mum and dad I wouldn't do drugs' she said squirming. She was acutely aware that at college she had a reputation for being a goody-good girl. She felt pained that she wasn't considered to be one of the cool set and was often the butt of jokes because of it.

'Oh, I promised my mum and dad' Tracy mimicked, her tone deeply sarcastic 'really, Sal, when are you going to chill, uh? I mean, it's only ecstasy for God's sake, everybody does it.' She placed her hand on her friend's arm 'the bloke I got 'em off is an old friend from school, he wouldn't sell me crap.'

'You've had this stuff before then?' Sally asked surprised, Tracy nodded, a naughty twinkle in her pretty brown eyes 'yeah, a couple of times and it was great Sal, I was lit up like a Christmas tree all night. God, what a buzz.' She pulled on Sally's arm and leaned in. 'Look, why you don't just try one, OK? If you don't like it then that's it, you'll know for sure. Then you can say yup, tried 'em, don't like 'em, not for me, right?'

'Nah, I'll leave it Tracy, that stuff leads to trouble.'

'Oh gord, listen to the virgin queen' said Tracy rolling her eyes upwards. 'You're getting to be a bit of a drag you know Sal. I mean, I love you to bits, we've been mates since forever but, Christ, you're getting to be such a boring bitch.'

Sally felt close to tears 'what's got into you lately Tracy? You never said stuff like this before.'

'Before what?'

Sally blushed feeling embarrassed 'before.... you know... before you lost your virginity to that Waldo Williams guy' she blurted.

'Oh, so now you think I'm a slag, do you? Too good for me now, are you? You should try sex yourself Sal, there's nothing great about virginity.'

Sally started sniffling, feeling miserable, she hated confrontation 'oh, Tracy let's not fight, we're supposed to be going out for a good Time, aren't we?'

Tracy relented feeling sorry that she'd been so bitchy towards her friend. She put her arm around Sally's shoulder hugging her close. She loved her but wanted her to be worldlier after all, she thought, she's pushing eighteen and still a virgin for god's sake. Brendan Mostyn had told her that he'd slipped his cock into her hand when they were snogging after the prom and that she'd flipped, blushed beetroot and scurried off like a scalded cat.

'Sally darling, I only want you to be cool mate, you know? You're a great mate and I don't want to upset you, but you gotta chill girl, be more like the rest of us.'

'Oh, OK then if it'll shut you up' Sally said, feeling battered into submission by peer pressure 'but you've got to take one with me, OK?' Giggling mischievously Tracy produced the pills again, their brief argument already passing into ancient history; they each slipped a pill into their mouths and swallowed.

*****

Jack was watching the local news mainly to see the weather forecast for the following day. The keen archer and crossbowman was anxious to know about the likelihood of rain, the wind speed and direction, cloud cover and anything that could affect accuracy. He liked to shoot over longer ranges, he found the extra discipline and focus required rewarding. He was looking forward to a day's shooting at the club especially as there was a chance Sally would be there to give him some serious competition. OK, so they frowned on the crossbow, he couldn't use it at the club as its range was far too great for safety. But it had been almost a fortnight since he'd used his longbow due to his hunting of a pickpocket and he felt the need.

To his annoyance Jack's phone rang in the middle of the forecast. 'Hi, Jack, sorry to ring you this late but I've got some terrible news' said Vernon Allsop.'

'Hello Vernon, what on earth's the matter mate? Has the club burned down?'

'Have you seen the local news about the deaths?'

'The drug cases you mean Vernon?'

'Yes Jack' his voice broke and he began sobbing 'I'm sorry, so sorry, Jack, one of them was our Sally.'

Jack's breath hissed in through his teeth, he felt his heart lurch and miss a beat. Sally? His beautiful Sally? How could that possibly be? Jack felt a wave of shock and nausea engulf him.

'No Vernon, there has to be a mistake.... she's a good girl' he stammered unable to take in what he was being told 'she never took drugs, never. How?... Who? Oh Christ!' He sat down heavily in his chair feeling as though a giant fist had punched him in the guts, his heart pounding.

'She was here just this morning Vernon, laughing and joking in that madcap way of hers, drinking coffee and telling me off for not having the right biscuits.' His head reeled in confusion. His throat felt constricted and tears pricked his eyes. The images on the T.V. became blurred, the sound unheard. Sally, darling Sally, the child he and Joan had never had. They'd loved her so dearly, spoiling her whenever they got the chance and taking great pride in her achievements as she grew up. Vernon hung up, racked with sobs, unable to sustain the conversation.

Jack eventually dragged himself to bed that night but in spite of drinking most of a bottle of scotch sleep would not come. He kept seeing images of Sally at different stages of her young life. Her christening, although Joan and he were not practicing Christians they promised to do their best and they had. They had been present when she'd taken her first steps at her first birthday party. He 'd bought her her first bow, he had taught her to shoot. His heart ached and he felt physical pain compressing his chest as his silent tears flowed onto the pillow.

Over the next few days more details came to light. The police gave a conference asking for the public's help and announced that they expected developments soon but as the days dragged by this was beginning to look less and less likely in spite of a substantial reward being offered. The case was featured on television's Crime Watch programme but as time passed without results the story and accompanying hullabaloo dropped from the papers and news bulletins.

Detective Sergeant David Bardon knocked on his Inspector's office door.

'Come in Dave, have a seat'

'Thanks Ma'am, I've got the toxicology report on the two dead girls' he looked up from the papers in his hand as if wishing that what they contained could be changed 'It was the drugs ma'am, as we knew it would be' he sighed and shrugged his shoulders 'a rogue batch, five times stronger than normal and cut with a substance used for oven cleaning.'

In his twelve years as a detective Bardon had seen most things but it always depressed him when young people were the victims not only of the drug pushers but their own naivety, too.

Detective Inspector Jane Beaker-Rosen pushed the paperwork from in front of her 'Anything new since we last spoke Dave?'

'No Ma'am, I'm afraid not. We're sure it was Waldo Williams who sold them the drugs but, as usual with Khan's lot, there's a wall of absolute silence.'

'Every one of the people we picked up for questioning gave the same 'no comment' response throughout their interviews' Beaker-Rosen said her face tightening until a small muscle twitched in her jaw. 'A sure sign they've been got at Dave, but how do we break through it?'

'Dunno at this point ma'am, the reward is at twenty thousand pounds already.'

'It won't do any good putting it up by a few grand either Dave. If anyone was to talk they'd need to disappear forever and not even a hundred grand would be enough for that.'

'And we can't afford to go higher anyway' Bardon said his shoulders slouching. His long face and dull brown eyes gave him an air not dissimilar to a blood hound.

He glanced through the post mortem report again reflecting sadly that Sally Allsop had still been a virgin. Not even tasted the joy of sex poor little sod and now she's gone.

Tracy Anne Jenkinson had been about three or four weeks pregnant though she probably didn't know that at the time of her death. He thought about his own teenage daughter Becky and shuddered, God, he thought, feeling a chill run through him, this sort of needless waste is just so bloody awful. Two bright kids with all their lives in front of them. Shit!

Beaker-Rosen sat back and folded her arms beneath her ample breasts 'I believe MI5 may have an interest in Khan Dave though that mustn't go beyond these four walls for the moment.' She looked at him sternly 'this is for your information only, there's a suspicion he could be mixed up with the jihadist lot, arms, finance, that sort of stuff. He's been moving a lot of money lately, some of which has ended up with some suspicious charities.'

Bardon's eyebrows shot up 'bloody hell! I wouldn't have put him down as the crusading, fanatical type ma'am. Still, stranger things have happened' he paused considering the consequences of Beaker- Rosen's statement. 'Were news of MI5's interest to reach his ears' Bardon said 'Khan may well close up shop and clear off to the subcontinent, ma'am. God knows he must have enough money by now to enjoy a comfortable life back home.'

She unfolded her arms and fiddled with a pen on her desk for a moment as if lost in thought 'He's greedy Dave and an egomaniac to boot, that sort don't know when to call it a day so there's a chance he'll trip up yet. Say nothing to your team but keep your eyes and ears open with that in mind, OK?'

'Sure ma'am, I'll filter every bit of information with that a consideration.'

'We've got to keep the pressure up Dave, the Chief Constable wants a result badly on this one. As well as justice for those innocent girls there could be a hell of a lot more at stake.' She sighed, 'we need to be looking over their shoulders night and day to get these people behind bars where they belong.'

Beaker-Rosen stifled a yawn, suddenly she looked very tired. 'We know Khan has powerful political friends and I suspect he has a highly placed informants in the force Dave.' She paused looking straight into Bardon's eyes 'hence his seemingly charmed life. The raids on his shops last year produced not a damn thing, it was as if they'd been spring cleaned in honour of our visit.'

'Yes, then his sodding lawyers screaming loud and long to the media about police acting on rumour and gossip from vicious business rivals.' Bardon shook his head 'that didn't help our cause' he glaced through his notes. 'His charity work was pointed up and his poor-boy-made-good image burnished. All the usual crap.'

'Khan, when he's had a drink or two, likes to tell anyone who'll listen that he grew up on the streets of Lahore selling cigarettes to support his widowed mother. The truth is, Dave, he was the son of a prosperous businessman and had a private education.'

Beaker-Rosen felt a sudden anger as she said 'the smarmy bugger's lawyers will pile it on thick and heavy and of course play the race card. If we go near him again without damn strong evidence there'll be hell to pay. We can ill afford any more mistakes. If he has got a source in the force, and I'm sure he has, we'll have to play our cards very close to our chests.'

Bardon shuffled uncomfortably in his seat remembering his own connection with Khan. As a beat officer, some twelve years previously he'd often been called into one of Khan's takeaway shops to deal with drunks and trouble makers after the clubs closed. Sometimes he'd accepted a free kebab on a cold night.

Bardon had never taken money from him directly but Khan had 'arranged funds' as he termed it for special drugs and treatment for his daughter Becky when she was diagnosed with childhood leukaemia. The money came from one of the charities Khan sponsored. Becky was better now and Bardon had felt no guilt about accepting the favour. What father wouldn't be compelled to do all in his power to protect his little girl? Then, when Khan had asked for some relatively minor information, he had found it impossible to say no.

And so the process of the corruption of a good police officer had begun. Khan's brother-in-law owned a taxi firm which sponsored Bardon's son's junior football team. Then there was the use of a holiday villa owned by the friend of a friend in France at a very favourable discount. One thing led to another in a gradual, subtle process of seduction and soon he was providing a few more snippets of information to Khan. Recently Bardon had realised just what a precarious position he was sliding into and was now trying to extricate himself.

Khan can be a very charming and persuasive fellow, that's for sure ma'am.' Bardon said trying to keep his voice neutral 'and he does do an awful lot for charity, too, including the Police Benevolent Fund.'

'Yes Dave, and as we both know that's one of the tactics of a man with much to hide.' Beaker-Rosen said sourly 'that man is too sweet to be wholesome Dave, too sweet by far.' she added 'it's recently been rumoured that he likes underage girls, too, but there's no evidence to support that.'

Bardon's surprise showed in his voice 'really ma'am? That's the first I've heard of it.'

'The whisper came from a source very close to the Columbian cartel Dave so it's highly suspect. It's probably just a slur to divert attention from themselves' Her face hardened 'If there was the slightest bit of evidence I'd lift the bugger so fast he'd be dizzy.'

'I'll keep my ear to the ground ma'am but as you know there's a solid wall of silence where Khan's concerned.'

'Khan's organization have got be the one's who sold those girls the drugs that killed them' Beaker Rosen said 'no one else would dare work his patch. But how to prove it? All we can do is to keep chipping away Dave. Good, sound, basic coppering usually works in the long run.' She turned her attention back to the papers on her desk indicating the interview was over.

*****

It was two weeks after the funerals before Jack saw his old friend John Bryant again. He came into the archery club just to get out of the house for a couple of hours. His wife Eileen spent most of her days staring at the television taking nothing in, unable to accept that she'd never see her granddaughter again.

Occasionally she'd get up and make them a cup of tea then shuffle back to her seat. John had taken over most of the household chores and did his best but he was no cook, not that either of them had much interest in eating anyway. His loss of weight shocked Jack, he looked gaunt and drawn. Although John was a couple of years younger than Jack he now looked very much older. His eyes were dull and sunken with dark circles, his shoulders sagged and his voice had a hollow tone to it. Jack's heart ached for him.

Ordering a large pot of coffee Jack took his old friend over to a seat in the bay window away from the other members. After sitting in silence for a few minutes Jack cautiously asked 'How's Vernon and Sheila, any fresh news John?'

John looked at him, a bitter smile twisting his lips 'Vernon and Sheila are still unable to function Jack; they're totally lost. They had such great hopes and dreams for Sally.' He brushed his brow absently, a gesture that showed he found it painful to talk about it. 'The police have told us in confidence that they've narrowed it down to three possible dealers.' They keep saying they'll crack this case eventually but they never seem to get any closer Jack.'

'They'll have picked these suspects up for questioning then?' Jack queried.

'Oh yes, along with half a dozen others, but there's a wall of silence. No one's talking in spite of the reward offered and without evidence the police have their hands tied.'

Picking up his cup Jack took a long swig of his coffee letting the hot liquid burn its way down his throat. John's pain only served to bring his own to the fore. After a long pause to let the lump in his throat relax a little he asked 'any names, John?'

'Detective Sergeant Bardon, the guy in charge of the case, was a pupil of mine in my teaching days. He told us that one of the dealers, the chief suspect actually, went to the same school as Sally and Tracy. He was three years above them and had left to go to college but he dropped out to deal drugs full time.'

'Do you know his name, then?' Jack queried.

'Bardon couldn't tell us that of course so I asked some of Sally's friends. They knew who I was talking about straight away. His name is Waldo Williams, Jamaican father British single mother, twenty one years old. He rents a large flat and drives a damn great Merc sports car would you believe?'

Jack grimaced 'Oh yes, I'd believe all right, there's loads of money in the drugs game.'

'According to Sally's friends this Williams is a real nasty piece of work. He got one of his conquests pregnant and when she wouldn't have an abortion he dumped her.' John sighed deeply 'it seems that later, when she asked him for some child maintenance, he beat her half to death denying the kid was his.'

'He sounds a real charmer.' Jack grunted.

The weeks of numb stagnation, of living through the agony of the funeral, of the whiskey soaked nights when all he sought was oblivion, all this started to slide into the past. Now he had made a decision. He made up his mind up to meet this Waldo Williams character. At last he had a direction to move in. Something to focus on.

He said nothing more about it to John of course; it would have to be done with maximum discretion.

Jack changed the subject and they chatted about club activities for a while but it was clear John's heart was not in it. Presently he rose 'It's been nice to see you again Jack but I have to be getting back to Eileen. I don't like to leave her alone for too long, you understand.'

After John had left Jack sat deep in thought. This Williams guy might be innocent of course but he was a dealer and had knowledge of the local drug scene. If he didn't sell the bad drugs he probably knew who had so the use of a little non-standard interrogation technique was justified. No comment, eh? Jack thought to himself. We'll see about that, sonshine.

Driving home Jack found himself humming tunelessly, a habit left over from his Army days. He was going back to the work he knew best and some bastard somewhere was going to start talking.

Waldo William's flat was in block on the edge of the Shepherd's Bush area. Identifying Williams had not been difficult from John's description of him and the car he drove. The metallic purple Mercedes stuck out a mile. Jack had discreetly watched night after night from the roof of a multi-storey car park as the partying went on until the early hours. Rap music blared as people endlessly came and went in various states of inebriation, cavorted in the street and generally made a nuisance of themselves. He'd seen one couple making love on the top of a parked car, oblivious to the people walking the pavement near them. Waldo Williams never went anywhere without a couple of large thuggish looking youths with him; getting to this guy would not be easy. It took a tedious fortnight before Jack identified an opportunity.

Waldo left the party unaccompanied on Thursday nights about 11.30 p.m. to drive a few miles to a middle class housing estate. He parked his car and walked the last hundred yards to a well kept detached house in a cul-de-sac. Once there, he looked up at the softly lit bedroom window then, after checking all around, walked quickly down the drive and tapped the front door.

At the open end of the cul-de-sac Jack crouched behind a privet hedge training a small pair of binoculars onto the scene. The door opened to reveal a very pretty woman in her early twenties dressed only in a see-through negligee, she glanced quickly up and down the street before admitting Waldo.

Jack shook his head thinking to himself it won't be long before those two are caught out. Why the hell didn't he go around the back? Why does she think it necessary to glance up and down the street like that? Bloody amateurs, their body language positively shouted we're at it folks!

Jack waited, crouched behind the privet in the cold and damp, his legs stiffening painfully. When the bedroom light went out he slid out of his hiding place and walked to the house feeling the relief of the blood pumping in his legs once more. He went immediately round the back, soundlessly trying the back door. It was locked.

Next, he examined the kitchen window then went down the garden where he found an unlocked gate in the panel fence that led out to a service road. Excellent he thought, I'll have him next Thursday if her husband hasn't murdered the bastard first.

Waldo stripped slowly and paused for a moment to allow his partner to appreciate his well toned body and his magnificent manhood before he slipped into bed. Alison, his illicit partner for the night, looked at his nakedness and gave a small groan of desire 'Oh, you are such a big beautiful boy Waldo' she cooed. Taking hold of his penis she bent over it and kissed it, licking her lips before sliding it deep into her throat.

Jack didn't follow Waldo on his next date in the cul-de-sac, he knew where he'd be so there was no need to risk even a ghost of a chance of being spotted. He waited patiently until he was sure the nocturnal acrobatics were at an end then removed the haversack of tools from his car boot.

Making his way down the service road he checked himself at the garden gate jumping up and down to make sure nothing rattled. He felt the adrenaline coursing through his veins as he anticipated the night's action. God, he had missed this sort of stuff. Taking a deep breath he opened the gate and entered.

Stepping up on a garden chair Jack put the brace and bit on the bottom edge of the opening part of the top window. Steadily he turned the handle and the drill silently did its job until he had a half inch diameter hole under the window catch. Pushing a small screwdriver through the hole and flicked up. The catch bar slid up and he soundlessly opened the window. Reaching in and down he lifted the catch on the main opener. The window sill was crowded with plant pots and knick-knacks.

Stepping down off the chair, Jack replaced it to its former position. He smiled to himself as he placed an old leather wallet on the ground three feet outside the back door. Now for the fun bit he thought as excitement coursed through him. He opened the window wide and, using both gloved hands, gave a violent shove scattering the contents of the window sill onto the kitchen floor. The crashing noise seemed, after the silence of the operation so far, to be enough to wake the dead. He knew however that the neighbours were very unlikely to have heard it.

Jack paused until a light came on upstairs then stepped around the corner of the house. He drew a sock filled with lead shot from his pocket. And so it begins he thought.

Waldo and Alison were instantly awake. 'Oh no' she wailed 'he's back early. God, he'll kill me.'

'Shut up you stupid bitch. If it was him the lights would be on' Williams snapped 'It's burglars, we're being turned over. Bastards!' He leapt out of bed his heart pounding and slid quickly into his jeans, feeling in his hoodie pocket, he retrieved a flick knife and flew down the stairs barefoot. After glancing into the empty living room Waldo hurled himself into the kitchen flicking the light on. He saw the open window and the detritus on the floor. Putting two and two together he came up with five.

The clumsy bugger must have knocked the stuff off the window sill climbing in, he thought. Probably had it away on his toes by now but best to check. Opening the back door he peered out cautiously, staying back from the opening. In the pool of light from the door Waldo saw the wallet.

'Aha' he cried aloud 'got you now you silly bastard.' Stepping outside and reaching down for the wallet was the last thing Waldo Williams remembered for a long time after that.

Jack had unfolded the body bag he'd brought ready to receive its cargo. Swiftly he cable-tied Waldo's hands and feet, taped his mouth then rolled him into the bag zipping him up. He gripped the handles and heaved Waldo up into a sitting position then, crouching down with bent knees, he slipped him onto his shoulder and straightened his legs all in one smooth action. He found lifting the dead weight of his prisoner only just within his capabilities. As he staggered rather than walked to the garden gate his knees and hips hurt like hell, reminding him that age was not on his side. God, he thought, I'm getting too bloody old for this stuff.

Towards the end of the service road Jack dropped Waldo none to gently on the ground then went the few yards to fetch his car. Reversing into the alley he looked around carefully before heaving his limp load into the boot, tossing in his haversack of tools. Out of breath and sweating profusely his heart racing he drove away with a feeling of grim satisfaction for his night's work.

Waldo awoke in Jack's cellar stark naked, hooded and tied to a chair which was bolted to the floor. His head hurt like hell and he groaned. From somewhere nearby he could hear movement and smell fresh coffee. He groaned again and swore out loud 'Fuck man, whoever you are you'd better know what you're doing or you're one dead arse hole.'

The laughter had the ring of genuine amusement 'that so?' said the pleasant American voice 'Well tremble, tremble Waldo, you got me all shook up.'

Waldo was baffled; a yank? He didn't know any Americans, had never done business with them so he couldn't have upset anyone from over there. What the hell was going on? Losing a bit of his bluster Waldo said 'Listen man, whatever this is about we can sort it, yeah? We can do a deal. Who sent you man, her husband?'

His questions were met by total silence and Waldo began to feel panic rising 'listen man, I'm connected, right?' he said reverting to bluster once more. 'I'm one of Khan's boys, see? You know who Khan is don't yer? He runs things round here and he can make people disappear. Nobody fucks with Khan mate.'

This time Williams got a reaction in the form of a vicious backhanded blow across the mouth.

'Waldo' said the same calm patient voice 'nature gave you two ears and one mouth, that fact alone should tell you something.' There was a pause then the voice continued 'here's the deal Waldo: We know where you got the bad batch of drugs you sold those two dead girls. We need to know all about him, everything you know, and then you can walk. It's not you we're interested in pal but the main man, the wholesaler.'

Williams was shocked, how the hell could a yank be involved with that shit? 'Wha? What d'fuck you on about, man? It wasn't me that sold that shit, no way!' his voice was hoarse, his throat dry with fear. Again a stinging rap across the mouth jerked his head back. He spat blood from his split lips, cursed and wriggled at his bonds but they didn't give in the slightest.

After another pause the voice started again, this time close to his ear, this time low and sinister. 'Waldo, let me lighten your darkness a little. We know you sold those girls the drugs but you can only sell what your wholesaler sells to you, OK? Anything else would incur this Mr. Khan's displeasure, right?' The question was rhetorical and the voice continued 'He would take a dim view if you bought elsewhere Waldo, as you just said nobody fucks with this Khan guy, right?'

Jack was pleased. Waldo Williams had already given him the name Khan and told him he ran things without him even asking. It seemed his prisoner was none too bright, which would make his job easier.

Jack had perfected a Mid-Western American accent during his 'Green Slime' days. For one operation Jack's cover had been that of an American businessman sympathetic to the Provisional IRA cause. The Army got him a professional voice coach, an American lady, who proved an excellent teacher and even better in bed.. The

American authorities gave him a checkable background for his cover persona. He also spent a month in the States familiarising himself with the area he was supposed to come from, polishing his act. The operation had been a success. Three top terrorists were convicted, a boatload of arms and explosives seized and a major source of American funding cut off.

Jack's aim in kidnapping Waldo was threefold: Firstly, to glean information about the local drug scene. Secondly, to discover who the "Mr Big" was. Thirdly, to get enough info to mount an effective attack. Waldo had already divulged the first bit information without even realising his captor hadn't known who Khan was.

Jack wanted to spread fear and alarm within the organisation. The sowing of misinformation, half truths and well told lies was a tried and tested Green Slime technique. Introducing the buggeration factor into the enemies' lives made them uncertain, made them angry and angry people made mistakes.

To close the wholesale operation for good was a priority for Jack so he needed maximum detailed information. If he made his captive suffer some of the misery he'd so readily inflicted upon countless others, so much the better. It was time to up the tempo with some "Green Slime Therapy" or GST.

'Waldo, you disappoint me man, you really do' Jack drawled 'first you threaten me then you try to offer me some kinda bullshit deal.' Sensing the change of tone Waldo began to whine 'It's not bullshit man, I got money, man. I can pay you, honest.'

Waldo felt a rubber gloved hand lift his cock 'my but you're a big boy Waldo, no wonder that lady likes you.' Jack attached a bulldog clip electrode to Waldo's foreskin and heard him cry out in fear as the teeth dug in. Jack then quickly slipped his hand beneath the hood and fastened another to Waldo's ear lobe.

'Let me tell you what's going to happen Waldo' Jack said resuming his calm voice 'I've fixed up an electric shock machine to your delicate parts and now I'm going to show you what real pain is. Please feel free to scream as loud as you want.' Jack paused to allow this information to sink in before continuing 'this machine of mine can deliver anything from a very mild shock all the way up to barbecuing your balls Waldo.'

Jack watched Waldo's chest rise and fall rapidly in anticipation of the horror to come. He started to plead 'I don't know nuffink mate 'onest. Jesus mister, yer got to believe me. Please.'

Ignoring him Jack moved to his workbench behind his victim. The truth was the wires were attached only to a small hand cranked generator taken from an old Army field telephone. Turning its handle rapidly would create an alternating current needed to ring a phone at the other end. It produced a very unpleasant shock but nothing lethal. Jack knew that when using GST that half the pain came from the victim's imagination and anticipation of suffering; a sort of placebo effect in reverse. It worked very well and his former terrorist 'clients' could appear in court unbruised and apparently unharmed.

Turning the handle rapidly for five seconds Jack watched with satisfaction as Waldo arched his back as far as his bonds would permit and screamed in fear and pain. He waited whilst Williams subsided 'Good God Waldo, that was only the gentle end of the spectrum, we can do much better than that my boy.'

'Please mista, please, fer fuck's sake' Waldo pleaded rolling his head from side to side 'I don't know nuffink, please, no more eh?' In reply Jack turned the handle again this time much more rapidly and for a good ten seconds. Waldo screamed and writhed in agony. His genitals felt like they were being crushed and fried at the same time as knife was being thrust into his ear. Jack let his victim subside for a few moments before saying 'Now, Waldo, about these drugs?'

'Oh, Christ man, please, I'll tell yer what yer want man, anyfink, what do you want me to say, man?'

Jack recognised this stage of the proceedings and knew he was making good progress but, for now, Waldo was still thinking rationally, he would say anything to ease his situation. What Jack wanted was the truth therefore he had to break the man completely. He turned the handle again this time prolonging the pain for twenty agonising seconds. Williams screamed throughout. Jack then moved to the second act of his play.

Taking a hook attached to a block and tackle on a ceiling beam he fastened it to Waldo's wrists which were pinioned behind his back. He then cut the cable ties that were securing Williams to the chair and began slowly hoisting. Waldo's arms stretched up behind his back painfully before taking the full weight of his body. He began to scream once more. Being suspended like this, Jack knew, is hideously painful even fatal if carried to extremes. He had no intention of killing his man, others would do that soon enough.

'Just hang in there a while Waldo' Jack said 'I'll be back real soon, OK?' He doubted he'd been heard as the hanging man was screaming in agony his legs thrashing. Jack had no fear of the neighbours hearing as he'd long since soundproofed his basement workshop to a very high standard. Joan had not liked noise.

In his kitchen Jack fed Mischief before making himself a sandwich and heating some soup. After his simple lunch, he watched the one o'clock news whilst Mischief sat purring contentedly on the arm of the chair opposite as she licked her already glossy black coat. 'What do you reckon Missy?' he asked her 'do you think he might be a bit more subdued by now? No?' Well, perhaps a little longer then.'

Jack switched off the TV and sat back allowing his mind to drift back to the time he'd been recruited to this line of work. He'd been a young Corporal in 14th Company of the Army Intelligence Corps when he'd been approached by a Major who told him he was looking for a certain type of person and wanted to interview him for the possibility of a special mission.

The Major had worn no hat but on his uniform jacket were the red collar flashes of a staff officer. His name, he said, was Frank. He was to address this officer only by that name. So unusual was this that it had grabbed Jack's attention immediately. During the interview 'Frank' asked all sorts of questions that didn't make much sense at the time. Finally, Frank asked him to talk about his parents. To that question Jack replied in a voice devoid of emotion 'Fuck off!'

Frank had paused looking at him quizzically 'Why do you say that?' he'd asked calmly.

'Because you've read my file, you know I grew up an orphan, a Barnardo's brat,.' Then Jack had raised the stakes by adopting an aggressive attitude. 'Listen mate, when the Army pulls a stunt like this it's usually for some real shit job or something bloody dangerous. Which is it pal?'

'Dangerous.'

'How dangerous?'

'Sixty forty says you won't live to the end of your two year tour once operational.'

He had listened as Frank told him about certain people who were literally getting away with mass murder and how they had to be stopped. He was hooked. 'Well now, Frank, I've no one who'll weep for me, so why not?'

*****

Jack checked his watch it was time to talk to Waldo Williams again. Returning to the cellar he gave a satisfied grunt. Waldo was hanging, his head slumped forward, his breath coming in shallow gasps as the result of his compressed chest muscles tiring. He was moaning softly, a puddle of piss beneath his feet.

Jack moved over to the pulley and lowered his prisoner, guiding him back into the chair and securing him once more. 'You ever go to the movies Waldo?' He didn't wait for an answer 'you know, I just love that James Bond fella you Brits have, he's such a source of inspiration.'

He paused to let Waldo respond but all he did was whimper. 'I remember' Jack continued conversationally 'in one film the bad guy had a sort of iron hand with pincers. He was threatening to snip bits off Bond, you know, fingers and toes a joint at a time. Wonderful idea, don't you think?'

'Please man, please, I need water' Waldo croaked weakly 'then I'll tell you everythin' I knows, alright? Everythin.'

'Well now, we'll see about that real soon Waldo but first you need to listen to my idea, OK?' Jack said 'I noticed that magnificent cock of yours hasn't been circumcised yet and I have here a suitable implement for just such an operation.' Jack produced a set of garden secateurs and stroked Waldo's cock with them lightly watching him flinch in terror. He then stretched the foreskin and closed the blades lightly on it. He started to squeeze very slowly.

'Oh, Christ man, no' 'Waldo shrieked as the blades started to bite 'I've said I'll talk man, please, please!' His voice was a high pitched screech now as total panic engulfed him. Jack continued to slowly apply pressure until blood started to ooze through the skin then he stopped but kept the secateurs in place.

'I'm going to ask you some questions Waldo' Jack said 'some of which we know the answers to, some we don't. If I catch you in a lie man, I'll not hesitate to carry on with my surgery, no warning, no second chances. That clear?'

'Look mate, I ain't gonna lie to you, I swear man, I swear' Waldo felt the sharp pain from his privates above the intense dull ache from his arms and shoulders. Total terror seized his mind leaving him no option but to blurt the truth.

Jack then asked his questions: How did he buy his supplies? How were they delivered? Where did Khan keep his stash? He continued in this vein for a good half hour until he was satisfied that the dealer could tell him no more. Finally, with a light squeeze on the now bloodied foreskin, Jack stated 'And it was you sold those girls the bad stuff' Waldo had no more resistance left in him.

'Yeah man, it was me, but I didn't know it was bad gear man, you've got to believe me.' He paused, trying to clear his parched throat 'those bastards wouldn't give no refunds man, just told us to get it off the street as it was bringing too much heat. We burned the shit like they said. Nobody crosses Khan man, nobody.'

Jack removed the secateurs and paused for a moment deep in thought 'Then it's high time someone did, Waldo.'

Rational thought began to replace hysteria and it occurred to Williams that this bloke, having got his information, might well kill him and dump his body somewhere. 'What you gonna do with me man? Please let me go, I gotta kid man, I gotta a little kid. He's only a year old.'

'A kid whom you have never even seen and deny is yours, right?'

Jack made no effort to keep the contempt from his voice. 'You even beat his mother up when she asked you for a little money.' Jack felt a sudden surge of wild anger flood through him. He kicked the whining Waldo hard in the shin, his Oxford brogues cutting the flesh to the bone. 'You snivelling piece o' shit.'

Waldo screamed, he was on the point of hysteria again, the searing pain from his leg adding to the agony of his tortured body 'please let me go mista, please. I'll pay for 'im I swear and his mother, too' he sobbed.

Jack went to the end of the workbench and poured a coffee to give himself time to calm down. Getting angry would not help his cause. Much as he would have derived great satisfaction in putting Waldo Williams out of everyone's misery the man had a purpose to serve. Jack poured himself a second cup regarding Waldo dispassionately. He had subsided into a softly blubbing hulk slouched in his bonds, a totally empty shell.

'Relax Waldo, if I was going to kill you I would have removed the hood and let you see me do it.' Jack took a water bottle he'd prepared earlier and fed the plastic tube up under Waldo's hood.

'Drink' he ordered and heard the sucking slurping noise as the bottle's contents rapidly disappeared.

He left him then and returned at dusk. He brought a bottle of ether and the pad of bandage. 'Before I let you go Waldo, I want to tell you how lucky you've been. One of those girls was a relative of a good friend of mine, I wanted to kill you, I still do want to kill you but her family said no so I gotta respect their wishes.' He left a few seconds then added 'It's that Khan bastard we really want Waldo not minnows like you. I would have been here sooner but family business stateside delayed me and in our family, Waldo, you gotta take care of business first.'

Having planted the suggestion that Waldo was dealing with the American Mafia, Jack moved quickly on. 'You are now out of the drugs trade forever my friend, you understand?' Waldo nodded briefly 'if we hear of you pushing shit again I'll personally hunt you down and slice you into one inch cubes starting with your dick, you got that?' Waldo started to babble 'Yeah man, I got it, I got it. Please man untie me, I won't say nuffink man.'

Jack had gleaned from Waldo the little he knew of Khan's wider operation. It made sense that a man like Khan would not share the inner workings of his business with anyone who didn't need to know. Certainly not with the likes of Waldo Williams. That he was up against a highly organized, highly intelligent and ruthless criminal with a powerful organisation was very clear. Williams had told him that Khan had informers in the police. That Khan had spies everywhere Jack had no doubt whatsoever. Khan would find out about Waldo's interview and if he didn't Jack would find a way of letting him know. It was, however, better by far that the drug baron found out from his own trusted sources.

Khan could do the dirty work of disposing of Williams after extracting a pile of misinformation from him. Waldo would convince him that there was an American dimension in all this and keep him on the wrong foot whilst Jack made his preparations. Waldo Williams would suffer yet again before finally being dropped down a disused mineshaft somewhere or into the sea. Bugger him, he deserves all he gets Jack thought dispassionately. The fact that Waldo Williams didn't have much information troubled him though. He needed to get more if he was to deal with Khan effectively.

Waldo Williams woke up in darkness at the side of a deserted country lane his head throbbing with the worst hang over he had ever known. He groaned and stretched out a hand only to have it recoil instantly. He was lying in a bed of young stinging nettles stark naked. He moved again gingerly and again the agony of the potent nettles stabbed him. He sat up straight from the waist. This hurt a little less so he stood and waded his way onto the lane ah's and oo's escaping his pain-racked body. He limped painfully down the lane from one sharp place to another cursing under his breath. His skin was on fire from nettle stings, his arms felt like they'd been ripped out and stuck back in again and his leg was burning with pain from Jack's kick.

At last Waldo saw a ray of hope. Creeping cautiously into a Farmyard, praying he would not disturb any dogs, he stole a shirt from a washing line. He found a pair of white Wellington boots in a nearby milking shed. He staggered back to the road as a dog in the house began to bark. The shirt hung on him like a limp flag around a pole and was a bit short in the body but it would have to do. The Wellington boots were a size too small and hurt his feet like hell. After a mile Waldo sat down at the junction of the lane and a main road, his thinking confused and unclear. What to do now? He had no idea where he was or how he'd get back to London. If Khan got to know of this he was in deep trouble.

He found a public phone box but it had been vandalised. As he huddled in it for a few minutes trying to organise his thoughts he recalled the number of public phones he had robbed and vandalised just a few years earlier. The irony was not lost on him. Maybe if he could flag a car down on the main road he could spin some tale and blag or bribe his way back home. It was starting to get light and the traffic was building up. He made the mistake of trying to hitch a lift. After half an hour of thumbing Waldo, clutching the shirt tails between his bare legs like a character out of a West End farce, was picked up by police patrolling in an unmarked car. He told them it was a party prank gone wrong and that he was just trying to get home.

When the officers had finished laughing they called it in and had Waldo's details checked. Although he had no I.D. he was able to give details of several past arrests and convictions that only he and the police could have known. At the police station, they gave him antiseptic ointment to sooth his nettle stings and bound the gash in his leg. They didn't believe a word of his story of course but had no evidence of any crime.

They found him an old pair of trousers and a T shirt but no shoes. A local taxi firm was called to take him home after he reassured them he had money at his flat to pay. Waldo's adventure was now logged in the police system. Not only that but it was an amusing incident to be shared with colleagues, it wouldn't be long before Khan found out.

Ishmail Khan

'Hello Muszra, has the shipment arrived yet?',

'I've just had a call from the driver Mr Khan, he's stuck on the M25 he reckons another two hours at least.'

'Shit. Well, nothing to be done' he replied then his voice took on a slightly strained tone that Muszra Azziz had come to recognise 'I will be visiting friends in Camden Town, contact me only if very urgent.' Khan hung up, took a Viagra tablet and started his car.

Azziz put away his phone and poured himself a coke, a worried expression on his face. 'Friends in Camden Town' he knew was a euphemism for a visit to a certain guest-house-cum-brothel that specialised in providing underage boys and girls to a wealthy clientele. Recently, Khan had become besotted with a blonde thirteen year old and saw her as often as his time allowed.

Azziz had no qualms about under aged sex, his own mother had married at thirteen and his sister at fourteen so he couldn't understand why Westerners were so against it. What did concern him was that Khan might get caught and jailed. These underage sex things had a way of surfacing when least expected and his boss was going far too often lately.

Azziz was onto a good thing working for Khan but he knew that if the boss were to go down then his gravy train would pull out. The Columbians would move in and take over. He didn't fancy the idea of taking on those people. It was Khan who had all the suppliers abroad. Khan alone had the influence with the authorities. Azziz lit a cigarette and inhaled deeply, a worried frown creasing his face.

*****

'Suite twenty three Mr. King, she's waiting for you.' Khan smiled and handed over several high denomination notes. 'Thank you, Mrs Grey.' He went for the stairs without further talk, his excitement mounting with every step.

In the room, the girl was lounging on a lace covered king sized bed that emphasized how small she was. She wore only a pink see through shortie nightie, her young face made up far beyond her years. Her childish attempt to look older only served to make her look pathetic and vulnerable. She smiled her greeting, sticking out her half tennis ball breasts as she had been taught. This was exactly the look that turned Khan on.

'Hello, my dear' he crooned leering at her, feeling himself becoming erect 'I've brought a present for you.'

He handed her a pill which she took and swallowed eagerly. At least if she was high it would be less of an ordeal. She slid off the bed and stood before him her arms in the air. He slipped the nightie off over her head. Her slender waif's body was now fully revealed. She did a slow pirouette as he stared down at her, his eyes bulging. 'Help me undress' he croaked.

She moved obediently, her nimble young fingers deftly unbuttoning, unzipping with practiced ease until he stood naked then, at his signal, she knelt before him her pretty mouth receptive.

Ishmail Khan had been born in Lahore the only child of a prosperous businessman. He had received a private education and was being groomed to take over the family business. He'd been sent to London to do a masters degree at a business oriented university. He attended lectures and studied assiduously but never went home to take over this father's business. He had developed a taste for aged malt whisky, underage girls and the drugs business.

At first, he simply supplied drugs to his fellow students for kicks. It was an act of rebellion against his straight-laced father. Being ambitious by nature and seeing the vast profits to be made, he started to expand. Khan had put in years of hard work building up both his licit and his illicit businesses and in cultivating influence in high places.

In the early days, almost all of the profits were ploughed back into establishing a network of restaurants and takeaways in London, Birmingham and Manchester. Some of these establishments he used to distribute his drugs and all of them to launder his ill-gotten gains. A careful and utterly ruthless man, Khan never moved against an opponent until he was ready. He then struck with skill and lightening speed. He would first identify the hierarchy of opposing dealers, study their routine and then take out the leaders. They simply disappeared. Their followers would then either join him or die wishing they had.

At forty-five Khan was smooth, cultured character. He had married a girl of good family in London and had a son now fifteen at the same school he had attended in Pakistan. His daughter, twelve, was educated at a lesser establishment. He had sent his wife and daughter to their mansion in Lahore. Things were reaching a critical level in London with the fruition of a terror plot getting ever closer. If he had to run or hide afterwards he didn't want to be encumbered with family.

Downstairs he spoke to the madam jerking his thumb backwards 'She may need a little attention Mrs Grey, I'm afraid she didn't want to anal. I had to persuade her.'

'Don't worry Mr King I'll see to her, although it will cost extra.' Khan's eyes flashed and his mouth turned down at the corners in a mean scowl 'How much?'

'Two hundred.'

As he paid up she eyed him speculatively 'Do you like redheads? she asked casually.

He paused, his wallet still half way to his pocket 'maybe, how old?'

She could tell from the look on his face he was interested. Mrs Grey's cold blue eyes sparkled 'She's just twelve and still a virgin at the moment, four feet eleven tall, hazel eyes, very pale skin, slender and leggy. I can have her ready for next week.'

'I'll admit I'm tiring of the blonde bit now so how much?'

'We'll discuss the price next week Mr King, I don't know what my expenses will be yet.' Grey, a retired prostitute, was as avaricious and amoral as Khan. There was no way was she going to talk money now, she knew he'd try to bargain her down. Next week, however, when he was rampant again and with the girl in front of him he'd willing pay a premium. She knew her business.

Khan had a maxim he lived by 'Never let greed lead' by that he meant that gain was not the only factor to be considered in any deal. He always evaluated the risk involved, what were the chances of being cheated, betrayed or being caught by the authorities? Only once had he ignored this rule and now he was regretting having done so.

Bhakti had contacts in Afghanistan and had offered extremely attractive prices for the supply of high quality drugs. In return, Khan would make an initial donation to a small madrassah, a retreat for young Muslim men who were in danger of being corrupted by Western values. The UK branch of what was then a small extremist group called ISIS would be running it. Khan believed in those days that Al Queada was the only major player in the international terror game. These ISIS people were mere upstarts who would soon be put in their place. In the meantime, though, the price they were offering enabled him to make twenty percent more profit even after giving them their cut.

Now Khan was assailed with fears as to what would happen after the planned terror strike had taken place. He had known nothing of it when he made the deal with Bhakti, believing the Imam was simply lining his own pockets.

Ali Mansoor had told him of his nephew becoming involved after being recruited at the madrassah. It worried him greatly. They would no longer need him after the strike, of that he was certain. He would then be a loose end to be disposed of. Also, the authorities would be using every trick in the book to track down all connections.

Did he know too much to be allowed to live? Certainly. He knew Bhakti was involved and the man would need to protect himself. These ISIS people were utterly ruthless and difficult to deal with, yet he must keep them sweet for the moment. He'd keep his ear to the ground for more information. Could he could gather enough evidence to prove Bhakti's involvement and blackmail him? Khan sighed, he was riding on the back of a tiger. He didn't want to be there but if he got off he would be eaten.

*****

Jack let the last notes of Mozart's Requiem fade away; he paused for a moment before opening his eyes, when he did they were slightly damp. He'd had an excerpt from the work played at Joan's funeral as it was one of her favourite pieces. He thought of Sally and that last time she'd called on him so full of life, so beautiful. His heart ached.

He turned his thoughts to Joan. How long ago had it been now? Three years and five months, the time had dragged endlessly until things had suddenly changed between himself and Indira a month or so previously. She was rapidly becoming the new centre of his life. They had no immediate plans to live together yet, each being an independent soul. However, he knew even at this early stage in their relationship that he loved her.

Lifting and carrying Waldo Williams had told him that, despite the gymnasium three times a week, the swimming and the long walks, he was not getting any younger.

He pushed the thought aside at once as a picture of Sally's smiling face came to his mind once again.

If I should die ridding the earth of just a fraction of the murderous drug dealing scum that infested it then I would die in a good cause he thought. His anger surged again, a cold terrible fury that demanded vengeance. The people who were responsible for the death of his beloved Sally would pay the biblical price of an eye for an eye. He would destroy them. He took a deep breath 'yes, an eye for an eye, you murderous bastards' he said aloud.

Sitting upright on the floor Jack crossed his legs in the lotus position, it was time to calm all rage, put aside all thought with his daily meditation. Closing his eyes, he began to breathe slowly and deeply for a few minutes focusing on the cool air as it entered his nostrils and on the warm breath as it left his mouth. He began silently repeating his mantra.

As he focused on the centre of his forehead he saw brilliantly coloured patterns start to slowly move. Blues, reds and a deep purple all floated before him like wraiths of smoke. They seemed to be projected onto the inside of his forehead. Imperceptibly, the mantra slipped away, the colours disappeared and all conscious thought ceased. He was not asleep but totally still and completely at peace, devoid of all conscious thought for the next twenty minutes. When he returned to himself he knew what he wanted to achieve. How he would do it he didn't yet know but do it he would or die in the attempt.

Jack had previously Googled Khan and found him easily enough, a prominent Asian businessman with a string of restaurants and takeaways across London, Birmingham and Manchester. He also owned a food and spice wholesalers according to Waldo Williams. Strangely, it was not advertised anywhere and had no website. Most odd unless of course Khan wanted it that way to supply only his own business. If he was carrying out illegal activity there he wouldn't want customers calling.

Khan owned various homes up and down the country and a large house in Lahore. He was listed as a patron of several charities and he dabbled in local politics, too. On the surface Mr. Ishmail Khan was a rock solid citizen. Jack wanted to meet the mighty Mr. Khan personally to assess the kind of man he was dealing with, though that was easier said than done.

One piece of information Jack had extracted from Waldo Williams was that Khan visited a takeaway just four hundred yards from his home. He went there on the last Thursday morning of every month presumably to discuss the performance of his drug business. He kept tight control of his illicit empire and this shop was a major distributions centre. It was in the keep of one of his trusted lieutenants a large brutal man by the name of Muszra Azziz and his assistant the head chef called Ali Mansoor.

Jack planned his visit with care. Walking up the alley behind Khan's takeaway, Jack felt a nervous twitch as he approached the back of the shop. He could see the security cameras were state of the art and had infrared capability. When he was sure he was within camera range Jack started poking about under the numerous dumpster waste bins that lined the alley, with his bamboo walking stick. He looked around with the air of a man searching for something that may have been underneath the large steel receptacles. He peered into the back gates of the various adjoining businesses.

He was almost at the back of the shop when the gate in the adjacent premises opened behind him. Two Asian men one, a large fellow in traditional dress accompanied by a smaller man in Western clothes, approached him. The smaller of the two men didn't bother to hide the suspicious scowl on his rat-like features. The man's looks were not helped by the thin moustache under his pointed nose.

The big man spoke quietly 'Hello my friend, can we help you? Have lost something?'

Jack smiled disarmingly, 'oh hello, er yes, yes' he said in a vague manner 'I've lost my cat, Mischief, she's been gone two days now and I'm rather concerned for her you see.' he scratched behind his ear and looked about rather vaguely. 'She's getting on a bit and I do worry about her.'

Rat face spoke in a slightly falsetto voice 'Well, as you can see she is not here' he said sharply. He opened his mouth to say more but he was interrupted by the large man.

'What does she look like sir?' he enquired politely 'we do get quite a few strays around here because of the food waste bins.'

Jack pulled a sheaf of papers from his pocket 'well thanks for your interest. I've made some posters with her picture.' He peeled one off and handed it to the big fellow 'I'm going to put these up in the area and ask the local shop keepers to do the same.'

The big man looked at the poster and smiled 'Why don't we put one up in our shop, sir? Please, come through the back here.' He put a strong hand on Jack's shoulder and guided him to the back gate of the shop. Although the man's pleasant demeanour never changed, Jack knew this wasn't a request but he allowed himself to be led into the back yard.

This was better than he'd hoped for. If they had ignored him in the alley Jack would have called at the front door where he might have been simply ignored. By arousing their curiosity watching his antics on CCTV, he stood a better chance of achieving his purpose. This way they'd found him for themselves. He was there by their invitation.

'Why thank you, that's so kind of you' Jack enthused with a broad smile. Rat face fell in behind as if to block any escape.

They entered the shop down a corridor, the kitchen was off to the right with a storeroom opposite. The entrance to the shop was directly in front through a beaded curtain. In the kitchen a chef was busily preparing food, his back towards them. 'Through here please' said the large man leading Jack into the shop. 'let me introduce you to Mr. Khan, the owner.'

At a side table, where customers could eat in if they chose, sat a tall athletic looking man who was in his mid to late forties by Jack's appraisal.

He's sure not short of money Jack thought, that suit is Saville Row, the shirt pure silk. As he stood up and approached Jack he noticed the man's expensive handmade shoes. Khan's face held an expression of polite enquiry as he said 'hello, I'm Khan, what can we do for you Mr…er?'

'Ellis, Jack Ellis Mr. Khan. I'm looking for my cat you see…' He was interrupted by the large man who rapidly explained in his native tongue that he'd found Jack snooping around in the alley. Khan listened intently giving Jack a chance to study his clean shaven face in more detail.

He thought his original guess of Khan's age to be between forty five and forty nine years of age accurate. Khan's large piercing eyes were like pools of liquid tar and were quick and intelligent. His look was direct and intense, almost a stare. His mouth had a sharp cruel look to it caused by the slight downturn at the corners. This man was clearly the boss as evidenced by the big man's deferential body language. Jack felt a slight shudder run down his spine. He's certainly no mug Jack thought; I'll have to be very careful around this one.

The big man finished speaking and Khan nodded before turning to Jack his face suddenly illuminated by a broad smile. 'These gentlemen are my shop manager Mr Muszra Azziz and my head chef Mr Ali Mansoor.'

Jack smiled and nodded politely to each in turn 'pleased to meet you Muszra, Ali.'

'Well Jack my friend' said Khan in a slightly too familiar way 'we will certainly put up one of your posters in the shop and will ring if your cat turns up.' He then switched off the smile as rapidly as he had acquired it. He didn't know why but there was something about this older man that made him feel nervous. Maybe it was his pale grey eyes or the cool confident way he stood. He looked like a man who had killed, or could kill.

'Tell me, Jack' asked Khan 'what on earth makes you think your cat would come around here?' There was an interrogative edge to his voice that warned that any lie would need to be a good lie.

Jack had anticipated this sort of question, he smiled disarmingly 'she's a greedy animal and she loves curry, it's her favourite. I live only four hundred metres away so she could quite easily have been attracted by your waste bins.'

'I see' said Khan who now appeared most concerned. He paused before continuing 'Jack' he said in a sombre voice 'I don't want to sound alarmist but that alley at the back of here really isn't safe you know.'

'Really?' said Jack a look of surprise crossing his face 'Why ever not?' 'There was a vicious mugging there quite recently' Khan said frowning 'surely you must have heard about it?'

Jack remembered a report of a local mugging some weeks previously 'Oh yes, yes, now that you mention it I do remember something in the papers' he said, 'was that this alley, then?'

'It certainly was' Khan replied looking deeply into Jack's eyes as if trying to make his mind up about something. 'You know an older gentleman like yourself who relies on a stick would be a big temptation and an easy target for the muggers. They show no mercy you know.'

Khan was trying to see if Jack scared easily, he didn't want people wandering about around the alley and maybe witness a dealer coming to collect his supplies.

Jack adopted a worried expression 'Oh dear, thank you for the warning. I'll not be going down there again, that's for sure.' He could act the meek and mild little old man expertly, he just hoped this sharp eyed fellow found him convincing.

Khan pondered for a moment then decided to use flattery. 'Are you fully retired now Jack?' he asked sounding politely interested. Jack told him he was and Khan went on to ask why a fit looking man like him needed a walking stick. Jack answered that he had to use it most days now due to an arthritic hip.

'Ah, I thought it might be an old war wound' Khan said smiling.

'War wound?' Jack said sounding incredulous 'I've never been near a war in my life' he laughed 'I was a Trading Standards Officer for forty years, quite boring really.'

The TSO role was one he'd learned about in detail in order to fend off awkward questions about his job in security. He practiced until he could drone on for ages about rules and regulations if he had to. Most recipients of this information on the rules and regulations rapidly became bored enabling him to change the subject.

After a bit more subtle probing disguised as small talk Khan called out to the chef in the back who had already anticipated his boss's request. He came to the serving hatch handing through a paper bag. Rat faced Ali, as Jack had named him in his mind, took the bag and handed it to him forcing a smile.

'A small gift Jack' smiled Khan 'just some samosas, one of our many specialities you know.' Once again oozing charm he picked up Jack's walking stick from where he'd propped it against the table. He hefted it almost imperceptibly as he handed it over.

He led Jack to the front door reassuring him the poster would be put up promptly and that he would ensure all staff were informed to keep an eye out. Jack thanked him profusely and left.

So that was the famous Khan he thought, a real slippery bastard if I've ever met one. Jack then called at all the other business in the row handing out his leaflets, keeping up his act of the elderly man worried about his missing pet.

As the door closed behind Jack Khan turned back to his colleagues deep in thought. 'Silly old fool' said Mansoor, his voice filled with contempt 'what sort of a man keeps a cat anyway?'

Khan spoke sharply 'shut up you fool, have you learned nothing from me?' He may be all he says he is but he has very intelligent eyes and the air of an ex military man no matter what he says he was. He also looked far too fit to need a stick.' He paused thoughtfully the bamboo walking stick had been too light to be a swordstick, gun or club. The man's purpose for being in the alley had seemed genuine with his sheaf of reward posters but still he felt a sense of of unease. He waved his hand dismissively. 'Anyway, to business, I haven't got all day.'

Strike One

Indira Bhatti was a librarian. She was also a polyglot speaking no fewer than five of the subcontinent's languages fluently and had a working knowledge of a couple more. A comely widow of fifty eight she always dressed herself smartly in Western clothes for work and the sari for her leisure time. Normally a shy, self-effacing person, a couple of months previously she had determined that she would get to know Mr Jack Ellis a little better.

'Hello Jack, have you read all those books already?'

She smiled warmly and took his returned books 'My goodness' she said 'you are overdue on this one and I must have you arrested immediately if you do not pay a twelve pence fine.'

Jack laughed, he liked this attractive mature woman with her jovial smile and kind eyes. Handsome lady he thought. Yes, that's the correct word for her, handsome. 'I'll see if I can scrape it together' he said with mock seriousness.

In selecting his new books Jack took time and care, life was too short to waste reading rubbish. He returned to the counter and Mrs. Indira Bhatti. Ah, she thought, one on Indian recipes. Seeing her chance she said. 'I see you like Indian food Jack, do you cook much?'

'I try Indira, but I'm no expert, mine always seems to come out quite differently from the pictures in the book.' he gave a rueful smile 'they probably taste nothing like they should either.'

She laughed. 'As it happens' she said, tilting her head to one side in that attractive way Indian women have, 'I was going out to a rather special restaurant tonight but the lady I was going with has cried off at the last minute.' She lowered her eyes demurely for a moment then looked up through fluttering lids 'would you think me too presumptuous if I asked you to escort me?' she then smiled sweetly, a picture of respectability and decorum 'you'll have an excellent example to judge your own efforts by.'

Jack looked at her closely feeling pleasantly surprised but also bemused by the formality of her request. A shy grin stole across his face. It had crossed his mind to ask her out in the past but the thought that it might spoil their friendship scared him. He only saw her every couple of weeks and loved their chats. It was the fear of jeopardising them that had held him back.

'Oh, well, yes I don't mind' he said then, noticing her frown, corrected himself at once 'that is to say yes, yes please, I'd be delighted Indira, what time? Where shall I pick you up?'

On the walk home Jack felt like punching the air as a feeling of joy changed his mood completely. He'd had other women show an interest in him since Joan died of course, but always he had suspected their motives. He owned his home outright and it had sky-rocketed in value over the years. He drove a nice car and was financially solvent, well off in fact. One of the women he'd met had, on their first date, asked unsubtly 'Do you have an accountant, or do you do your own tax?' She had been blown out sharpish.

Indira was different. In all their chats she had never shown the slightest interest in his finances. He knew from their talks she took holidays back to her beloved India at least twice a year, so she wasn't short of money not that money mattered to him if he met the right woman.

Indira had not invited him to her home but to a restaurant, neutral ground, good for them both. It would be a pleasant change to put aside his work for an evening. He'd been spending a lot of time in his cellar lately planning and making things he thought he may need to deal with Khan.

The restaurant turned out to be a revelation to Jack; it was an Indian vegetarian one. 'I've never eaten in a vegetarian restaurant before' he said studying the menu.

'Be prepared for a real surprise' Indira said.

Jack, who saw vegetables as supplementary to meat, prepared himself for a disappointment and to go home hungry. Not only was the food that Indira had recommended some of the best he'd ever tasted but he came away happily replete both physically and spiritually.

As he dropped Indira off, she leaned across the car and thanked him. Her perfume was both subtle and at the same time heady, filling him with a desire he had not felt so strongly for a long time. She kissed him lightly on the cheek and fixed him with a dazzling smile

'It's been the most wonderful evening, Jack' she told him 'please, let's do it again soon, OK?' He had readily agreed thereby opening a whole new chapter in his life.

*****

'Hi Muszra, I'll have a lamb tikka masala with boiled rice, a couple of those great vegetable samosas of yours and some lime pickle please.'

'It'll be about ten minutes Jack, will you wait or come back?' Azziz asked.

'I'll wait, thank you.'

'Did your cat come back, Jack?'

'Yes Muszra, she did thanks, but not until this morning. She smelled of engine oil.so she'd probably got herself locked in someone's garage.. I found her on the doorstep looking bedraggled and she was starving, too, but otherwise she seems fine.'

Jack looked at the big man assessing him carefully. None of his huge frame was surplus fat, obviously this man worked hard on his body.

'Great news. Right, I'll pop your order through' and with that Azziz went through the beaded curtain to the kitchen.

Jack sat down at the table and looked casually around the shop, his expert eye taking in every detail. It was early evening and he was the only customer. He noted that the camera which covered the entrance and most of the shop was above his head and he was out of its angle, so far so good.

Slipping his hand in his pocket he brought out some loose change and started counting it, he then dropped a coin on the floor and bent to pick it up. In doing so he stuck a listening bug to the underside of the table and with a deft move checked that it was firmly fixed. He then sat up and continued counting his loose change. There may not have been a hidden camera looking inward from the front door but why take chances? Ten minutes later he collected his food and left after taking down his missing cat poster and thanking Azziz for his help.

In the Army, it'd been drummed into him over and over that an ounce of precaution was worth a ton of mending. Operations he'd subsequently been involved with proved this to be very true. 'Just 'cos we're the clever guys' his instructors had told him repeatedly, 'don't assume that we're the only clever guys, that way leads to disaster.' They also had another saying more typical of the Military: The seven "P's" 'Poor prior planning produces piss poor performance.'

Dialling into the device shortly after the takeaway's closing time that night Jack recorded three members of staff sitting around the table drinking coke and chatting before going home. Of course he didn't understand a word of Urdu but he knew someone who did if, that is, he dared to involve her.

He was surprised to hear the word jihad mentioned three or four times and his own name mentioned twice but the latter he put down to the news of his cat being found. After ten minutes, someone farted loudly and they all laughed and made what he assumed were the usual bawdy remarks men made on these occasions. Then they left the shop and Jack cut the call and checked the recording.

As a lone operator Jack knew he had to be cautious, there was no room for mistakes. If he was to inflict maximum damage on Khan's drug empire his strike had to be fast and effective. He'd only get one shot at it. If he was caught they would kill him.

Disinformation

Waldo Williams sat in Khan's North London home staring into the deep dark eyes of his boss. Azziz stood behind him arms folded across his massive chest looking down with cold indifference.

'Honest Mr. Khan, I told the cops it was a party prank, that I'd passed out drunk and me mates did it for a lark.' He shuffled uneasily in his chair 'That seemed easiest, most believable, like.' His voice trembled slightly, betraying the fear that was raging through him.

Williams had thought Khan would find out sooner or later. He hoped it would be much, much later. He'd hoped to have had enough time to track down the Yank and kill him and by doing so his story would be the only version. If Khan found out about him he was finished.

'None of your men would dare to pull such a stunt Waldo, so what really happened?' Khan felt his paranoia rising.

'I was in bed with this bird Alison; she's a great shag, I give her one while her husband's away on business. He came home early and caught us at it. He clobbered me with something heavy while I was still asleep, the twat.' Williams paused and rubbed his head 'I've still got a bloody great lump on me head' he looked at Khan trying to gauge if he was being believed or not but it was impossible to read his impassive face.

He continued 'next thing I knew I woke up somewhere out in the sticks stark bollock naked and freezing me arse off in a nettle bed. Stung to fuck I was. I managed to nick some gear off a clothes line and was getting back home when the Filth stopped me. I didn't mention it to any bugger boss 'cos it's nothing to do with the business and I would have lost respect.'

Khan nodded his eyes boring into Waldo. He knew all about Alison of course. He made it his business to know everything about his main players. He suspected there was something Williams was not telling him. Maybe it was just his embarrassment at being caught off guard but he needed to be sure.

'This husband, what are you going to do about him? Presumably you'll want your revenge?'

'Yes, but not straight away Mr Khan sir' said Williams, a flash of inspiration coming to him 'I've learned a lot from you sir, like not drawing attention to myself.' He smiled slyly 'I'm going to wait a few weeks then, when he's least expecting it, he'll have an accident.' He hesitated and added deferentially 'with your permission of course, Mr Khan.'

Khan smiled and nodded knowingly as if accepting Waldo's story. By using flattery Waldo Williams had ramped up his suspicion that his man was hiding something. 'That cock of yours will get you killed one day Waldo' Khan said jovially. Then he turned suddenly serious again 'OK, Waldo, we'll leave it at that unless there's anything you want to add...?'

The few seconds pause seemed like an hour to the petrified dealer but he shook his head in the negative. If Khan knew he'd given information about the business to some strange yank he was a dead man.

'OK Waldo, but if I find out later that you are hiding anything from me….' He left the sentence unfinished, he looked at his huge thug 'show him out Muszra.'

*****

Although he had recorded almost an hour of conversation from the takeaway over three nights Jack had no idea of the content as he understood no Urdu. He knew of course that Indira was fluent but was reluctant to ask her. What if there is criminal information, the knowledge of which could put her in danger he thought?

His second concern was that he feared Indira might think he was a user, that his friendship was motivated by his need for sex and her interpretive services. He could not, of course, pay a translator as that would be too high risk. He could simply hand the material to the authorities. However, without knowing what was being discussed it could seem like a hoax. Then, later, when he relied on them believing him, he would be dismissed as a crank. He had to admit, too, that there was a large place in his heart that desired a personal involvement in wreaking vengeance on these people.

Going over the information he had extracted, Jack knew that drugs were stored in the empty shop next to the takeaway. How the drugs got into the country and how they were then distributed was a mystery to Waldo Williams. This made sense of course, a man as shrewd as Khan would never divulge such information. Williams knew the stuff arrived at the shop weekly on Thursday afternoon in a wholesaler's delivery van.

When he wanted to buy more drugs, Williams would either call in person or he'd order a takeaway meal which would be delivered with his supplies C.O.D. The other method used was the taxi firm just down the block that was owned by Khan's cousin one Mohammed Ul Haq.

Williams also told him that he believed Khan had some high powered protection both in the police and politics as well. He always seemed to know what was going on, where the drug squad would raid and when but Waldo was, as expected, short on facts.

Jack knew that if he merely informed the police Khan would get to know and shift his stuff long before the drug squad could organize a raid. All he would achieve using that tactic would be to slightly inconvenience the man. That wasn't nearly enough.

His thoughts turned to his sweet young Sally and he saw her face before him, her tinkling laughter ringing in his ears. Damn these bastards to hell he thought as he felt his gorge rise. His clenched fist trembled, his knuckles showing white as a spasm of intense anger shook him. 'No,' Jack told Mischief, 'I want to cause these slimy bastards some serious grief. I want to destroy them, to drive them to distraction then to destruction.'

Jack's urge to break Khan before taking him out was overwhelming. He wanted maximum vengeance. For Khan to suffer a quick crossbow bolt in the head would not be sufficient. Besides, others like Azziz would take over immediately and the carousel would go on turning. He needed to strike real fear into their hearts before obliterating them.

Just how to do it? was the foremost question in Jack's mind. The security was damn tight around the shop. There was no way anyone could just walk up and steal the drugs short of having a small army and he was alone.

Jack sat in deep meditation for forty minutes that evening letting go of his problems and all conscious thought. He then went to bed and slept soundly.

As so often happened when he directed his sub conscious to find a solution an idea came to him. Not all at once but first a bare bones solution. Jack worked on the idea over the next couple of days. For this first part he wouldn't need the recordings translated. This bit he could do with the information he already had. That it wouldn't be easy he knew, but with careful planning he could execute his ideas. He felt daunted not having done anything remotely like this for years. Fear gripped Jack for if he slipped up, if they even suspected he was behind it, he would die.

He thought of Indira. What a woman, so beautiful, so gentle, so intelligent, it was wonderful just to be around her. The thought of losing what he had found with her filled him with dread. Then Sally's pretty face again came into his mind, yet again he was haunted by her laughter, saw her smile and a single teardrop formed. 'How can you not try?' he asked himself aloud. 'What are you, Jack Ellis? A scared old man?'

Firstly, Jack bought some light aluminium tubing then went to work on some powder he hadn't made up for years. A few other simple items finished the job. Jack then drove out to the New Forest and, making quite sure he was alone, tested his device. It worked more spectacularly than he could have hoped; now for the hard bit.

Having done reconnaissance of the streets adjacent to Khan's takeaway Jack saw the best solution was to gain entry to the derelict St Martin's church two streets and almost seventy metres from the back of Khan's premises. Entry would be fairly easy as vandals and rough sleepers had done severe damage. The building, long stripped of its roof lead, was in such a bad state of repair that even the rough sleepers had abandoned it of late. It was a very unstable building so skill, luck and caution would be needed.

On the next Wednesday night just after eleven o'clock, dressed as an old tramp, Jack shuffled up to the security fence that surrounded St Martin's, an old haversack on his back. He squeezed through the gap in the chain link fence with its danger warning signs and made his way to the door. Once there he looked around and waited in silence, crouched in the darkness of the porch. After listening for five minutes he heard nothing but the sound of his own soft breathing and a distant buzz of traffic.

Drawing a short crowbar from beneath his coat he prised off a board that had been nailed over a smashed door panel in a vain attempt to keep out intruders.

Once inside Jack switched on a small torch and made his way to the bell tower. The door to the stairs had long ago been wrenched off its hinges and used as firewood, giving easy access. Fortunately, the stairs were made of stone. He crept up and tested the floor cautiously. Some planks were missing and others rotten. By staying close to the wall he reached the stone slatted windows. The view was as expected and the flooring seemed to be firm despite the thick layer of pigeon droppings. He checked that he had a clear view of the back of Khan's takeaway. He left the building as surreptitiously as he had entered it replacing the board on the entrance.

Fire, Fire.

Jack watched from a small café, a hundred metres from Khan's takeaway, it was Thursday afternoon and if Waldo's information was correct a wholesaler's van should be calling quite soon to deliver supplies along with a substantial consignment of drugs.

Sure enough, as Jack finished his third cup of coffee the van drew up. He felt excitement quicken his heart but stayed outwardly calm. The driver, a large muscular man, spent the next five minutes carrying boxes into the shop. He acted casually, taking his time looking exactly like what he was supposed to be, an ordinary delivery man.

Jack made a note of the business address on the van's side. Right, he thought, let's see what they have there. He left the cafe and drove to the address. He surveyed the building from a distance at first, it was a large industrial unit on a small trading estate. He kept his distance so as not to arouse suspicion,sweeping the area with binoculars. The building was fitted with a floor to roof roller shutter door across its entire frontage. At the sid,e a normal entrance door. At the back was an emergency fire exit. The ground floor windows had all been bricked up. Drug dealers were cautious people.

Jack checked his watch then drove off to a DiY store where he made a few purchases before returning. This just might turn out to be easier than he had expected so best be ready to take advantage.

At five o'clock two men left the premises. He could tell by the way their jackets hung they were carrying guns. One was carrying a small hold-all the other a large plastic bag from a supermarket. So, he thought, they're off for the night not just nipping out for a takeaway. They drove away in separate cars.

Jack watched and waited, surely a night watchman would arrive soon? At five twenty the van he'd watched earlier pulled onto the forecourt. The burly driver, a caucasian of about thirty five, climbed out and went to the roller shutter door and operated the opening mechanism. He then drove the van inside and lowered the door unaware that a man with a pair of cold grey eyes was watching him.

Jack guessed the driver would emerge from the side entry door. He donned his haversack, picked up his walking stick and moved quickly to the far side of this door, pulling on a full-face silk balaclava. This was too good an opportunity to miss.

He didn't have long to wait before the door swung outwards hiding him from the departing worker. As the guy turned to close the door Jack struck. The hollow bamboo walking stick now contained a solid lead insert and he swung it in an arc at the man's head. The driver's eyes widened with shock, he tried to jump backwards but he was far too late. He went down emitting a slight groan. Jack grabbed him under his shoulders and with great effort dragged him back through the door; he then went outside to retrieve his walking stick and haversack.

Back inside the alarm the man had set continued to beep its count down. He knew he didn't have long before it started screaming. Jack had laid the driver down inside the door and had just walked passed him when his legs were snatched from under him. He fell with a crash onto the concrete, knocking the breath from him.

Inwardly he cursed himself for not securing his man immediately. The shock of the fall jolted him badly and pain shot up his back. The powerful driver was hurting bad but managed to crawled up Jack's prostrate body, pinning him down. He wrenched the balaclava off Jack's head.

'Jesus,' he exclaimed in surprise when he saw his opponent was an older man.

The driver pinned Jack's legs and lower body with his weight he then struggled to his knees still groggy from the head blow. Straddling Jack, he leaned forward and grabbed a lapel with his left hand pulling back his right to deliver a punch 'Right you old bastard' he snarled 'you're dead.'

Jack groped around desperately for his stick his fingers closing on it just as the driver dragged him up into a sitting position in order to hit him as hard as possible.

As he was pulled upright, Jack used the momentum to swing with all his might, sheer desperation lending him strength. He brought the weapon down hard on top of the man's skull, hearing the sickening thud and crunch of fracturing bone. The man's eyes rolled up into his head and he fell forward on top of him pinning him to the floor, thin streams of blood were oozing from the driver's ears and down his nose. The big man twitched convulsively, his feet shook briefly then he was still.

Struggling out from beneath the guy was difficult but Jack managed it just as the alarm kicked off screaming. Shaking at his near miss, he staggered cross to the door and locked it. If the alarm was connected to a monitoring service then a phone in the building would ring very shortly. If he answered it they'd want a code word. If it went unanswered, then they'd send a security guard. He had time but not much.

No phone rang. Jack knew hardly anyone passing by would take notice of a burglar alarm, treating it as just another everyday nuisance. If someone did come and check the premises they would find the doors locked and no sign of forced entry and just assume it was another false alarm.

Looking around the windowless warehouse the only light came from skylights and one small panel high up at the top of some stairs where there was an office on a mezzanine floor. There was floor to ceiling shelving units along three sides and and down a centre aisle. They were packed with huge catering sized jars, sacks, tins and bottles stacked from floor to ceiling mostly on wooden pallets. The air was pungent with the smell of exotic spices. At the far end of the unit was a butane powered forklift truck. Jack moved to it swiftly. Starting it up, he tried the various levers to see what they operated. Satisfied, he put the vehicle into gear and drove it slowly around the side of the van placing it carefully, he then adjusted the forks.

Jack accelerated the forklift into the van's side smashing through the outer skin and hitting the fuel tank, splitting it wide open. The fuel gushed, spreading far and wide. Climbing down Jack opened his rucksack and took out the half gallon of mentholated spirits he'd bought. He doused the fork lift and laid a trail to the fire door that would be his exit point.

Jack soaked an old cleaning rag he found in the spirits and put a light to it then threw it to the floor. The spirits caught instantly, the blue, almost invisible flames, racing to the edge of the spreading pool of diesel. It caught the fork lift first which started to blaze. The diesel caught not with a whoosh but slowly, gradually spreading boiling black smoke. The alarm continued its banshee screech. It was time to go.

Killing the driver at the warehouse had not been part of Jack's plan. He had meant to drag him out again after firing the building. He regretted the death only in as much as that he'd been careless and cursed himself for not using his cable ties on the guy straight away. Getting careless in your old age, he told himself.

The man had seen his face and the first rule of engagement in his old profession was no witnesses. The death didn't weigh on his conscience, the man was part of the organisation that had killed his Sally. It was just his bad luck Jack thought. If he hadn't chosen to be in the drugs game it wouldn't have happened.

Now he had to get rid of everything he had been wearing. Driving into his garage he laid an old tarpaulin on the floor and stripped off whilst standing on it. He then went into his house naked, showered and found some old clothes. Putting the tarpaulin bundled clothes in his garden incinerator Jack piled some old branch cuttings on top and soaked everything with petrol and lit it. He stood over the blaze poking it to ensure every thread was destroyed.

*****

Khan received a call from his warehouse manager informing him of the fire at the business. He rushed there at once and was gutted by what he found. The place was a blackened shell, the roof mostly missing. The office, a wooden structure and the mezzanine floor, was totally gone. He'd just had a container delivery with this month's supplies of drugs most of which were still in the warehouse awaiting distribution the next day. The timing could not have been worse.

The firemen were still damping down, moving about in the ruins with sprinkler hoses spraying hot spots that could potentially reignite. Khan found the officer in charge hoping they had not found any split cans of chickpeas.

'As far as we can tell at this early stage sir it looks like it was just a tragic accident' the officer said sympathetically 'It would appear your worker driving the fork lift crashed into the van splitting the fuel tank and igniting the fuel. We found what was left of his body by the side of the forklift truck poor devil.' He went on reporting what he knew and informing Khan that an investigating team would be calling next morning.

The police asked for details of the casualty's identity, next of kin, whether Khan was insured etc. Khan answered in a daze, too stunned yet to function properly. What the hell was that idiot doing driving the forklift? One thing he knew though, he had to get his people in that night to remove evidence of drugs. The police put his vagueness down to shock and kept the questions to a minimum.

Khan felt faint and sat on a low wall, his drug import system had worked well up to now but it could all come undone by this fire. His next consignment was on the high seas with no way of speeding it up. Someone gave him some hot sweet tea that revived him a little. He rang Azziz and told him to get all the men and vehicles he could muster and be ready after midnight to shift evidence. The drugs were imported in catering sized cans of chick peas, if any had split he could be in big trouble.

At two a.m. on Friday morning, Jack again donned his tramp disguise and left his car making sure he was not observed. He entered the church again and made his way to the empty bell platform, to the broken slatted openings that had once let out the sound of Sunday. A small flock of pigeons took umbrage and flew out in a loud flurry of flapping feathers. Even though he knew this would happen Jack's heart still leapt.

Taking his torch, Jack emptied his rucksack and assembled the crossbow, fixed the sights on and cocked it. Fitting one of the thick aluminium incendiary bolts he'd so carefully filled with magnesium powder and other ingredients, he moved to the side of the tower overlooking the rear of the takeaway. As expected the place was in darkness, even darker was the building next door which was his target.

The terraced building was old and had huge sash windows four feet wide and eight feet high. The ground floor windows and door had metal shutters to deter intruders but the upper floor fenestration still retained its ancient glass.

Jack knew he could not afford to miss. He waited, staring at the target for a while until the light wind subsided. Taking careful aim he squeezed the trigger gently and took up the first pressure. It was then he had a stroke of luck. A stray cat jumped up on the alley wall triggering the security lights and floodlighting the dark building. He fired at the top of the window knowing the bolt would drop. He saw the middle pane shatter as the bolt flew through. He quickly reloaded and fired again at the next window and again had the satisfaction of watching his bolt penetrate into the dark interior.

At first nothing seemed to have happened then he saw the glow of the fire as his bolts began to do their work. Each bolt would burn for about a minute generating a local heat of over three thousand, two hundred degrees. Quickly, Jack put another bolt through each window. He didn't fire the shop because he knew Ahmed, a chef, lived above it in a small flat. He thought he would interview him at a later date.

Back home Jack poured himself a large Bushmills, feeling a sense of satisfaction. Khan would know straight away is was no accident and start a vengeful hunt for those responsible; it would drive the man to distraction. He might even start a war with other dealers he thought responsible. Great, let the bastards wipe each other out he thought.

*****

Earlier that Thursday evening, before news of the warehouse fire had reached him, Azziz had sent Ali Mansoor to visit Alison. Waldo Williams had already contacted her and told her that it was very unlikely anyone would ask but just in case she was to regale them with the cover story of her returning husband catching them in bed and beating Waldo senseless.

Poor Alison had sworn she'd stick to the story and had wanted to do her best but she was no match for Mansoor when the nasty little man had knocked on her door. She'd answered it thinking Waldo had changed his mind and was visiting her after all. Her eager anticipation rapidly turned to fear as Mansoor barged in and clamped his hand over her mouth. He kicked the front door closed behind him telling her to keep quiet or else.

Mansoor spoke in his slightly falsetto sing-song voice which seemed to lend extra menace to it. 'You are a very good looking woman Alison, I would like to give you the chance to stay that way so listen to me carefully.' He paused to make sure she understood. When she nodded numbly he continued 'understand this: You have only one chance to get this right. We Asians have ways of dealing with women who displease us, OK?' Alison was trembling visibly; all she could do was nod. 'If you lie to me then firstly you'll be raped by at least half a dozen men. One of these men is a very large fellow who loves taking women anally; he's not a pleasant man.'

As Alison sank to her knees totally terrified, Mansoor continued his intimidation, enjoying himself immensely 'then, before we leave you to the tender mercies of the medics, we'll give you a facial with battery acid.'

He smirked at her, revelling in the terror he was causing. 'Oh, please don't worry Alison' he said with deep sarcasm 'we'll only do half your face and one eye that way you'll always be able to see what you once were and what you have become.' Alison, kneeling on the carpet started sobbing and losing all self control 'please mister, please' she pleaded 'I'm a married woman. We want to have a child next year, Waldo is only an acquaintance, a bit of rough on the side, please, what do you want me to do?'

'I want you to tell me exactly what happened the last time you bedded Waldo, you kuffar whore.'

The cover story went out of the window before a word of it was uttered; totally terrified she told how Waldo had gone downstairs to chase a burglar. Then it all went quiet so she'd gone to the back bedroom window and looked out in time to see some bloke carrying what she assumed was Waldo in some sort of sack or bag leaving by the back gate. She had not dared to call for help but had waited an hour then gone down and locked the back door then she had cleaned up the mess in the kitchen. After twenty four hours Waldo had contacted her and said he was all right but refused to offer any explanation as to what had happened, simply stating it was private business.

'OK, so why don't you ring him and ask when he's coming around?' Mansoor said handing her the house phone.

'I already tried but he's not answering.' she wailed.

'Try again, whore.'

She dialled his number from memory and waited as it rang. Finally, the automated voice started to tell her 'the person you are calling is not available…..' She cut the call.

Mansoor had eyed her closely all the time she had been talking. She was too frightened to lie he was certain of that and she couldn't tell her husband or anyone else for that matter. It would give him great pleasure to torture and kill this woman he regarded as a slut but that went beyond his instructions. It would only add unnecessary complications to an already uncertain situation and Khan would not like that.

'Right, one more thing before I leave then you are home free' he said with a sneer. He grabbed her hair and drew her to him. Pulling down his zipper he ordered her 'take it out and suck bitch and make sure you swallow all of it.' Meekly she obeyed.

The fire brigade was delayed reaching the blaze at the shop. Firstly, because of the late hour, it was a good five minutes before anyone noticed and rang it in. Then the local fire engines had been called away by a man with an American accent from a public phone box on a hoax call at the far end of their patch. The backup crew from the next district took a further thirteen minutes to arrive. By this time the building was well ablaze from ground floor to roof. Khan took the call from Ahmed the chef. Ahmed told him he'd been in bed less than half an hour. He was exhausted from his long shift in the takeaway and then by being dragged away by Azziz to clear the warehouse. He'd seen and heard nothing.

'What?' Khan barked 'How the hell is this possible?'

'I don't know Mr. Khan sir, the crackling of flames and the light through the window woke me up then the fire engines took ages to arrive.'

Khan dropped the phone and sat down heavily on his bed. He sat with his head in his hands for a long time trying to think. His stomach heaved, his head felt an almost intolerable pressure at this news of the second fire in a few hours. Over two million pounds worth of drugs had been destroyed earlier that evening and now two hundred thousand pounds worth had likewise gone up in smoke.

Someone was hitting him, but who? He had a truce with the Columbians, not that he trusted them, but they knew that a turf war was unwinnable by either side. It would be just plain damn bad for business. No one else was big enough to challenge him so what the hell was going on? He staggered to the bathroom and puked down the pan.

This had to have happened now he believed the Flame of Truth were finalising their attack plans. Hassid would not be pleased by the news but he had to tell him in case it affected their plans. He could not deceive The Flame of Truth and live. Even a suspicion of betrayal was enough for them to order a beheading. Mansoor had told him it was only because they needed his nephew's specialist knowledge of modern communications systems and that he had humbly pleaded for forgiveness that he had been spared.

Khan lit a cigarette, trying to clear his head. How? It had to be sabotage but who for god's sake? Who and why? It couldn't be Bhakti. He knew the Imam hated him but how could it be in his interest to destroy his business?

These questions went around and around in his head. He had, with his usual care and attention to detail, had the wiring replaced when he bought the shop next door to his takeaway. He had taken massive precautions to keep it burglar proof. In the attic, he'd had firewalls built so that fire would not spread from other buildings along the attics. He'd stopped short of installing a hugely expensive sprinkler system as it might draw attention to the fact that high value goods were kept there.

It had to be sabotage, one fire could be an accident, but two? How the hell could it have been done? How was it possible?

After what seemed an age Khan stopped pursuing these thoughts, dressed and left his house driving through the almost empty streets of North London. Arriving at the shop his worst fears were confirmed the whole building had been gutted from basement to roof. Wisps of smoke still floated out of the empty window frames and through the black hole in the roof.

'What happened Ahmed?' he asked, his normal sharp tone subdued 'what the hell happened?'

'I don't know Mr. Khan' said the chef looking as stunned as his boss 'I simply have no idea how it could have started although the firemen said it started on the first floor where we store the packaging for the shop.' He waited to see if Khan would respond then continued 'they'll be returning tomorrow to dampen down and start an investigation. They wanted to know if you were insured sir.'

Khan glowered at Ahmed ignoring the question, that sort of stuff was of no consequence to him now. 'Later Ahmed, you must ask your handler if this was anything to do with them, OK?'

Ahmed looked dubious 'OK, but I can't see why MI5 would attack us, we give 'em too much info.'

Khan's problems were twofold, first the brothers would want £200,000 in cash by the end of the month, secondly, he needed fresh supplies for his people or they would drift away and buy elsewhere. Demand wouldn't stop simply because he couldn't supply it and his next shipment wasn't due for another three weeks. Fear only went so far in holding his empire together and there were plenty others willing to take his place at the first sign of weakness.

The rest of the night Khan spent sitting in his car chain smoking, deep in thought. At seven a.m. he rang Hassid to report what had happened. Finally he asked 'do you think Special branch or MI5 could possibly have had anything to do with this?'

Hassid paused before answering 'I'll see what I can find out, I can't see how but I'll ask my contacts, in the meantime I'll inform the brothers. They'll still expect the next instalment of their funding, though, be in no doubt of that Khan.'

Khan tried to sound positive 'There won't be a problem with the funds sir' and with that he rang off.

The Undoing

'Get out you bastards, get to fuck out of my place' Waldo Williams sceamed, chasing all the runners and hangers-on out of his flat, lashing out at those slow on the uptake. 'Piss orf the lot o' yer's, yer freeloading bastards' he roared, booting the last pair out of his door. He needed to grab his stash and get out while he could.

Spain, he thought, might be a good place to spend some time while things quietened down. He'd then have to start all over again, Khan was not the sort to forgive and forget. He went to his bedroom and lifted the carpet then put his knife blade under a floor tile and flicked it up. Opening his floor safe, he grabbed large bundles of cash and stuffed them into a hold-all. After packing a few clothes, he phoned a taxi. When it arrived he jumped in 'Harwich docks mate, a sharp as yer can.'

'Harwich?' the startled driver queried 'bloody Harwich mate? I don't go that far on me holidays.'

Waldo was in no mood to argue he drew a bundle of cash from his pocket 'there's five hundred quid there mate, take it an' let's go.'

The driver hearing what sounded like desperation in his passenger's voice made the mistake of trying to up the ante 'Well, I dunno mate' he said hesitantly 'I've got a wife an' kids to feed if you could up the price a bit...'

Waldo's knife flashed open with a vicious click an inch from the driver's eye. 'Listen you chiselling bastard, you can either take me for the five hundred or I'll gut you and drive myself.' That ended all resistance and the driver hurriedly put the car in gear and drove off.

Williams knew that Khan would check his story. He didn't expect Alison to hold out for long against whomever Khan sent to question her but he'd hoped for a few more hours to arrange more funds.. Now she'd sent him a text that read: "Fine friends you have. He threatened me with acid and gang rape then made me give him a BJ. It's over. Fuck off and don't come back. EVER."

Waldo couldn't go to any of the airports; Khan would be having them watched. He figured Khan's second guess would be him taking the Eurostar Express to Paris or a train to Dover to catch the ferry via the shorter route to Calais. Williams had even considered using his own car but dismissed it at once. The vehicle was a bright metallic purple Merc. It stood out a mile, no way was he going to risk weaving his way through London's painfully slow traffic in that.

A longer, slower, but far less obvious escape route would be the ferry from Harwich to the Hook of Holland, once on the continent he could pick and choose which airport to fly from. All he had to do was hold his nerve. As a plan thought up under pressure it was a good one.

The driver dropped him off at the ferry terminal half expecting to be mugged for the five hundred but the man simply picked up his bags and walked away.

The driver, well out of radio range, then rang his boss to tell him where he was and what had happened. He'd switched off his radio and phone for fear of annoying his passenger and ending up with a blade in his ribs. The unusual story was soon circulating on the taxi airwaves and was picked up by a driver who worked for Khan's cousin.

Khan wasted no time getting in touch with one of his contacts in the police. 'I believe he is responsible for a murder and two serious arson attacks on my places' he lied 'see what you can do Bob it's rather urgent, I will be most appreciative.'

Khan didn't have to say anything else, Sergeant Bob Oliphant, long used to doing favours for Khan in return for substantial reward, got onto it right away. He contacted the Harwich police with Waldo Williams' mug shot implementing a protocol usually used for terrorists, impressing upon them the gravity of the case. A man dead and two buildings torched.

The ferry was about to sail when Williams saw the gangplank being put back into place and a group of uniformed policemen come aboard. His heart sank.

Taken back to London, Williams was interrogated on suspicion of murder and arson. He told the police he'd done it in order to stay locked up out of Khan's way but he could furnish no details of how it had been done.

Ahmed came forward and made a statement saying he had spent the evening of the fires at Waldo's place all night and that Waldo had never left the building and that Khan had been fed wrong information.

Khan withdrew his statement and Waldo was released. He'd raved about how Khan was going to kill him he confessed that the large amount of cash he was carrying was drugs money he intended to launder all to no avail. Cell space was short, the cops took his confession and released him on bail pending further inquiries. Azziz and Mansoor were waiting when he left the police station the next day.

*****

The Flame of Truth was Imam Bhakti's madrasah that operated openly but was secretly a British offshoot of ISIS. It was hidden in plain sight. They recruited exclusively home-grown young men and boys. Great care was taken in this selection. The young men had been sent to The Flame of Truth madrassah on a religious retreat. They were sent by devout families who feared that their young men were becoming too Westernised.

Those with criminal records or anyone with links to any terrorist organisation were not approached, nor was anyone with a record of poor mental health.

Those selected had to be 'terror virgins' with nothing about them to attract the attention of the authorities. The chosen ones were only approached after they had been observed for some time and had answered a questionnaire in a certain manner.

Young and impressionable, they were carefully indoctrinated and sworn to secrecy, told to await a great happening. It was early spring, the time had now come to recall the chosen ones for extended teaching. Every student at the madrassah now was one of the chosen. Imam Bhakti had been planning and preparing for his spectacular strike for over two years. Only the most zealous had passed final selection and this group of twenty eight were now in training to strike a blow that Bhakti had described as "Bigger than 9/11."

None yet knew what the target was or when they would strike but they trained with weapons and explosives. Mortars and bombs and rocket propelled grenades were also part of the plot, as were suicide vests. Only the Imam knew the whole picture but he promised a strike that would shake the 'Western devils' for generations and hit at the very heart of 'The Great Satan.'

The training camp was in the dense Kielder Forest in Northumberland in an area of deep, almost impenetrable pine plantations cut only by fire breaks and game trails. At its heart was a huge reservoir that attracted thousands of visitors in summer but that was a long way from the retreat.

An ancient gamekeeper's cottage and outbuildings had been bought, renovated, extended and converted into classrooms, a refectory and kitchen with offices and dormitory accommodation above. The track up to it was long, steep and in very bad repair so that it was impassable to all but off-road vehicles. The compound was surrounded by a chain link fence that incorporated a football pitch and a large open sided barn like structure that made weapons training possible without being observed from above by satellites or drones.

There was an assault type course, canoes and a dozen motorcycles. These were explained away easily enough. No one can study religion all day every day. Young men needed to burn off excess energy lest they drift into unholy personal practices. Hard physical training kept the body fit and the mind pure.

The centre had been opened with as much fanfare as Bhakti could muster. He knew that if he sought to open it in secrecy that its existence would soon become public knowledge. Then the press would descend like wolves probing and speculating. By opening the retreat publicly and announcing its purpose as that of a quiet retreat, a madrasah for religious scholars, he had drawn the sting of the conspiracy theorists. He asked that people did not visit accept by prior arrangement as the peace and tranquillity of this remote place was essential to deep religious study and contemplation.

After a short time weapons were smuggled in and secreted with great care. The weapons consisted of AK 47 assault rifles, automatic pistols, rocket propelled grenades as well as sixteen cut down sixty six millimetre mortars. They were stored in a secret and well camouflaged bunker outside the chain link fence.

Whenever the weapons were needed for training sentries were placed at the top and bottom of the only approach road with radios to give early warning of any intruders. The young jihadists trained until they could strip and assemble their weapons blindfold and exercised until they were as proficient as it was possible to be. There was no need to actually fire the weapons as on the operation their targets would be many and very close packed. Spraying automatic fire at waist level would be all that was necessary.

One of the retreat's instructors was a man called Muhammad Ali Hussein he had, before his religious calling, been an officer in the Pakistani Artillery. It was his job to zero in the sixteen cut-down mortars in the group's possession and work out firing positions, also deal with the technical side of the ammunition. The mortars they were to use had barrels less than half the length of a conventional weapon. This would of course severely curtail the range making them less accurate over a long distance but these mortars, he was told, were be used at a very short range.

The Army training area of Otterburn was a fairly short drive from the madrasah, its vast sprawling acres mainly empty since the Army cutbacks. This was all to the good because Hussein needed to test fire at least a few of the mortars. He would use unfused bombs of the same weight to test for accuracy.

When he had mentioned some of the technical problems of firing mortars with precision he had found Bhakti very knowledgeable on the subject. 'The range will be short, five or six hundred metres so the trajectory will be high.' Bhakti told Hussein 'the difference in ground elevation between the target and the firing point is negligible, the charge temperature will be constant at 10 degrees C and the winds on the day have, historically, been light from the west.'

Hussein had simply bowed and said 'very good sir, in that case we have no problems.'

It was a fine Saturday morning just after sun up when Hussein and six student helpers drew up in two camouflaged Land Rovers similar to the military ones. They were in a very remote area of the firing ranges where people rarely came because of the possible danger from unexploded ordnance. They quickly threw out some old wooden pallets from the vehicles and spread them on the ground. Next they planted a small flagpole with a bright yellow rag at its top. Remounting the vehicles then drove off to exactly five hundred metres. Hussein now surprised his helpers.

'Dig me a trench half a metre deep, half a metre wide and two point five metres long' he ordered indicating the direction of the trench. They young men looked puzzled but knew better than to question their superior. They took a spade each and began to dig.

When they had finished to their instructor's satisfaction he had the mortar tubes and their base plates brought from the back of the vehicle and had each fitted the electronic firing device. He then measured the bearing and distance to the flag with a laser rangefinder and did some calculations. After setting up four mortars in the trench and checked the bearing and elevation several times. The students were ordered to fill in the trench so that just the tip of the barrels protruded. The mortars were loaded.

The men retired a few yards then they were fired by a hand held device.

They made a coughing sound and a flat flash at the muzzle. Thin bluish gouts of smoke spread on the wind and dispersed. Now for the hard bit, watching for the fall of shot, not easy when there is no explosion to look for but they couldn't risk attracting attention. As it turned out they were in luck as one of the pallets suddenly leapt in the air in spinning shattered fragments. 'Allahu Akbar' they shouted in unison.

*****

Khan looked dispassionately at Waldo lying on the floor of his garage hands tied behind his back. 'So, Waldo, I give you a chance to come clean with me and you try to run away instead.' He paused and dug the prisoner with his foot. 'What do you have to say for yourself?'

Waldo blurted out the story of his capture by some American gangster who tortured him into telling what little he knew of Khan's operation. ''Onest Mr. Khan sir, the bastard damn near electrocuted me through me dick and me ear then he hung me up with me arms behind me for hours. He was going to cut me dick off! I've still got the scar if you want to look Mr. Khan sir?'

That was an offer Khan declined with a sour smile and a shake of his head. Gradually the whole story came out. When the terrified Waldo had finished he begged for mercy swearing on his mother's life he would work for Khan for free, kicking back all his profits until he considered the debt paid.

Khan retired with Azziz to the lounge to talk things over. They knew their prisoner was incapable of making up such an elaborate tale and Alison had seen her lover being carried off. On the night of the fires it was an American who made a hoax call that drew the fire engines away. Clearly there was something going on here that they knew nothing about and it worried them.

Khan said 'who the hell is this American? It couldn't be just vengeance on Waldo Williams he wanted, surely?'

'It seems a long way to come just to torture a man then let him go.' said Azziz, a scowl of his face. 'No, there has to be something deeper and involving the arson. We need to find out what it is fast or our lives could be in danger' he added, 'whoever he is, this American knows about torture and interrogation techniques, he's a pro.'

'So, you reckon the American authorities are taking an interest in our business?' Khan asked surprised.

'No, not on the drugs side anyway, they've got enough problems of their own to keep them busy. It's the jihadist stuff you're into boss. I reckon they may have gotten wind of something.'

Khan paused and reflected on this thought for a moment if this was the case he couldn't see where the leak was. He knew Ahmed was an MI5 informer, he'd turned him and his boss ages ago and besides, Ahmed could have learned nothing of importance of the jihadist connection unless he was exceedingly clever which, in Khan's judgement, he was not.

The thing MI5 was interested in was the drugs and money laundering. He'd been feeding them low to medium level intelligence for a couple of years now to keep them sweet. It was a good way to get rid of opposition and the feedback he got from Ahmed along with his police sources kept him a free man. So what the hell was going on? Whatever it was it involved this unknown American. He must be identified at all costs. Who was he? What did he know? Who did he report to?

His thoughts were interrupted by Azziz asking 'Should I get rid of Waldo now, boss?'

'No, not just yet Muszra, he may know something he doesn't even know he knows and we can't un-kill the bastard later' he paused then said 'let's go back and have another word.'

They found that Waldo had wriggled into a corner of the garage trying to rub his bonds on the wall.. Khan laughed. 'That only works in the movies Waldo so save your strength.'

Waldo started to whine and plead and Khan silenced him with a vicious kick to the body. 'Shut up and listen you cretin.' He stared at his victim for a few seconds 'Azziz here assures me you're a good man and would never grass in normal circumstances so I'm going to give you a chance to live Waldo. One chance only, you understand?'

Waldo, badly winded, simply nodded his understanding.

'Good, now listen to me. I want you to go over in your mind everything that happened to you from being taken to being released, OK?'

Waldo nodded again.

Take your time, if you can give me any detail, no matter how small or insignificant you believe it to be and it helps, then you will be spared. Is that clear?'

'Yes' Waldo managed to croak.

'Good, well you just get a good night's rest on my garage floor and I'll see you in the morning.' Khan laughed but there was no mirth in it.

In his bedroom Khan showered, put on a fresh robe and poured himself a large scotch. He lay on his bed smoking and thinking.

After an hour he put the light out but sleep would not come. He kept going over in his mind the possibilities. Mafia, CIA? MI5? He never came to any plausible conclusion.

The payment to the brothers was also a concern. It was a contractual obligation and it would be due soon. He could get the money together of course, but it would involve moving funds and large sums moved quickly always left a trail.

Khan's next problem involved new supplies of drugs. The Columbians would do a deal, but they would squeeze him on price until the pips squeaked. These matters went round and round in his mind until finally sheer exhaustion caused him to doze off into fitful slumber.

Waldo Williams was cold and stiff and damned uncomfortable. His wrists felt like they were on fire from the chaffing where he had constantly wriggled in a desperate attempt to free himself. Azziz was an expert at tying knots and not a millimetre did they give. He also wracked his brains for anything that would keep Khan from killing him, anything at all. He concocted several stories during the long night but discarded them all. Khan was no fool, he would see through his lies in a moment.

At seven the door opened and in walked Azziz with a glass of water. He let Waldo have a few sips then poured the rest over his head. 'I want you nice and fresh for the boss Waldo, but I think you'll be mine.' He grinned at the hapless man, anticipating killing him brought a sadistic joy to his heart. Over Azziz's shoulder Waldo saw Khan enter and his spirits sank. He began sobbing softly to himself.

'OK Waldo, Mr. Azziz here has some pliers in his pocket and I need to get your undivided attention my friend.' He looked at Azziz and said in an exaggeratedly polite voice 'Mr. Azziz, would you be kind enough to show our friend here how earnest we are?'

Azziz's eyes glinted, he looked as happy as a vulture with fresh road kill. 'Certainly Mr. Khan, happy to oblige.'

With that the big man rolled the terrified captive on his back and sat his massive frame on his chest. Waldo opened his mouth and screamed and Azziz thrust in the pliers locking them on one of his front teeth, pushing his head to the floor with his free hand. With a swift twist left and right Azziz yanked the tooth out of Waldo's head. The screams were muffled by a small towel being stuffed into the open mouth. Khan didn't want even one drop of Williams's blood anywhere in his house.

Waldo's agony was intense, his mind was reeling as waves of pain flowed through him, tears streaming down his face. All he could do for the next few minutes was scream in pain and terror. Khan and Azziz stood eyeing him dispassionately until he at last began to subside.

'Now that I have your undivided attention, Waldo' Khan said coldly 'I want you to go through the evening of your capture a step at a time, leave nothing out, not a single movement.'

Waldo began slowly thinking of the events of that fateful Thursday night, choosing his words with care. When he got to the wallet on the ground Azziz nodded grudging approval and muttered 'the guy's a pro' all right.'

'Did you see anything under the hood Waldo?' Khan asked patiently. Waldo thought for a while 'yeah, just once when he gave me a drink of water, I saw a floor tile, a grey floor tile with black streaks.'

Khan went and fetched a laptop, searched for grey floor tiles and ran through several dozen patterns until Waldo at last said 'Yeah, that's the one there.'

Khan made a note and they continued step by step until at last Williams had finished. Azziz was bending over him when he suddenly said 'oh yeah, and there was a cat there.'

Khan, who had turned away, stopped in his tracks 'A cat? You heard a cat?'

'No sir.'

'Then how the hell could you possibly know that?'

'I'm allergic to cats and I was sniffing and my eyes were running too. I didn't really notice until I got home 'cos I was hurting like hell from the torture and felt hung over from the gear he knocked me out with.' He waited for Khan to say something but when he didn't he continued 'my arms had red blotches and I was itching like hell. I thought it was the nettles at first, then I recognised what it was. I had to take a double dose of antihistamine tablets.'

After what seemed an interminable pause Khan said 'you've done well. I'm going to have breakfast now Mr. Williams then I shall consider your fate.'

In the kitchen Khan made omelettes whilst thinking about this new information. He thought about the old man and the lost cat, a coincidence? Khan didn't believe in them.

'That old fellow, Jack Ellis, who supposedly lost his cat, do you think he could be connected, Muszra?

Azziz rubbed his chin 'It's possible of course, but I can't see how. Do you want me to pick him up for questioning?'

Khan considered the facts for a moment without answering the question. 'We're supposed to believe that, several weeks after those girls' deaths, a guy comes all the way from America for vengeance and doesn't follow through? Bullshit! This out-of-the-blue visitor also has access to a remote workshop where screams wouldn't be heard? With a hoist and a shock machine, a welding set probably. Where would he get such facilities?'

'Maybe' Azziz ventured 'he made all the arrangements before coming and that's why it took so long for him to get here boss.'

'That could, of course, be the answer Muszra, but somehow I

In the back of Khan's mind a very uneasy feeling was taking hold. He was up against a clever enemy that was for sure, one who knew about his shipment or had guessed from what he squeezed from Waldo Williams. He had acted on it quickly, too, destroying not only his uninsured buildings but drugs with a street value of well over two million pounds all in a single night.

'Do you think that old Ellis fellow has anything to do with this American guy? Azziz asked. 'As you said, he looked a highly intelligent sort to me and too fit to need that stick.'

Khan nodded, remembering the feeling of unease he'd had when Jack visited his shop. 'Probably we're clutching at straws Muszra, but it's all we have.'

'I'll pick him up for questioning, shall I?' Azziz asked again.

'Like hell you will. I want to check this guy out first. I need to find out just what we're dealing with and who, if anyone, he's connected to' Khan took a gulp from his coffee not really tasting it, his normally calm mind buzzing. 'If he does have anything to do with it Muszra then he'll have back-up from somewhere. He can't be working alone. No one man could achieve what's been done alone.'

'Shall I have him watched then?' Azziz asked 'If it's him he's a pro' so it will be damn difficult if not impossible to keep him under surveillance permanently without him spotting us.'

'If he's involved Muszra, the last thing we need is to let Ellis know we're on to him. To pick him up only to have the cavalry charging in to the rescue would be catastrophic. I shall make further inquiries first.'

Khan's own protection could only be assured if he conducted his drug business discreetly. He must of course report these happening to Imam Bhakti through Hassid and seek his guidance. The interview would be an uncomfortable one but the consequences of being caught being less that forthright with him were unthinkable. The Imam, Khan knew, had influence in the highest Government circles. He could obtain information and favours from ministers desperately anxious to flaunt their multicultural credentials. He may be able to resolve this problem.

'You and Mansoor get rid of Waldo today, no fuss, no mess, he just quietly vanishes, OK?' Khan ordered the murder as casually as he would order a coffee and cake 'oh, and tell that Jonny Burke fellow he's now got the Williams' franchise.'

Azziz nodded 'It will my pleasure, I think I have just the end Waldo deserves, I never did like the flash bastard.'

'Fine, just make sure it's very painful and prolonged and that he is fully conscious when it happens, OK? I hate grasses.'

Later that day in a copse on a remote hill Waldo lay bound and gagged whilst Azziz and Mansoor took turns at digging his grave. The terrified man just hoped it would be quick and clean, a bullet to the head would be best. He lay whimpering and paralysed with fear watching transfixed as the work progressed. His bowels moved involuntarily.

The two assassins finished their work and sat smoking, Azziz a cigarette and Mansoor a large spliff, they were in no hurry; the longer it took the more Waldo would suffer. This was private farmland and worked by a dealer so they were not going to be disturbed.

After a while Mansoor went to the car and lugged two large sacks, slashed them open and threw the contents down the hole. Waldo's nostrils were assailed by a familiar smell that he couldn't quite place. The two then threw lit newspaper into the pit and all became clear as he recognised burning barbecue lighter fluid as the smell.

Azziz took a large machete from the vehicle and walked into the woods returning with his arms full of dead wood, making three more trips before he was satisfied. While he was doing that, Mansoor was chopped down a stout sapling. Finally satisfied, the men walked over to where Williams lay choking with fear.

Azziz regarded his victim for a moment relishing every minute of his sadistic pleasure 'Waldo, my dear friend' he said expansively 'You have caused me and Ali here a great deal of hard work.' He paused eyeing the man as if he were meat on a slab 'You see we have been arguing, I wanted to bury you but Ali here prefers cremation. It was quite a problem so in the end we decided to do both.' He smiled icily 'You see the trouble we have taken over you?' He ripped the tape from Waldo's mouth, he wanted to hear his man die screaming.

Williams, hysterical with terror, began crying for help, shouting for his mother and babbling for mercy. The two men got hold of their wriggling bundle and threaded the sapling through his bound legs and between his wrists. Next, they fastened his belt around the pole drawing Waldo's midriff close to the spit, like a pig for the roasting. With a nod from Azziz they lifted him and carried him over the pit in the bottom of which the charcoal was now a dull grey. They lowered him until he was suspended over the roasting heat five feet below him.

'I'd like to eat a slice of your arse when you're cooked Waldo' sneered Mansoor 'but I'm a good Muslim, I can't eat pig!' He screamed the last word and spat on him.

Waldo took a long time to die screaming his lungs out and struggling all the while he slowly roasted to death. When at last he succumbed they casually cut the pole and let him fall into the pit. Azziz then piled his firewood on top of the corpse and then he fetched a 25 litre plastic can of petrol from the vehicle. Removing the top Mansoor slashed the can above the fuel level. Azziz carefully lifted the container then heaved it into the pit, ducking back as it caught with a great whoosh.

The murderers then sat relaxed chatting and smoking, Mansoor with yet another large joint. Azziz produced a flask and they enjoyed coffee whilst discussing the possibility of another victim coming their way. The old man with the cat, they could think up some novel ways of killing him if it turned out he was involved.

When they were satisfied Waldo was now just charred bone and ashes they drove to the farmhouse and ordered their man to fill in the hole.

Plots

Jack and Indira had dated for almost a month before she had invited him to her home for a meal. Her home, Jack saw, was an eclectic mix of Eastern and Western styles that somehow managed to blend in complete harmony. There was a hint of incense recently burned that he found stimulating. After an excellent vegetarian meal they were sitting on her couch each replete and contented when she asked 'are you still active, Jack?'

Jack should have been surprised if not slightly shocked by her directness. However, he had learned in a very short time that Indira, for all her demure ways, didn't beat around the bush on issues important to her. 'As in bedroom active?' he asked with a broad grin, knowing full well what she meant.

She lowered her eyes blushing slightly 'yes' she said quietly. Jack slid his arm about her waist and drew her to him, he kissed her full lips for a long time before he answered her question with one of his own 'Would you like to find out?' he said in a gently teasing way.

Making love to Indira wasn't like it had been with his late wife Joan in the early days of their relationship. Then, they had practically thrown each other around the bedroom in what they called a knock-down, drag out fuck fight that had left them both satisfied and exhausted. In those days each had been anxious to satisfy the other as quickly as possible so the next round could begin. They had of course mellowed with age but their love making was always vigorous.

With Indira it was a slow, gentle build-up of feeling. Rivulets of anticipation ran shivering through him as she deftly stroked and fondled. She seemed to read his desires as if by telepathy and performed the next act exactly when needed. He in turn used all his experience to please her, seeking out her erogenous zones with delicate fingers and probing tongue. He took things slowly, a step at a time, listening to and feeling her responses. He was rewarded by her soft moans of pleasure.

When each could stand it no longer he entered her with long gentle strokes gradually building up speed, encouraged by her whimpers of pleasure. Her fingernails scratched his back in light circles sending shock waves through him. He bent forward and gently nibbled her ear lobes discovering that this sent her into near delirium. They, along with her hard nippled breasts, were her greatest pleasure zones. Her legs clamped around his back as they rode to a mutual climax. They were eventually left each clinging each to the other in a state of sighing satisfaction.

This development in their relationship made it all the more difficult for Jack to ask Indira to translate the recordings from the takeaway. Ask he must, but not tonight.

*****

Imam Bhakti sat on the silken cushions scattered about the edges of his spacious living room listening intently to the Minister of Security, James Jason Hunter, a career politician.

'You have done very well Imam to arrange things the way you have' he said sincerely. 'Had you built the madrasah in such a remote place then not publicized its existence the press would have viewed it with great suspicion. They would have said it was a secret training camp or heaven alone knows what else. As it is, this press article of which you quite rightly complain, is most unhelpful.'

'We have nothing to hide Minister, our humble madrasah remains open to the appropriate authorities to inspect at any time' he paused taking in a long sighing breath 'such a retreat for deep religious study is best kept far away from the noise and distractions of towns and cities.' He paused to gauge what effect his words were having on Hunter. Seeing the man nod in sympathetic understanding he continued 'Kielder Forest is ideal for just such solitude. This ludicrous accusation in the press that we have military style training there is just wild speculation. It does nothing to promote understanding between our communities.'

Hunter smiled ruefully 'Yes Imam, as a politician I have myself been a victim of such irresponsible reporting.' There was no hint of accusation in the Minister's voice as he asked 'but was building an assault-type course really a wise choice, Imam?'

Bhakti let his breath explode through pursed lips in a sound that conveyed both contempt and protest. 'These students are young fit men Minister with a great deal of energy. We seek only to build their confidence and expend their surplus energy in a positive, character building way. Not even the most devout Muslim can study and pray twenty four seven.'

Bhakti spread his arms in appeal 'we even consulted the Army as to its construction and gained permission of the planning authorities. Nothing was hidden, we have no ulterior motive.'

He paused to pour more tea for them both and offered Hunter a biscuit, when the man declined he continued 'we have canoes for the lake, we have a football pitch, we have a large covered area where the men can exercise in inclement weather.We even have a few motorcycles for the recreation of our devout young men.'

Bhakti's face was a picture of moral outrage 'not one of these excellent facilities were mentioned in this malicious article, Minister. Only the confidence building course, which this journalist portrayed as a military style assault course.'Bhakti expelled a long sigh 'It really is intolerable that these people can spread malicious rumours against Islam and devout Muslims with impunity.' He raised his arms in a gesture of helpless indignation.

Hunter smiled obsequiously, his constituency had become a marginal one in recent years. It had a very large and influential ethnic population two thirds of whom were Muslims; he could ill afford to offend these people.

'I shall at once issue a press release Imam to denounce this ill judged and ignorant article as rampant Islamophobic propaganda' he adopted his 'deeply concerned' look normally reserved for press conferences. 'Please leave this to me Imam, I shall denounce this article in the strongest possible terms.' he smiled reassuringly 'and please rest assured the views expressed in that vile article have nothing whatsoever to do with this Government or my party.'

'I understand Minister' said the Imam sounding mollified 'it was kind and considerate of you to visit me at such short notice since I couldn't get to The House. Now that our formal business is concluded James, may I offer you some more substantial refreshment? My wife has prepared a modest lunch.'

The Minister smiled broadly, relieved that the embarrassing interview was over. Eastern food was a favourite of his and the Imam kept a superb table. 'Why thank you Ibrahim, that would be most welcome.'

Imam Bhakti had carefully laid his plans and executed them with great care over the last two years. Nothing must be left to chance if he was to strike the blow for jihad that he had in mind. To strike at the very heart of British, nay, Western society in an area where security was tightest the greatest care was needed. He had vowed to achieve this in way that would never be forgotten.

Bhakti thought Bin Laden had done a brilliant job on the Twin Towers of course, but that was a long time ago now. The man had promptly gone into hiding, a spent force living on past glory. The Americans had inevitably found and killed him, though it had taken them an inordinate amount of time. Al Qaeda, he believed, was now in decline, it had lost a lot of its former initiative and momentum; it no longer spoke for devout believers everywhere.

The people needed a new direction and that direction was ISIS of which he was an ardent but secret member. He would make the world tremble and nothing could stop him.

Through his brother-in-law Uthman Hassid, Bhakti had kept his distance from ISIS and their extreme views and actions. Bhakti, using intelligence from ISIS, had recruited Khan, a whisky drinking, drug dealing paedophile whom he held in the utmost contempt to raise the necessary dark funds for the project.

The dealer had the saving grace of ruthless efficiency and a seemingly respectable front. Khan kept faith because he was making great profits and he feared the terrible consequences of double crossing ISIS. He had stuck rigidly to their deal. Now, though, he was causing problems which must be nipped in the bud as soon as possible. Whoever the American responsible for the arson attacks was he must be found, and found quickly. Who he was and to which organisation he belong to had to be established. He needed to know what he knew before eliminating him. It was highly unlikely he had discovered anything of his plans of course, but Bhakti wasn't prepared to take even the smallest chance.

Of the young jihadist recruits, every one of the radicalised men was a contact of Uthman Hassid or one of his minions, not himself. To all appearances Bhakti was a peaceful moderate, a leader of his community who had given talks on radio and television on the need for tolerance of all views. He had very cleverly hidden his jihadi's in plain sight.

Bhakti had run four twelve week courses a year for the last two years. Not all the students had been suitable for a variety of reasons. Some were considered weak and too timid, corrupted by soft Western ways. Others had relatives with connections to various terror groups. These had all been allowed to finish the course and return to their homes ignorant of the madrasah's true purpose. The chosen one's were offered a follow-on course. As a result of this painstaking process his dedicated group of willing jihadi's were all well below the security radar. Even now they were at the madrassah doing weapons training.

The time to strike was drawing near when a journalist from a national daily went sneaking around the madrasah looking for dirt to dish. The man, Cecil Truegood, had been politely but firmly ushered from the area, it was after all, private land and he had no invitation. Truegood had retaliated by writing an article full of unfounded speculation, expertly playing to the fears and prejudices of his readership.

Bhakti could do without this sort of negative attention so near to the fulfilment of his planned coup. Now he had other worries, firstly the deaths of two teenage girls linked to Khan's organisation and then the appearance of some mysterious American who was prepared to use extreme violence in order to gain information about Khan. Clever, he thought, very clever to use this Williams creature to spread fear and alarm instead of simply killing him for revenge. This way he had forced Khan to do the killing for him.

But who was this American and for whom was he working? CIA or Mafia? Both were possibilities and dangerous ones, too. He had no doubt whatsoever that Khan would give information in order to save his worthless skin if it came to it. The Imam mulled this possibility over, he knew that Khan had no hard evidence and that he, Bhakti, had built up a benign public image and had the confidence of high Government office holders. There was no need to panic but things had to be put back on an even keel as quickly as possible.

This American person, whoever he was, was clearly a cool thinking, ruthless individual. The arson attacks which had been so expertly done that, in the case of the shop, the authorities still had no idea how it had been achieved. A huge amount of drugs were destroyed which could delay next month's payment even though Khan had given assurances that it would be paid. Large amounts of money had to be moved with extreme care if they were to stay invisible.

Bhakti decided to contact Rizah Nawaz the Security Minister's private secretary, a man with a secret life he wanted to keep secret. He was his link to sensitive information from the highest offices in the land. He had to identify this mysterious American and eliminate him if he was a criminal or neutralise him by political means if he was CIA. He would pray for guidance. .

Khan had orders via Hassid to sort out his business quickly, find out who was attacking his interests and eliminate the threat. If he discovered it was the CIA or some other Government agency then he was to do nothing but report back. This was to be his only priority, no other concern of business or personal life was to distract him. The message was delivered in such a manner that Khan was left in no doubt that his masters considered this a matter of the utmost urgency.

Khan put out the word that he was interested in information on Jack Ellis plus any Americans that had moved into the area recently. He also told Ahmed the chef to ask his boss at MI5 to search out any information. He thought it unlikely that this old fellow Ellis was involved with any of the secret services at his age but in the name of thoroughness he had to be investigated.

Results soon started coming in. Ahmed reported that there was a very old file in the name of Jack Ellis in the MI5 catalogue but that file was classified 'Top Secret/Ministerial eyes only,' the highest possible level of security. Ahmed's handler, even though a senior MI5 agent, couldn't even look at it without the written approval of the Minister of Security himself. Coupled with this information it was reported that one of the street pushers had a blind beggar customer who used to be a top pickpocket until he ran foul of an old man who fitted Ellis's description and who had said his name was Jack.

Freddy the ferret travelled by taxi to see Khan, he'd been told there was five grand on offer for useful information. His pusher had told him about an old bloke they were interested in and it had struck a chord with Freddy. He had no real idea who Khan was, only that he was some big time drug dealer with plenty of money.

The pusher had set up the meeting through Jonny Burke and Freddy travelled to see Khan eager to get his hands on some easy cash. When he had been a pickpocket he had money, a flash car and a lap dancer girlfriend. She had left him soon after he was injured selling his car and clearing out his savings before she went.

'Well mate' Freddy said in his mangled English 'dis geezah wos abhaat sixty, fit lookin' an' wiv a big hooter, like. He had weird grey eyes wot stared straight through yer. He told me to retire or he'd retire me then he chopped me in the guts the bastard.' Freddy looked towards Khan with unseeing eyes expecting a sympathetic response, when none was forthcoming he continued. 'I reckon it must 'ave been 'im slipped me the cigarette lighter wot blew me bleedin' 'and orf.'

'You're not sure it was the same man who slipped you the lighter?' Khan queried sharply.

'Nah, not at first 'cos I only saw him from the back but afterwards, when I'd fort abhaat it I reckon it woz 'im orlright but disguised, dressed up like an RSP.'

'RSP?' Khan was having difficulty understanding Freddy's coarse street language; he found it deeply irritating.

'A Red Sea Pedestrian, a yid, a frummer' said Freddy sounding exasperated. 'A Jew boy! Jesus mista, doncha understand English?'

'And I suppose I'm a Paki bastard behind my back' Khan said bitterly. He'd no love for the Jewish race but he hated the way these ignorant East London white boys thought the colour of their skin made them superior to all and any of a different ethnicity.

'Listen my friend' Khan said 'if you want the reward you'd better speak plain English, I'm becoming very tired of you.'

Azziz gripped Freddy hard by the back of the neck. 'Speak plain or I'll break something' he growled, shaking the man vigorously. Freddy immediately started whining 'Please guv'nor, I'm just a poor blind man wot is trying ter 'elp yer. I reckon it woz 'im slipped me that lighter wot blinded me and blew me 'and orf.'

At a nod from Khan Azziz released his man. 'Did the man whom you met in the café have a walking stick? Khan asked.

'Nah, but the Jewish gent had one' Freddy said trying his best to speak correct English 'it was made of bamboo.'

Khan addressed Azziz. 'Give him a thousand and get his number.' He turned away showing no further interest in the matter.

'But my dealer said five grand' Freddy protested.

'You're a blind man, you can't give us a positive ID' Azziz said stuffing a wad of notes into Freddy's pocket 'you're damn lucky to be getting that much you ungrateful little bastard.'

Freddy's heart sank, he'd rashly promised his dealer five hundred pounds as a reward for putting him onto Khan. He knew his dealer would insist on payment. His frustration boiled over overwhelming his good sense 'Go on then, cheat a poor blind bloke yer rotten bastards an' I've travelled miles to help you lot, taxi cost me twenty five quid it did.' Freddy said bitterly 'Paki twats.'

Khan turned back, eyes flashing dangerously, a feeling of cold rage consumed him.

'He's right Azziz, we should be more considerate to our blind friend here. Call my brother-in-law's taxi firm, we'll pay his fare home, oh, and give him a free fix, too. After all, he did his best' he said with mock sincerity as he made a cut throat sign. Azziz nodded 'certainly Mr Khan' he pulled out his phone and called the cab then produced a small bag of almost pure heroin. Who'd ask a lot of questions about a blind junkie who'd accidentally OD'd?

'Here you are Freddy, it's the best I can do, sorry' said Azziz ' Freddy clutched the bag of drugs like it was gold dust and stuffed it into his pocket without a word of thanks. The taxi soon arrived.

'Well Azziz, it looks like that old man is in this up to his neck. I have to report this to Hassid before we can move, but I think you and Mansoor will be getting more work very soon.'

Azziz was delighted 'It'll be my pleasure to deal with that crafty old bastard and his interfering American partner, too.' His sinister smile made even Khan shudder inwardly.

Jonny Burke's men had reported two new non-tourist Americans in the area, one was a top diplomat who rented a lavish apartment in Holland Park Road, way outside the budget of any CIA operator. The other was, allegedly, a businessman who was staying at a four star hotel.

He'd had them followed; the supposed businessman spent a lot of time at the American Embassy. This man, one John Westaway, seemed to fit the mould of CIA. Neither man had seemed like Mafioso. He reported his findings to Hassid who told him to await further instructions.

Hassid had to move with care, get it right first time. Picking up Jack Ellis for questioning too soon could be as dangerous as doing it too late. If he were indeed connected to any of the secret services then great care was required. He also had to pick up the American and Ellis at the same time or the absence of one would alert the other. He could of course simply have them killed, but dead men can't answer questions and he had to solve the puzzle of the American connection. How much did they know? What were they doing about it? Would the strike end in disaster as they walked into a trap?

It seemed likely to Hassid that a man with such a highly secret file as Ellis, no matter how old, would still have contacts at the highest level. He also had to bear in mind Khan's assessment that the mysterious American who'd tortured Waldo Williams was a pro. That Ellis and he were working together was a certainty, he believed. They had both come on the scene at the same time, too.

It never occurred to him for a second that they could be one and the same man.

All Khan could do for the present was to await Hassid's instructions. His head whirled with confusion. Everything in his world, once so well ordered, was now a challenge and a dangerous one at that. He needed a drink and something to distract himself from his problems for a while. He would ring Mrs Grey and book an appointment to see a little red head.

*****

The day that Freddy had seen Khan, Jack had at last broached the question of translating to Indira. He told her it was probably nothing but these people were suspected of high level drug dealing and that it had caused the death of those two young girls, one of whom he had loved very dearly, regarding her as family.

Indira was reluctant 'But I don't want you involved in this Jack, it sounds very dangerous.'

Jack explained the trouble the authorities had to go to obtain permission for a bug plant. He also said, quite rightly, that these people had informants in the police and would get to know.

'Look Indira, I won't get involved other than to prepare a report for MI5. I'll even hand it in anonymously.' his tone was pleading 'if I go to the police these dealers will know within the hour.'

'How do you know that Jack? How can you be certain? It all sounds so very strange to me.'

Jack felt bad lying to her but he could hardly tell he he'd tortured a man. 'I overheard one of their people boasting. It may have been just an empty boast but I cannot take the chance.'

She looked at him her luminous eyes filled with worry 'please Jack, if I do this, promise you'll not get involved, OK?'

Jack promised her he wouldn't get involved other than to hand the evidence to the relevant authority anonymously.

Indira reluctantly agreed and spent an hour listening intently and making notes. She summarized them for him: 'They seem to think you may be some sort of spy although they are far from certain. A man called Ali obviously holds older people in great contempt. He believes you wouldn't be capable of any effective action.

Then there is some madrasah in the Kielder Forest called The Flame of Truth that Khan funds. The young men there are training for a jihadist mission of some sort but they don't know exactly where or when other than it's to be soon and in London. They do seem quite certain though that a massive blow will be struck in London very soon' Indira looked deeply worried 'then there is an awful lot of chat about their families, about the drugs business and how prices on the street are falling due to oversupply.'

Jack pondered this information for a moment, the mention of Jihad, a holy war, was a completely new and worrying facet of the situation. It could be all hot air of course but he would need to find out more about this madrasah. It was an added complication and nothing to do with drugs.

Jack had a growing feeling within him of danger looming. He recognised the same feeling as when he'd been on his last assignment in Northern Ireland all those years ago. Things were not right then and he'd sensed it. His senses told him they were not right now.

Talk of a terror strike in London added a worrying new twist to the situation. How soon was soon? And was it even a real threat? It was unlikely that Khan would involve himself in that sort of action; drug dealers like him were not religious men, their only interest was self interest. He'd have to look into it, though, PDQ such attacks were a growing threat and an ever more likely possibility. Jack's personal belief was that a massive attack in the Capital was a matter of when not if.

'Jack what is going on?' Indira queried a worried look on her face. 'I don't like the tone of these men one bit and I don't want you mixed up in their business' her big brown eyes were serious and pleading 'Please Jack?'

Jack hated to deceive Indira but the fact was he didn't know what was going on himself. He was determined to find out though so he said 'Look Indira, I started off just trying to gather information on local drug dealers to hand to the police anonymously, that's all. These people killed my Sally and her friend and think they can get away with it. Well they can't.' His passion and determination radiated from him and his whole body tensed. 'It seems these people are into far more than just drugs.' He paused and looked into her big beautiful eyes trying to gauge the effect he was having on her. 'If you listen to the rest of the stuff tomorrow I can assess it and pass it on to the relevant authorities, OK?'

'OK Jack, but please don't involve yourself with these men, they sound very dangerous.' She looked extremely unhappy with the whole scenario but she agreed to go on for his sake. They went to bed that night and held each other close but neither of them felt like lovemaking.

Next day Indira rang Jack sick with worry. 'Jack these people are pure evil' she told him 'they're psychopaths Jack. They were talking of roasting someone called Waldo to death and it didn't sound like a joke either, Jack. They even mentioned killing you.'

Jack tried to calm her by telling her they were probably high on drugs and boasting of stuff they'd like to do, but she was having none of it. 'They talked about checking you out with MI5 Jack some guy called Ahmed is a double agent or something. They were frustrated because they couldn't access your file. Have you got a file Jack?'

Jack decided he must divulge some of his past, he'd never told Joan about in all their years of marriage. 'Indira, I used to be with Army intelligence' he told her patiently 'of course I have a file but it's classified at a very high level, they have no chance of gaining access. Anyway, even if they did, it's all ancient stuff now concerning the IRA. There's nothing there of any use to anyone.'

'The guy called Ali spoke of the Kielder Forest again and something about it all will come to pass very soon and London will never be the same again.' She paused and he heard her sobbing, her breath coming in gasps. 'Ali apparently has a nephew who is one of their chosen ones.'

'OK Indira' listen to me, don't worry yourself. I have no intention of approaching these people. I know they're dangerous and I'm already formulating a report for MI5.'

He paused to let her respond but she stayed silent. 'If I approach the authorities with what sounds like some cock and bull story accusing seemingly respectable citizens like Khan of being involved in terrorism without evidence I'd be laughed at. These people may then get the time they need to commit God alone knows what atrocities.' His voice took on a note of desperation 'please, Indira my love, be patient a little while longer, please?'

'But they already suspect you of involvement Jack, they could attack you at any time, aren't you afraid?'

'Yes, of course I am afraid, but I can't let them murder god knows how many innocent people without doing something about it Indira. Preparing a sound case and giving it to the authorities is what I'm going to do and quickly, too.'

They talked for a few minutes more and she hung up feeling far from reassured. Jack determined to pay a visit to this so-called madrasah and ascertain a few facts for himself. He researched it on line and was impressed by the professional web site and the stated aims of the establishment.

It all looked very worthy and respectable, even slightly boastful in the way it portrayed its facilities. There were photographs of smiling young men extolling the virtues of the place. It had been founded by one Imam Bhakti a leading moderate cleric and a pillar of British Islamic society. Jack recognised his photo; he'd seen the man on TV a number of times preaching moderation. There was also a picture of Khan who was portrayed as a philanthropist and benefactor. He'd contributed substantial funds to help set up and run the madrasah. If this place is as straight as Khan he thought, then it needs looking at real soon.

Jack went to his cellar to prepare the kit he thought he'd need for surveillance. The strange sense of foreboding increased. Next day Jack was up before dawn preparing for his visit to the Kielder Forest. He selected his clothes with care and took all the precautions he would have done if spying on the IRA in the old days. The drive up was long and tedious but he completed it stopping only to refuel and grab a hasty meal.

Leaving his car in a walkers' car park over a mile and a half away from the madrasah, Jack walked through the afternoon light up a broad track for half a mile then turned left up a rough steep track with a large sign that told him it was private property and to keep out.

It was gloomy under the close packed pines and Jack felt a sense of apprehension at the silence and stillness of the place. He made patient progress toward a point on his Ordnance Survey map where he could rest up from the steep climb and prepare his kit. He checked with his GPS every now and again comparing it with the map. Three hundred metres from the school and still out of its sight he left the track and headed cautiously through the trees to the hill that rose behind the complex.

Progress was now painfully slow in semi darkness as the trees closed in even more tightly. It was then that disaster struck.

Jack's foot caught under a root and he fell forward sliding ten feet down a steep bank. He plunged the last three feet into a shallow ravine landing hard on a protruding rock with his left thigh.

The pain that shot through him was intense and it was all he could do to stop himself crying out. He lay there for several minutes gasping for breath in absolute agony. At first he thought he'd broken his femur but he breathed slowly and deeply letting the pain subside. Checking himself out for broken bones he found none. He could move the leg but it hurt like hell. His fingers touched something that crunched.

Feeling in the map pocket on his thigh he discovered his phone was broken. The screen was shattered and the body bent. He cursed silently until he realised the phone had spread the impact of the sharp rock and had saved him from a broken leg. But it meant he had no means of communication and no camera.

He knew his mission had to go on however much it hurt, there was too much at stake. He lay where he was for half an hour massaging his injured limb and calming his mind. At last he felt a little better 'C'mon Jack' he muttered to himself 'sort yourself out' but it was easier said than done.

Crawling slowly from the gully Jack used a tree to pull himself upright. He stood leaning against it for a moment to allow the pain to subside a little then he continued at a snail's pace, every step sending a stab of fire though his thigh.

Sally's pretty face came smiling into Jack's mind. It's not just for you now my darling he thought, there's a lot of other innocents that could be killed.

Eventually he heard the steady hum of a well silenced generator. Going belly down he crawled the last few yards down the steep incline dragging his injured leg until he could look down on the compound.

 Just ahead of him grew a clump of thick gorse and he headed for it and lay behind it waiting until full dark.

As the stillness of the night enveloped him Jack heard the murmur of voices as the men read aloud from the Holy Qur'an then all went silent and the lights came on. At eleven o'clock the lights went on in the upper storey. Half an hour later the main generator cut out leaving the place in darkness except for an out building near the gate which had a small generator of its own. Jack soon saw why as the door opened and a young man walked out clutching a walky-talky to stand guard by the gate. Why, he wondered, would an innocent school require a guard? It rang alarm bells.

Jack's position was OK for now but not for daylight so he slowly and silently tunnelled into the gorse cutting sparingly here and there to shift the odd awkward branch. He suffered scratching to his hands and face as he silently and patiently bored his way in. These things could not be rushed. It was a full hour until at last he could see through the leading edge of the gorse.

Taking the camouflaged netting scarf from around his neck Jack hung it over the small observation hole he had made then rolled out a lightweight sleeping bag. Stuffing it under him a bit at a time he didn't get into it but lay on top for this night was not for sleeping. Backing carefully out of his hide Jack inspected it in the glimmer of pale light of the quarter moon that had struggled through the tree canopy. He then crept away some fifty metres and took out a plastic bag using it as a toilet. When he had finished he took a cable tie and closed the bag tightly. With his hunting knife, he dug a hole as deep as possible under a bush and buried his waste. The last thing he needed was some curious animal giving his position away.

Returning to his hide Jack carefully wormed his way back into it, pushing his rucksack in front of him so that he made the smallest possible hole. Lying on his back he closed the entrance with his feet as best he could; now for the long night ahead.

The guard changed every two hours promptly as a succession of young men kicked stones around the compound in bored resignation to their duty. Every so often the guard would switch on a flashlight and shine it around the perimeter. There goes his night vision Jack thought.

A dark shape moved near the chain link fence behind what he'd identified as the kitchen due to the large gas bottles standing in a row against the wall and oven vents through the roof.

Training his binoculars on the movement he saw it was a deer ambling along the fence grazing. It stopped and rubbed itself vigorously on one of the fence posts. No security light came on so the small generator powered only the lights of the guard hut, that was good to know. The animal, oblivious to his presence, continued on its way to a small stream that ran diagonally under the corner of the fence. There it paused and drank before vanishing into the forest. Thank you, dear deer he thought to himself you've helped me a great deal.

Dawn came early on this May morning and the compound rose from its slumber. As the sound of men at prayer floated up to him it began to rain gently and Jack was glad of his Gore-Tex clothing. He was shivering with cold and his leg had stiffened up considerably. It still hurt like hell but there was nothing he could do but suffer it.

What happened next came as a shock to Jack. As prayers ended a senior looking man in the robes of a cleric came out of the building with two young men. The young men turned down the track towards the road carrying hand held radios and the cleric turned through the gate in the opposite direction down a footpath to what appeared to be a great tangle of fallen branches and gorse.

He bent behind a tree and took a rope with a small grappling hook attached and threw it over a tree branch with practiced dexterity.

He hooked one of the fallen branches and began to pull. The whole tangle attached to a base of wooden pallets rose swiftly into the air revealing an olive green roller shutter door of a carefully camouflaged underground bunker. The man secured the rope then rolled up the shutter and called to the main building.

A shout went up and young men in double file ran out chanting some sort of military song. On joining the man at the bunker the men were each given an AK 47 assault rifle. For the next hour Jack watched as they drilled under the barn-like structure stripping and assembling the weapons blind folded. They also exercised without the rifles shouting slogans as they clambered over the assault course and ran around the football pitch. Jack wished he could have filmed them on his phone that would have been all the proof he needed. That they were very fit and dedicated was beyond doubt.

Training his binoculars on the bunker as the men finally returned their weapons Jack caught his breath. Now in full daylight he could see to the back of the bunker. Almost invisible in the gloom, were the shortest barrelled mortars he'd ever seen. Also, there were unidentified boxes that puzzled him. They weren't mortar ammunition he recognised those boxes, they hadn't changed from his Army days.

What the hell were these people doing with mortars? He needed to report this but to whom? From the recorded conversation, it was obvious that Ahmed was a double agent. He fed MI5 with information on rival dealers and sacrificed a few loudmouthed so-called radicals who were all talk and no action. He fed Khan with valuable information on MI5 operations in return.

Jack knew that any MI5 agent who ran an informant only received information they never gave it out unless it was for a specific, limited purpose. The only logical conclusion was that the agent was, as suggested by the recordings, on the take. Who was this person? What level did they work at?

Jack felt worried and puzzled. He'd promised Indira he'd not get involved and here he was being sucked into a situation against his will. If this information got into the wrong hands Jack knew he could be signing his own death warrant and that of Indira, too.

He was confounded for the moment, every avenue seemed blocked to him. The Police and MI5 couldn't be trusted so who the hell could he tell? What hard evidence had he got anyway? The tapes could be put down to bragging among work colleagues trying to impress one another. There was nothing specific on them, no targets, no dates no method of attack, nothing. One thing was clear in Jack's mind, these people had to be stopped.

Jack could not move from his hide until after dark, he was a bare fifteen metres from the compound fence on a steep forward slope. Any attempt to move back up the hill and away could easily be spotted from the madrasah. He spent his time making a detailed sketch of the compound, the bunker and the guard house. Everything he could see he drew with meticulous attention to detail. It was just like the old days in Northern Ireland when he'd lie in a ditch or under a hedge for two or three days eating cold rations and drinking only water with plastic bags for a toilet. His job was watching and waiting, noting the movements of people, recording vehicle registrations and gathering crucial intelligence.

In mid afternoon Jack thought he detected a sound off to his left a cracking branch he thought. He was at once alert, animals don't crack branches. He put his binoculars in the direction he thought the sound came from. After a minute, he saw a bush move slightly then a long lens poked through the foliage. So, someone else was suspicious of these people, but who? Had they got photos of the arms? It was hours since they'd put the assault rifles away so Jack reckoned they hadn't otherwise they'd have fled by now.

Whoever it was Jack needed to speak to them but the person was in grave danger of being spotted. He's so bloody clumsy thought Jack. God, why didn't he take more care? The lens disappeared and the bushes were stilled. Half an hour later the doors of the Madrassah opened and the men came out in track suits and made their way to the assault course.

Jack glanced to his left. Again, he detected slight movement and the lens came out once more. The sun broke through the clouds and Jack saw to his dismay that the camera lens was now shining. He groaned inwardly as a shout went up. One of the men was pointing and gesticulating. The men all started running around the outside of the compound fence in the direction of the cameraman.

Jack saw him then, the man looked in his late thirties as he got up and shuffled off into the woods. With his paunch overhanging his trousers and a heavy camera round his neck he was never going to get far. Jack groaned in dismay as he saw the guy was dressed in street clothes and shoes. It was a short chase. The man was dragged back to the compound shouting 'you can't do this to me, I'm Truegood, national press. The public have a right to know.'

They ignored him and continued to drag him into the compound. They halted not twenty metres from Jack. Two men held the journalist's arms, another two stood behind him. The senior looking cleric who'd earlier issued the arms came and stood before him. He signalled the men and they released him. Truegood stood glowering balefully at them.

'You were warned last time you came to stay away for good were you not, Mr Truegood?'

Truegood began to bluster 'I don't ask anyone's permission to do my job, the public have a right to know' he repeated as if the hackneyed phrase was some kind of get out of jail free charm.

'The cleric's face was stony 'Your editor was instructed to order you to drop your witch hunt I believe, did he not tell you?'

'Mallinson? That wimp? Yes, he told me but I don't take orders off him. I go where my nose leads me and my nose leads me here.' He looked defiantly at his interrogator 'I know you're up to no good here and I intend to find out what it is.'

The cleric rubbed his beard thoughtfully for a few seconds 'so how did you explain were you were going to your colleagues? Aren't you afraid they'll inform on you? This unwarranted intrusion could cost you your job, don't you realise?'

The cleric's voice was calm with no hint of threat or even annoyance but Jack saw the trap at once. For Christ's sake tell him everyone knows you're here, you damned fool he thought.

But the journalist, full of self-importance and righteous indignation, said 'I don't let those story stealers into my comings and goings. I'm a senior correspondent.'

'So you came alone? That was very brave of you. Didn't you think that might be dangerous if we are the villains you fear we are?'

'You wouldn't dare harm a senior member of the National Press' Truegood blustered 'over two million people read my column every day so if I can have my camera I'll be on my way, thank you.'

Jack groaned inwardly. Oh Christ, he thought, the idiot's full of piss and wind. He's a dead man.

'This way if you please, Mr Truegood.' said the cleric and turned towards the madrassah door. He nodded towards the woods where Truegood had been hiding and whispered an order as he passed one of the men. Jack's heart sank, he knew exactly what that order was.

They came in line abreast five metres apart sweeping though the woods prodding bushes with sticks, the man in charge five paces behind them closely supervising the work. Jack pulled his binoculars under his body then tugged his hoodie up and put his face down lest the white of his skin gave him away. He drew his knife. If they find me I'll take at least two of the bastards with me he thought.

The pair who explored the gorse patch where Jack lay hidden were two very different characters. One man was prodding and poking with great vigour, the other seemed reluctant to get too close to the prickly gorse.

The enthusiast's stick came nearer and nearer to Jack one prod missed his face by two inches, the next would surely find him. Then a voice spoke impatiently in English 'Hamza, you couldn't get a rat in there it's so tight and thorny. Move on, catch up with the others quickly, it's almost time to eat.'

Jack's hand relaxed on his knife handle as the tension drained from him and his nerves stopped jangling but the sweat continued to drip from his brow. The voices receded until, satisfied, they finished their sweep and returned to the compound. He heard one of the four by fours start up and drive around to the front of the building. A trussed up Truegood was carried out struggling violently his mouth taped over. They threw him unceremoniously into the back of the cab and two burly men climbed in after him. Truegood was taking his last ride.

Jack watched as steam started to rise from the kitchen telling him they were now preparing a meal. He unwrapped a couple of high energy bars and began to chew slowly on them. He then had a few sips of water after which he dozed for a few hours whilst the sound of the students reading aloud was a constant drone in his ear, he would awaken at once the droning stopped.

In early evening, he awoke suddenly alerted by a faint sound close by. He didn't move a muscle; his hand gripped the hilt of his knife as he lay listening intently his heart pounding. The sound came again and he relaxed, it was a deer grazing nearby. Jack hoped the animal didn't suddenly get his scent and take off, startled. After a few minutes the sound receded leaving him to breathe more easily. One minute later the chanting ceased.

After their dinner, the students went to a building out of sight round the end of the main building to Jack's right. There came the sound of motorcycle engines and then they appeared by the front gate a rider and a pillion passenger on each machine. They set off with a roar down the track and then took a new direction. Jack checked his map there was a firebreak or another trail which led off into the woods. They were gone for about half an hour before they returned to ride around the football pitch a couple of times whooping and waving before disappearing from Jack's view again to store the bikes. He knew the bikes were a part of the plot, probably to deliver the men rapidly to their targets.

The young men came back and played football, dashing about shouting to each other as they kicked the ball and scurried after it. Some of them were quite skilled Jack noticed. It was hard to believe that these young men who were shouting and laughing with such obvious enjoyment had such deadly purpose. They played for about an hour then a whistle blew and they went inside and the chanting resumed.

As it grew into twilight Jack heard voices close by. Two men emerged along an animal track below him and sat down on a fallen tree. They were a bare three metres away and he could see and hear them clearly. They lit cigarettes and smoked in silence for a while. Finally, one man addressed the other. 'They are to drown the fool in Wastwater Farooq, then put him in his car and drive it in. If he is ever found it will look like an accident'

'Why drive so far Hamza, surely it would be easier to bury him deep in the woods?'

'We take no chances, besides, Wastwater is the deepest lake in England. It will be many months if not years before he's found.'

'Serves him right, he was warned not to return. The arrogant kuffar has brought it upon himself.'

Jack knew the body of Truegood would probably be found that same weekend as dozens of scuba divers descended on the lake. He'd dived there himself in the past, it was a very popular venue. So, these bastards can make mistakes he thought, and that thought brought him some comfort.

'The time draws near Farooq I can sense it, why else would Hassid himself be visiting us? Whatever the target is I will endeavour to do my best and die bravely.'

Farooq didn't answer for a few seconds, drawing heavily on his cigarette then he said 'I will miss my family of course, but Inshalla, I shall achieve martyrdom fulfilling God's will.'

They sat in silence smoking for a while then got up to go. Farooq turned and looked up the hill and for a moment it appeared to Jack that he was staring straight his eyes. 'Such a beautiful place' he said then turned to his friend 'it's nearly time for salat alisha Hamza, let's go.'

Finally, full darkness fell and Jack crept out of his hide making sure nothing was left behind. He carefully closed the entrance again and exercised his stiffened leg. He winced as he did some slow painful squats. After a few minutes, the pain eased and he could use the leg a little better. He made his way slowly down to the perimeter fence and the stream where he'd seen the deer drinking. The fence ran straight over the top of the stream leaving a gap underneath which had been filled with coiled barbed wire. On checking the wire he found it had simply been thrown into the stream and was not fastened down. Thank God for lazy bastards he thought.

Continuing around the fence away from the guard post, Jack reached the arms bunker then waited until the lights in the madrasah had been out for half an hour before he retrieved the rope. It took him three tries to get it over a branch but at last he was able to uncover the cache and try to look inside. It was locked with a strong security lock that he had no equipment with him to defeat. One rifle would be all the evidence he needed but it was not to be. There was nothing he could do about it for the moment he had to get to London he needed to get to a trusted person in MI5, but who?

Jack ruled out reporting to the local Northumberland police they would be seriously undermanned at this time of night and the fire arms unit, if it could be made available at short notice, would be far too small to deal with all these guys. Whilst they were still following police procedures, doing risk assessments and trying to negotiate they'd have their box ticking, rule bound arses blown to hell. No, he decided it had to be London. This job would need at least a full Sabre Squadron of the SAS.

The drive was long and Jack had to fight against sleep the whole way. He rang Indira from a call box in the motorway service station; she was beside herself with worry. 'Jack where on earth have you been for the last twenty four hours?' Her voice sounded anxious but not angry. He explained as briefly as he could, leaving out all reference to Truegood. He heard her burst into tears on the other end of the line. 'You promised me Jack that you wouldn't become involved. You promised me.'

'I haven't become involved darling' he said soothingly 'I've simply been gathering the facts so I can put in a cohesive report to MI5' he sighed feeling deeply sorry for her, how the hell did he ever think involving her was a good idea?

There was a long pause 'I think I should go to the local police and tell them what I know and hand over the transcripts' she said at last 'let them deal with it.'

Jack's voice became at once urgent. 'Please Indira, please' he begged 'you don't know the size or strength of Khan's influence. If you go to the police he will find out within an hour. You'll be signing both ort death warrants and there's nothing on those recordings that can be used as hard evidence' His voice conveyed such seriousness that her resolve faltered.

'What are you going to do then, Jack?'

'First, I'm going home then I'm going to grab a couple of hours sleep, I'm falling off my perch with fatigue' he said wearily 'then I'm going to Millbank to report to MI5.'

'O K darling, but please take care, I love you and now that I've found such happiness I'd be totally lost without you.' There was helplessness in her voice that conveyed both acceptance of the situation and a dread of things going wrong. It made his heart ache. 'Be very careful Jack' she pleaded.

Indira was a very sweet lady and the truth was he'd be lost without her, too 'I will be really careful my love, I promise.' He hung up feeling very low, he knew what he must do and knew it would hurt her immeasurably if she thought he hadn't told her the whole truth. Suddenly he felt a burning hatred flood his senses. 'God damn you Khan and the whole bloody lunatic bunch of you' he muttered.

*****

Ahmed was not a trained MI5 agent he was merely a clever criminal who happened to be a trained chef that MI5 believed they'd recruited to spy on Khan. He'd been playing both sides for a couple of years now, knowing it was a dangerous though very lucrative game. He in turn had eventually introduced his handler to Khan who had made him a relatively rich man in return for information as and when requested. Ahmed had family in Pakistan and knew one phone call from Khan would be all that was needed to have them disappear or be arrested on some trumped up charge.

Khan reported what he had discovered to Hassid there was no point creating suspicion by trying to hide anything. Hassid said he had done well and that there was another channel to explore which could throw light on the Ellis conundrum. 'I'll call you soon' he told Khan.

Imam Bhakti rang the security Minister's private secretary Omar Rizah. The man was a British born citizen of Arabic extraction and, on the surface, a devout Muslim. Rizah was a man much troubled with a dark secret, one that could bring the deepest shame on his family. He liked men.

Bhakti, a shrewd man, had sensed what his real problem was when Rizah had gone to him for spiritual guidance. The man had made subtle allusions to being cast from a high place. This had been confirmed by Khan who had contacts in very many places. One of these places was a male only massage parlour called Studz where Rizah was a frequent customer. Khan made it his business to know of every place were drugs could be sold. Places like Mrs. Grey's paedophile guest house where he'd first met Waldo Williams and recruited him to his business.

Bhakti used this knowledge to blackmail Rizah into spying for him, feeding him with information, gossip and proposed plans in Whitehall. He now needed to call Rizah for certain highly secret information. 'You will obtain the file on this man Jack Ellis' he said as casually as if he'd asked for the time of day.

'But you don't understand how difficult that is' Rizah had protested nervously 'the Minister has no reason to send for such documents.'

'Then you must forge his signature and obtain them' was the harsh reply 'with luck, they'll be back in the archives before anyone queries their withdrawal.' Bhakti was seething with anger although he controlled it well. He needed to know urgently what he faced and if he had to sacrifice Rizah in the process then so be it. Nothing could be allowed to endanger his plans.

'The Minister receives a list of all classified documents he's called for at the end of every week' Rizah said his stomach churning with fear 'it's both a security check and a reminder of the documents he holds so that nothing gets overlooked.'

'Then you'd better do it today and get me a copy as soon as possible, your life and the lives of your entire family depend upon it.' The phone went dead in Rizah's hand and he sat at his desk trembling for what seemed an age.

It was Wednesday. The Minister was in the House of Commons for Prime Minister's question time that afternoon so he would do it then but he'd have to be careful. He realized his career was over and that he would probably go to prison but that was better than himself and all his family being butchered.

The Minister was extremely careful in his handling of secret documents. Unlike some other Ministers, he never took them home to work on. His laptop used for this work had a password known only to the Minister. The machine was encrypted, but even so it never left his office. There had been too many scandals lately and careers had come to an abrupt end when people had left laptops on trains or had them stolen from their cars.

Rizah decided he had no choice but to comply to protect his family. He then would take his own life if discovered rather than face the shame of arrest and trial. A plan came to him that offered a glimmer of hope, it wasn't much but there was at least a slim chance of it working. He'd have to act very quickly.

The Ellis file was an old paper based one, it had not been microfilmed nor computerised. It simply lay gathering dust with other obsolete files. Rizah withdrew it without difficulty and copied page after page, ninety seven in all, and placed them in his briefcase. He returned the files to the archive immediately afterwards telling the archivist they had been withdrawn by mistake and were not needed after all. Because the documents had been out for such a short period and had been declared withdrawn in error he hoped that would be enough to keep them off the official check list, but he doubted it.

When the minister returned from the House he had much to do and kept Rizah very late so it wasn't until after eleven o'clock that Bhakti received the information.

That same Wednesday morning Khan had received a phone call from one of his restaurant managers in Manchester. There had been a fire overnight and the damage to the kitchen was quite extensive. The manager hadn't rung earlier because he's been tied up with the police and fire brigade and had wanted to gather as many facts as possible before ringing. The cause of the blaze was at that point a mystery.

When Khan heard this his paranoia went into overdrive. So professionally had his shop been torched the authorities still didn't know how it had been achieved. Now he was being attacked again, this time in the North. What the hell was going on? He was being systematically destroyed by someone and had he to find out who was doing this and fast. Khan's normal calm logic deserted him and something akin to panic took its place. Hassid had told him to concentrate all his resources on his orders. But this was his business built over twenty years of careful work and he had to know what was going on.

Khan expected a wait of at least a couple of days before hearing from Hassid so he took off immediately for Manchester. Shortly after he arrived it was discovered the fire was purely an accident. Some idiotic waiter had left tea towels to dry too close to an electric heater in store room off the kitchen overnight. The damage was, as reported, quite extensive but there was no malicious intent evident. Tired and frustrated he had retired to his Didsbury house and went to bed. Four hours later Hassid rang his mobile his voice urgent.

'Khan, the Imam has managed to access the file on this man Ellis it seems he was formally known as Belthorn, a professional assassin for the British Army's Intelligence Corps in the seventies. He had to be given a new identity when an operation went wrong. He was a highly trained and very dangerous operator. Pick him and that American fellow up at once.'

Khan was stunned, his head spun and he climbed out of bed and sat down heavily in an armchair 'What?' he gasped 'Do you mean to tell me we've been given the run-around by some damned geriatric has-been? He's working for the Americans?' His mind was reeling, unable to evaluate the consequences of what he was being told. 'I'll have them eliminated immediately' he said, his confusion now giving way to blind rage.

'You'll do no such thing you fool' Hassid said 'we need to find out how much they know and who they have told.' He paused listening to Khan's uneven breath the man's anxiety was palpable.

'You must supervise their interrogation personaly, Khan. Ellis is an old man and I don't want those sadistic goons of yours killing him before we know everything, OK? Report to me every hour until we know all there is to know of their activities and connections. We need to know everything they know and fast.' The urgency in the man's voice was unmistakable. 'The act is to take place this Saturday morning, if we have to adjust our plans we need to know Nothing must be allowed to jeopardize it Khan, nothing!'

Khan quaked inside, his throat was dry and his hands clammy it would take him well over three hours to get back to London. He could risk bluffing and ring Hassid every hour telling him they had failed to find their men but with his resources Khan knew there was every chance he would not be believed.

To be found out in this deceit would mean a painful death. If he told the truth now they would be angry but may well overlook this one mistake when he and got the required information and eliminated the problem. If he then paid a heavy financial penalty and made a grovelling apology they might well be appeased, providing the strike was successful. Running away with his millions and hiding was not even worth considering, it would merely be a delayed death sentence for himself, his wife, son and daughter.

'I'm in Manchester at the moment on a matter most urgent sir, I will immediately return to London, in the meantime I'll have my men pick these fellows up and hold them.'

There was a long pause whilst Hassid took in what Khan had said 'I told you Khan that no concern of business or family was to get in the way of your total concentration on this matter, did I not? His voice was low and soft and filled with menace.

Khan felt faint, the tremour in his voice was audible 'yes sir, but....but I didn't expect results so soon. It really was a very urgent matter sir..I…'

'Be silent' Hassid snapped 'we will talk about this later, in the meantime you know what to do so get on with it.' The phone went dead and Khan's head sunk into his hands his emotions in turmoil. Fear, anger and hatred for these men who had caused him so much trouble all fought for precedence. He would make them pay dearly for this interference, very dearly indeed.

*****

Returning home as the sun broke the horizon filtered by the city smog, Jack was very tired yet some primeval urge cautioned him not to go to bed just yet. His subconscious had whispered 'poor prior planning produces piss poor performance.' Why that came to him now he no idea but he acted on it.

Going to his cellar he opened a drawer under the workbench. He withdrew what looked like a piece of copper plumbing pipe and some monofilament fishing line. Back in the hall he took up his walking stick and removed the rubber end piece. He then threaded the fishing line through a tiny hole under the handle down the hollow inside. Taking the end, he tied it to a metal loop on top of the copper tube then inserted it in the stick fitting a hard rubber locking ring around it. Making a small knot under the handle he gave it a tug and watched with satisfaction as a razor sharp eight inch blade flashed out and locked into position with a satisfying click. Jack smiled and reloaded the blade and replaced the end cap. The walking stick was returned to the hall stand. He then took a quick shower, set his alarm and went to bed falling at once into a deep exhausted sleep.

*****

John Westaway sat at a pavement table at a Costa coffee shop near Sloan Square. It was his first day off since taking up his new liaison post and he was familiarising himself with the streets of the British Capital. At least that was what he set out to do early on this fine spring morning but for the last hour he'd had the feeling that he was being watched. He hadn't seen anyone behaving suspiciously but he never ignored his instincts; they'd saved his life more than once.

He sat with his coffee and a newspaper on a street front table surreptitiously scanning the street. He looked relaxed dressed in loafers, chinos and a blue turtle necked sweater over a check shirt; the quintessential middle class idler.

Why would anyone be interested in me? he thought. I've only been in London for two weeks. He felt a sense of puzzlement. He could think of no reason why his British counter parts would follow him. Maybe he was getting paranoid in his old age?

He put his paper down stretched then seemed rubbed his eyes like a man recently out of bed. To the observer it looked for all the world that he was unsighted. An ideal time for a watcher to change position and sure enough, fifty metres up the street a young white man stepped from the deep shade of a shop doorway and approached the cafe. Westaway picked up his paper again, shook it into submission and continued reading. The guy went inside and ordered a coffee. Westaway could have moved then but that could have alerted the man to the fact he'd been rumbled.

Twenty five years in the field had honed Westaway's instincts to a fine edge. He would play the dummy and see what happened. The guy returned with his coffee and took a corner table as far away as he could get from him, took out his phone and began texting. Ah, he thought, he's taking my picture, now what does he want with that? He was intrigued as he was not involved in any active operation, he'd barely been begun working with his British liaison team who had no reason to suspect him of anything. This guy didn't look like an agent anyway. If he had been forced to make a guess he'd probably say the guy was a conman looking for a mark. But why me? I don't look like a tourist.

Westaway started like a man slightly surprised then reached in his pocket and took out his phone, quizzing the screen. He then put the phone to his ear and turned towards the street 'Yes Mack? Oh, fine thanks, and you? Good. He listened for a while then said 'oh OK, I'll see you tonight then. Yup, you too, bye.' He slipped the phone back in his pocket and lifted his coffee.

*****

Jack had been asleep for two hours when he awoke with a start as bright daylight came flooding into his bedroom blinding him temporarily as someone jerked opened the curtains. To his horror he saw the huge figure of Azziz standing over him on one side of the bed with Mansoor standing on the other side sneering at him. Azziz held a gun and Mansoor a wicked looking flick knife. Azziz grabbed him roughly and dragged him out of bed. 'Get dressed' he ordered in a flat emotionless voice 'be quick and be quiet or I'll kill you right here, right now.'

Jack obeyed looking dazed but his head was clearing fast. He saw the time 07:29 one minute before his alarm was due to go off. Cursing under his breath Jack did as he was bid, choosing black jeans and a light loose fitting dark blue jumper, socks and a pair of black Nike trainers finished the job. He switched off the alarm when it started to beep. He was ordered downstairs into the hall towards the front door. He didn't have to affect his limp as his leg was still stiff. 'I'll need my walking stick' he told Azziz.

'To hell with your stick you old fool. You'll need more than a stick when we've finished with you' Mansoor said with an evil leer.

'Give him his stick Ali' Azziz told Mansoor in Urdu 'It's a busy street even at this time of day and local people are bound to know this man.'

Mansoor hesitated, looking sullen at being overruled.

'If nieghbours see him leaving his house with two strangers they may be curious. If they see him leaving with us limping and without his normal walking stick then they may become suspicious.' Azziz gave an impatient grunt 'Attention to detail Ali and for God's sake smoke less of that skunk man, you're getting sloppy.'

Mansoor was furious at being told off, his eyes glinted dangerously. Just then Mischief came out of the living room. She was a very tame animal and, seeing strangers, thought she'd make friends. She rubbed herself against Mansoor's leg purring for attention.

'No Mischief, go away' Jack said urgently. Mansoor gave Jack a look of pure evil, bent and grabbed the hapless animal behind her neck. Thrusting her into the air he slit her throat with a single vicious stroke of his knife then threw her writhing body down the hall, the lifeblood pulsing out of her.

'There you are' he mocked 'one halal cat.'

Jack felt deeply shocked and an ice cold rage consumed him at this needless cruelty inflicted on a harmless animal but his face remained stony, his eyes cold as tomb stones. Azziz had put the gun away now and had drawn a knife.

'You will walk to the car at the pavement, don't hurry, don't look around, you get in the back. Do you understand?'

Jack nodded still glaring at Mansoor.

'If you cause us any trouble I'll stick you on the spot, that clear?'

'Yes.'

'You've caused us a lot of trouble Ellis and now we have nothing to lose' he lied 'one wrong move and it's over for you.'

Jack didn't believe him, he knew that if Khan wanted him dead he's be dead by now but there was nothing he could do at the moment. They could wound him that was for sure and being wounded would lessen considerably his chances of escape.

They walked to the car Mansoor opened the rear door and held his hand out for the stick. Jack got into the back as instructed and his captors got into the front after closing his door.

'Child safety locks are on and the windows are switched to driver control' Azziz told Jack unnecessarily, he'd already figured that out.

The ride was short, they pulled up outside the takeaway and Mansoor got out and opened the door then Azziz accompanied Jack inside. Once through the door Azzziz walked ahead, Mansoor pushed Jack violently ahead of him to the store room.

The room was dimly lit by a single naked bulb and Jack struggled to accustom his eyes after the broad daylight of the street. It was lined on three sides with shelves upon which various tins and bags of catering stuff were stacked. In the empty space in the middle was a single dining chair. Laid out on a side table were an electric chain saw, a hammer drill, some pliers and what looked like medieval thumb screws. There were several meat hooks and instruments Jack couldn't put a name to. His blood ran cold.

Mansoor threw Jack's walking stick into a corner. 'You won't need that again Mr. James fucking Bond' he scoffed. 'We've seen your file mate we know all about your hitman activities. Who knows, when we've finished with you, we might sell what's left of you to the IRA.' he laughed sadistically at his own joke.

Jack was forced into the upright dining chair and Azziz produced some long cable ties handing half to Mansoor. They started at his legs fixing them firmly to the chair. Then, as they were securing his hands to the chair's back legs the shop door entry warning ping ponged.

The men froze. Azziz recovered first slamming his hand over Jack's mouth and glaring at Mansoor. 'Didn't you lock the bloody door Ali?' his face was a mask of fury.

Mansoor paled 'I.. I'm sorry.' he stammered.

'Go and get rid of whoever that is you damned fool' Azziz hissed 'and be quick about it.'

Mansoor hurried off to deal with the newcomer. Azziz produced a roll of duct tape and fastened some across Jack's mouth before following Mansoor.

In the shop, a dishevelled man who looked the worse for drink stood swaying 'Hi mate, can I order a curry?' he slurred.

'We're closed sir, I'm sorry' said Mansoor sounding flustered 'We open at five thirty.'

'But I'm on me way 'ome an' I want a curry now, Abdul me old mate' the man swayed looking around Mansoor trying to see through the hatch into the kitchen. 'Yer've got enough chefs, ain't yer?'

Mansoor's voice rose 'Do you know what time of day it is? he asked irritably 'No takeaway is open at this time in the morning just go, OK?'

'No need to get upset Abdul me old mate. Keep yer hair on.'

Mansoor move towards the man his self control exhausted.

Azziz appeared from the rear his huge frame filling the kitchen doorway. He, too, wanted to grab this drunk and throw him bodily through the front door but that could cause complications.

With a great effort he controlled his voice 'I'm sorry sir, but we have had a gas leak and we've had to close the kitchen' he said apologetically. 'You know what these service engineers are like they said they'll be here between 9 a.m. and 2 p.m. so we just have to wait.'

He walked over, brushing past Mansoor who stepped back to let Azziz deal with the situation. He placed his huge arm huge arm around the man's shoulder and smiling in a friendly manner he was far from feeling guided him to the front door. 'Please come back tomorrow and say Azziz says you can have a free nan bread with your curry, OK?'

The man gave a drunken lopsided smile 'OK mate, thass good hov yer' he hiccupped and staggered away.

Mansoor looked disgusted 'drunk at this time of day, the decadent kuffar bastard.'

Azziz ignored the remark, his face remained impassive 'You should have locked the door behind us Ali, do I have to think of everything?'

Mansoor looked crestfallen but his ego wouldn't let him apologise for his fundamental mistake. 'I need a smoke' he said heading for the back door.

No you don't Ali, Azziz thought; you are smoking far too much of that shit these days and you are beginning to slip my friend. It looks as though I'm going to need a new partner soon. Fifteen years we've been a good team but you're getting past it mate.

Azziz made his mind up to kill Mansoor as soon as this job was over, their supposed friendship meant nothing to the cold psychopath.

Azziz went into the kitchen and made himself a mug of tea, carrying it into the shop he settled at the table then took out his phone and rang Jonny Burke 'Pick up the American guy as soon as possible.'

'OK Boss, I'll organize it.'

'Good, but quietly, no witnesses, OK?'

'Sure.'

When Khan had asked Jonny Burke to investigate any American's other than tourists new in the area it hadn't taken long. He'd put the word out to the porters and other hotel staff who sold his drugs to the tourists. Westaway had stood out, he had no cameras or video equipment, he didn't go on tours and went to the American Embassy by taxi most days. Sometimes he went to estate agents, too.

Jonny Burke wanted to get closer find out what the guy was up to. He wanted a photo to put about so others could report his movements, too. Where did he go? Who did he meet when not at the embassy? Khan had put a big pay packet on this one and Burke had no intention of giving it to an underling who might mess it up and bring down the wrath of drug baron on his head.

*****

The American finished his coffee, folded his paper then went inside to the toilets. Burke affected to ogle a girl in a tight sweater sitting just inside the doorway. He could keep an eye on the door of gents from here and also see if the guy tried to slip out the back way. A couple of minutes later Westaway emerged and nodded goodbye to the baristas before casually sauntering back to his hotel.

Burke need not watch any longer, the hall porter was one of his pushers and would inform him if he went out again. Yes sir, this American guy wasn't going anywhere or meeting anyone without him knowing. He reported to Azziz.

In his room Westaway uploaded the video he'd taken of Jonny Burke and made a call. 'He might just be a chancer looking for a mark but until Abdullah's dead I'm not taking even the slightest chance' he said.

He hung up and took a shower then caught up on some background reading on the British etiquette of liaison for security staff, boring but essential.

Westaway had been extremely busy liaising with his British opposite number. The guy had annoyed him at first as he seemed too laid back, not taking terrorists threats seriously enough.

As they days rolled by he realised that Kevin Foster was very serious and professional indeed. It was just his natural reserve and tendency towards British understatement that made him seem casual. 'John, we've been working bloody hard these last three days and that hotel room can't be much fun. He smiled warmly. 'Why not come over for dinner with me and Sue tonight, we have a few other guests and you'd be most welcome.'

'Sure Kevin, that sounds real nice, what time?'

The party was indeed lively and Westaway was beginning to understand the British a bit better. They were a reserved bunch until they got to know you then, boy, they let their hair down with the best of them. It was a well fed, pleasantly inebriated John Westaway that finally weaved his way into a taxi at 1.30 a.m.

Next day he slept until 9 a.m, which was late for him. It was a day off so he'd gone out for a stroll, but now he'd had to check a certain stranger before he could call Bridget. He uploaded the footasge he'd taken and submitted his enquiry.

Two hours later he checked his watch. It was time to call home.

'I think you'll like it over here honey, they know how to party.'

She laughed 'well I hope they have good baby sitters because otherwise we'll be stymied.'

She wasn't due for another month and then she wouldn't fly until the child was six weeks or so. They chatted amiably teasing each other with light banter.

The call was over all too quickly and he turned on the TV. He found a Clint Eastwood Western he'd seen before, but he watched it anyway. He then he did some paperwork before he slept ,his hectic schedule had finally caught up with him.

At six o'clock he decided to go out for dinner and changed into slacks, check open necked shirt and a tweed jacket. Down in the hotel foyer his instincts started to trouble him again. The doorman looked up from some luggage he was handling and gave him a half smile, glancing away just a fraction too quickly. John thought the guy looked furtive.

Instead of going out he sat on a settee where he could see through the double glass doors to the street and a line of waiting taxis.

A couple went out and the doorman, his work with the luggage done, waved at the rank. The front taxi stayed where it was and the second in line pulled around it and picked up the couple.

Westaway was immediately alert. After a minute he got up and slowly wandered out and the doorman greeted him, his smile fixed. 'Taxi sir?'

'Yes please.'

The man waved and the front taxi pulled forward.

'Oh sorry, no, no on second thoughts I'll walk' he said.

The doorman looked discomforted beyond what John would have expected 'It's getting a bit like New York in London sir, always best to go by cab, sir.'

John thought nice try ass hole but we'll see what they do next. 'No, I'll walk, thank you' he replied firmly and with that he made off waving an apology at the Asian cab driver.

John had gone about two blocks and was passing a terrace of large beautiful white Georgian town houses. They had long been split into several dwellings and had steep steps leading down to the basement apartments. The pavement maple trees cast their deep shade on the sparsely peopled pavement. He was about to turn up a one way street against the traffic flow to give any vehicle pursuer a hard time when the taxi suddenly appeared and screeched to a halt alongside him. Two men jumped out and ran towards him making a grab for him with the intent of dragging him into the taxi.

Westaway sidestepped the first guy, putting himself between him and the second man. He knocked aside the man's grasping hand and grabbed his coat collar. Heaving hard, he twisted and swept the guy's legs from under him with his foot.

The element of surprise had been reversed. With a startled cry the man catapulted forward over the basement steps falling a good ten feet and landing with a meaty thud. The second guy was the one who'd followed him earlier. He had a knife. He grabbed John's jacket front holding the knife back from John's reach 'Get in the cab or I'll stick yer' he snarled.

Before either of them could move there was the roaring of a high powered engine then another car drew to a screeching halt behind the cab. The doors flew open and two men jumped out. Jonny Burke hesitated for a second, looking from John to them.

It was all Westaway needed needed, his right hand shot up under his opponent's chin and shoved him backward at the same time he grabbed his knife hand twisting it then seizing a little finger he forced it back sharply. He heard the man scream as the finger broke and the knife fell to the pavement.

Burke tore himself away and dived back the cab yelling 'go, go.' The driver reversed hard into the other car with the intention of disabling it so rendering pursuit impossible he then shot the wrong way down the one way street to the blare of angry horns and out of sight.

'Jesus John, you ain't been here five minutes and you try to get yourself kidnapped. What the hell is going on?'

It was Brian Greenwood, Westaway's immediate boss and one of the embassy's burly marine security guards in civilian clothes. When he'd reported the morning's events and they'd agreed they should watch his back until they had answers.

'The guy down the steps might have some answers' John suggested 'let's go wake him up.'

They walked down the steps to where the assailant lay motionless in deep shadow. The Marine bent and placed his fingers on the side of the man's neck then shook his head. A pool of blood was spreading outwards from the back of the man's head. He was permanently beyond giving information.

Westaway sat reading the file the British police had provided. They had identified the living kidnapper as one Jonny Burke, a mid ranking drug dealer with a string of convictions for dealing and violence. There was nothing current outstanding against him. He was puzzled as to why a British drug dealer would want to kidnap him. Greenwood put it down to a case of mistaken identity. John was not at all certain that was the case and moved into the embassy as a precaution.

His job now demanded much of his time but Westaway still wanted to get to the bottom of why Burke, who'd disappeared from his usual haunts, wanted to kidnap him.

*****

Making his way through the city centre traffic was not easy. Even at this early hour it was busy and road works hadn't helped. Khan had to force himself to keep calm and concentrate on his driving. He at last reached the M56 and was passing Manchester airport when he received the call from Azziz 'we've got Ellis boss he's safely trussed up in the storeroom. We are working on picking up the American. Any further instructions?'

Khan breathed a sigh of relief 'Well done Muszra, but don't touch the bastard yet, I want him fresh as a daisy. Have you got your usual paraphernalia?'

'Yes sir, blowtorch, hammer drill, pliers, a chainsaw and some new thumbscrews I'd like to try out.' His voice was as matter-of-fact as if he were discussing a routine DIY job. 'Mansoor has his knife of course and is anxious to practice his skinning skills.'

'Excellent, I'll see you as soon as I can in the meantime don't let the tricky bastard have any food, water or use the toilet. He might be old but he's very resourceful.'

Azziz made a guttural sound, half laugh, half contempt for the mere thought that this man could possibly escape now that he was in their grasp.

In the dim light of the storeroom Jack was rapidly assessing his situation. These people had obviously seen his file which meant there was a traitor at the very highest level but that was a moot point now. He tested his bonds, the right hand that Azziz had secured was tight and it hurt to try to move it in the slightest.

Mansoor had been in the act of securing his left hand when the door chime had alarmed him and he'd frozen in the act. This cable tie was nowhere near as tight as the right. Jack began tugging at it. It cut into the back of his hand but he ignored the pain, jerking his hand up and down sharply. The teeth of the cable tie cut deeply and skin came off the back of his hand. The pain was intense but the blood helped to lubricate the cable tie. After five minutes of frantic thrusting up and down Jack wanted to scream in agony but he kept going, the back of his hand like raw meat.

At long last the tie slipped over his bloodied knuckles and the hand came free. He didn't know how or even if a free hand could help him but as his instructors of old had banged into him repeatedly: "it ain't over until it's over."

Finishing his huge spliff in the back yard, Mansoor immediately lit another, his thoughts brooding. Who the hell did Azziz think he was ordering him about? They were supposed to be equals. What was he anyway? Just an oaf from the tribal districts on the Afghan border. He, on the other hand, had been born in Karachi. He was educated to a much higher standard than that ignorant peasant. He felt the knife in his pocket. Maybe after this job he should think about dissolving their partnership permanently but then there was Khan to consider; he wouldn't hear of it. He was stuck.

Mansoor's foul mood worsened with every drag on his spliff. That old bastard in the storeroom and his CIA friend were going to die as painfully as he could make it. He was going to enjoy torturing and killing them very slowly.

Finishing his smoke, he made his way back into the shop. Passing the open door to the storeroom he couldn't resist looking in on the prisoner to gloat.

'How you doing, shithead?' he queried sarcastically 'Still think you're a smart-arsed bastard, do you?'

Jack looked up and fixed him with an icy stare, he knew that if he was to have any chance of escape he'd have to draw this man very near. He hadn't a bigoted bone in his body but he had to insult Mansoor's pride, wind him up to fever pitch. Angry men made mistakes. 'Oh, it's you, the cat killing queer' he sneered, his voice oozing contempt. 'I thought you'd be with Azziz sucking his cock you squeaking little faggot.'

Mansoor's face turned a dull red and he made a choking noise in the back of his throat. He stepped right up to the chair slapping Jack hard around the face. He drew his knife; it opened with a vicious click. 'What did you say, you kuffar bastard? What did you call me?' This was the reaction Jack had hoped for; he had to get his man in really close. He knew he'd only get one chance, one punch and it had to count. He felt his left hand gripping the chair leg lightly, ready to strike as soon as his tormentor came within range. He needed to bait him beyond endurance, to keep his full attention on his face and not glance down at his free hand so he continued 'you call me a kuffar you whisky drinking, pork eating peasant. Why don't you free me you rag headed goat fucker? Just you and me eh? I'll shove that knife so far up your arse it'll make your eyes bleed.'

Mansoor choked back a scream gripping Jack by the lapel his eyes bulging. The knife flashed above his head and Jack thought he was a dead man but Mansoor balled his fist and sent it into Jack's face. 'You'll curse your pig whore of a mother for having you before this day is out.'

Jack almost lost consciousness from the force of the blow but shook his head to clear it. He thought just a little closer my friend, please, just a little closer. 'Without Azziz to back you up you're nothing but a snivelling little arse wipe. Just a cock sucking, goat fucking, lowlife *wog*!' he fired the last word with all the contempt he could muster and spat onto Mansoor's chest.

For a split second Jack thought he'd overcooked it. Mansoor dragged him upwards, the knife once again flashing high, his face a contorted mask of rage. He couldn't lift Jack's weight one handed so he was dragged down, his face two inches from Jack's.

NOW! Jack's subconscious screamed. His left fist shot upwards and outwards smashing into Mansoor's throat, crushing his windpipe.

The result was spectacular. Mansoor dropped the knife as both his hands flew to his throat and he dropped to his knees eyes protruding, choking, unable to breathe or cry out. He rolled backwards and fell to the floor. Jack looked about for the knife. It lay just out of reach.

He began rocking the chair by throwing his weight backwards and forwards. Managing to make himself fall forward, he thrust out his free arm stopping himself from crashing face first. At last he got his hand on the weapon. First, he freed his right hand and then his feet. He looked at the choking Mansoor through a red mist

'A promise is a promise Mansoor' he told the dying man. Setting the chair upright again, he gripping Mansoor's trouser belt and collar hauling him across the chair face down. He slashed at the man's belt and down his trousers baring his arse. Jack inserted the knife in into Mansoor's anus and pushed hard with the heel of his hand until all but the very tip of the handle disappeared. Mansoor jerked spasmodically unable to cry out in his agony as the blood gushed down his legs. 'That's for killing my cat you bastard.'

Jack took several deep breaths. It was essential he kept calm. The next problem was how to deal with Azziz. Jack knew this man was no pushover and far more controlled than Mansoor had been. He retrieved his walking stick from where it lay near the wall and slipped the rubber cover off the end. He checked it over and saw no damage had been done. He tried to put himself in Azziz's position. The man had a gun but he would only use that as a very last resort. He would rely on his huge strength and maybe his knife. Obviously, Khan wanted him alive or he would be dead by now, murdered in his bed.

Jack decided he couldn't go into the shop and confront his opponent not even with his deadly walking stick. As soon as Azziz saw it he would realise it was a weapon, this man was a practiced professional. Well now, Jack thought, if Mohammed won't come to the mountain then the mountain must come to Mohammed.

Pushing the door open to almost its full extent against the storeroom wall Jack switched the inadequate light out. He considered for a moment taking off a shoe and placing it behind the door with just the end of the toe exposed. He dismissed this as impractical. Azziz would have learned the lesson of Waldo's wallet and the shoe would then indicate his true position like a signpost. No, best to keep the bugger guessing he told himself, then he had a fifty-fifty chance of getting it wrong.

Jack lay himself flat against the wall on the opposite side to the door. Taking the stick in both hands, he pulled the line. The blade flashed out and locked. He then let out a piercing scream.

In the shop Azziz dropped his paper and jumped to his feet 'Ali?' he roared 'Ali you bastard, are you mad?'

He rushed to the storeroom and halted in the passage outside. In the dim light from the corridor he could see Mansoor lying over the chair. 'Ali?' he called cautiously. He was then silent and still as Jack expected he would be. Then the big man's shadow started moving menacingly left and right as he peered into the room as far as he could without exposing himself. Seeing the door as the only possible hiding place Azziz suddenly plunged into the room a knife between his teeth, slamming the door into the wall with both hands.

Jack pounced. Even with this advantage it was almost not enough. The big man instantly realized his mistake as the door thudded into the wall. He was already whirling round when Jack struck.

The thrust had been aimed at the man's kidney to deliver a fatal blow but speared him in the side of the gut as Azziz jumped backwards to be stopped by the door. He screamed with pain, his knife falling from his mouth. He dived for Jack and caught him round the throat digging his thumbs in deep. Jack thought his head would burst with the pain. He thrust again sinking his blade deep into his opponent's gut. Azziz gasped and staggered backwards releasing Jack and clutching his belly.

Even with two stab wounds Jack could see the man was not finished and was grabbing with lightening speed for the cane. Jack stepped back lifting his weapon out of reach in the nick of time.

Azziz swung a haymaker at Jack's jaw, grazing the top of his head as he dropped onto one knee and thrust upwards, aiming under the ribcage to the heart.

Again, Azziz partially evaded the deadly thrust by swaying back and sideways. Even badly wounded the big man had reflexes like a cat. The blade went in two inches deep and four inches below his navel on his left side. Jack slashed sideways opening a great gash across his belly.

Azziz finally groaned and slumped back against the door looking down in horror as his intestines started to slip out into his hands. The automatic fell from his belt and clattered on the floor. He slipped down the door as his legs splayed and gave way under him. He looked up at Jack his face puzzled, finding it difficult to comprehend his situation 'who the fuck are you man?'

Jack kicked the pistol beyond reach then looked at his victim dispassionately 'What's the target for the strike?'

'Fuck you.'

Jack stuck his blade into Azziz's left eye and twisted it. The man shrieked in agony as the gore ran down his face.

'What's the target?' he repeated

'I dunno, nobody does' he screamed.

'How did you get hold of my file?' Jack asked in the same calm voice.

Azziz realized he was dealing with a man without a shred of mercy, someone as ruthless as he himself. The pain was unbearable 'I don't know, that useless bastard Ahmed couldn't get your file, he said it was too highly classified.'

Jack rested the blade just under Azziz's good eye. 'How did Khan access my file?' he persisted pushing lightly until the blood started to prick through the skin.

'He has other resources, some Mullah called Hassid, I don't know for sure, Khan keeps everybody in the dark. Hassid has connections high in Government. Khan doesn't know much.'

Jack tweaked the blade and watched coldly as Azziz winced.

'What time are you expecting Khan?'

'I dunno.'

Jack lowered his blade and stabbed Azziz through the penis. The man shrieked in pain and horror 'another two hours you bastard, now finish it, damn you.'

'Good God, no way Azziz, no way man' Jack feigned surprise at the request 'why, you've got a good couple of hours suffering ahead of you yet my friend.' Jack thought of the way they'd killed Waldo Williams. The guy was a total tosser, yes, but did they have to kill him that way? Jack's wrist flicked deftly and he stabbed him in both thighs causing him to scream yet again 'You think you're the only psychopath in the game? Think again dick head.'

Azziz subsided into moans of agony, blood pooling around his backside in an ever-growing puddle. It was with great difficulty he asked 'who....who you with man? Who the fuck are you with?'

'Just me mate, I'm on my own.'

'You...you're on your own?' Azziz was astounded. 'No Government agency? But...but there's the new American... CIA' he broke off groaning.

'Nothing to do with me, sir' Jack said in his American accent 'Sure looks like you've added two and two and come up with five.'

Azziz'z jaw dropped as realisation struck home.'Just you? A fucking army of one?'

Azziz's puzzled face had taken on a bloodless look now and his limbs started shaking. He was going into shock from which he would not recover.

'An army of one, eh? I like that.'

Jack's thoughts now turned to Ahmed. 'where's the other chef?' Azziz rolled his eyes upward indicating the flat above. 'Right, I'll leave you to die in peace.'

Azziz looked pleading, his eyes dropped to his stomach 'please...'

Jack eyed him coldly, no way would he finish this man off.

'You'll be in hell soon enough, you bastard.'

Even if Ahmed wasn't home there could be some clue as to the intended target Jack thought or at least who his handler was.

Jack retrieved the pistol, it was an old Walther P38 9 mm with most of the blueing worn off the barrel. It looked well maintained. He cocked it, sending a round into the chamber then applied the safety catch. The hammer fell forward to the half cocked position with a well oiled click.

Going out of the back of the shop and up the steps to the flat Jack found the door open. Strange, he thought, slipping the safety catch and pulling the hammer back to full cock, then he slowly entered. The place was dark, heavy blinds were drawn as is often the case when people work late into the night and sleep long into the day.

He stopped to listen keeping his body flat against the wall feeling the hairs on the back of his neck bristle. Nothing. Just an eerie silence, not even the ticking of a clock. He proceeded cautiously into the living room. Ahmed was sat in an armchair by the window. Jack approached the still figure slowly. As he got nearer he saw by the dull light from the heavily curtained window that there was a small hole in his forehead. Someone had been covering their tracks. Drawing back the curtain Jack saw at once the place had been ransacked so there was no use him searching for a mobile phone, laptop or notes. Bugger, he thought, and turned his attention to the corpse.

The weapon used was probably a low powered .22 pistol. It would have just made a crack, not much noise at all. There was no exit wound. The great amount of blood that was spilled down the front of Ahmed's face and tee shirt told Jack that although the guy had died instantly his heart had continued to beat for some time afterwards. It occurred to Jack that although the flat had been searched maybe the corpse hadn't.

Unpleasant as the job was he pulled out the man's pockets, finding, some loose change and a small pocket knife. That seemed all he was carrying. Looking carefully at the body Jack could see the guy's belt was lying at the side of him so the body had been partially searched but the shoes were still on his feet.

Ahmed's corpse was still warm so perhaps his arrival with Azziz and Mansoor had forced the assassin to flee for fear of discovery.

Jack removed both shoes and studied them closely. With an 'ah' of satisfaction he twisted the heel of the right shoe hard. It swung outwards revealing a cavity with a SIM card. He figured there would be only one number on it. Whoever owned this number was the man's handler and killer. He couldn't ring it now, but with luck, maybe he could find out who it belonged to.

Jack made his way back down to the shop where Azziz had breathed his last. He retrieved the phones of both dead men and noticed for the first time a large key hung around Azziz's neck. He had seen such keys before in his Army days. They were usually for the safe in the Company Commander's office.

Jack took it and found the safe under the shop counter. Opening it he discovered an old canvass hold-all. Pulling it out and unzipping it he found it was stuffed full of cash. He whistled under his breath there must be about two hundred and fifty grand he reckoned. He took this and the shop laptop from the counter which he stuffed in with the money.

Jack felt incredibly hungry now the adrenalin had stopped surging around his body. He checked his watch then made his way into the kitchen where he found some lamb curry in the fridge. After washing the blood off his injured hand he made up a takeaway container then placed it in a paper bag, picking up his plunder; he left down the back alley, once more leaning heavily on his stick.

It was a part of his make up that when he'd been in action Jack felt starving afterwards whereas most other soldiers couldn't eat a thing. It was just the same after the action that had ended his military career.

Five minutes away from his destination Khan phoned Azziz, the phone rang and went to the answering service. Khan immediately knew something had gone terribly wrong. He pulled over and tried to calm himself. What the hell could be wrong? He rang Mansoor with the same result, finally he rang Ahmed. Nothing. His heart raced as adrenalin flooded through him and cold fear made him shudder.

In desperation, he rang Bob Oliphant. The Sergeant saw his number and killed the call. 'Bloody ambulance chasers again' he complained to his colleagues. Two minutes later he went to the lavatory and, checking he was alone, rang Khan back.

'Hi Bob, have your lot arrested my men Azziz, Mansoor and Ahmed?'

'No, not to my knowledge, they're certainly not here'

'Got anyone available to raid my shop?'

There was a pause before Oliphant answered. 'I was going to ring you' he said 'I've just found out we have a team watching your places now. It's to do with lost drugs needing to be resupplied. Word on the street is you lost all of your merchandise in the fires.'

Khan cursed inwardly, it was true he was out of stock and had taken urgent steps to obtain more, agreeing to pay well over the odds to the Columbians. The stuff wasn't due to arrive until noon that day. The money to pay for it was already in the shop's safe. That was the least of his worries now.

'Beaker-Rosen ordered maximum security, I only found out 'cos I overheard a conversation in the locker room. She's a shrewd woman that one, she must suspect someone here is passing info.' Oliphant paused he didn't want to offend Khan but he had himself to think of 'look, I'll have to keep a low profile for a while so please don't call me again. I'll call you, OK?'

So, thought Khan, the rats are beginning to desert already. 'Are you absolutely sure Azziz and Mansoor have not been arrested?' he asked again.

'If they have it's been quick and quiet, they've not been brought here. I'll see what I can find out Mr. Khan but I can promise nothing.'

'Do you know who's in charge of the surveillance operation Bob?'

'Detective Sergeant Dave Barden and two Detective Constables, but what their brief is I couldn't tell you.' Oliphant was growing inpatient now, another officer could walk in at any time. 'Sorry, I've got to go now, I'm needed at the desk.'

Khan's phone went dead he immediately pressed a speed dial button and was cut off by Barden. It was obviously a bad time to call. Five minutes later Khan was still weighing up possibilities when Barden rang back. 'Jesus, Mr. Khan you pick your time, I'm engaged on an operation at the moment, it's difficult to talk.'

'I know where you are Dave and what you're doing so cut the crap and listen' he snapped, then he paused. He had to be careful with Barden, the man was by no means in his pocket. He adjusted his tone at once becoming placatory. 'Sorry Dave, sorry, I didn't mean to bark at you my friend but I'm under quite a bit of pressure due to one thing and another.'

It was obvious Barden had been offended by Khan's tone 'you and me both Khan' he said stiffly 'my boss is doing a lot of sniffing around at the station and she's no fool.'

'Dave listen, please, this is very important. Have you seen anything of my employees Azziz, Mansoor or Ahmed?'

'Yes, Azziz and Mansoor are in the shop right now' he paused feeling very uncomfortable, not wanting this conversation, reluctant to be giving Khan any information that could end his career with a prison sentence. He knows why we're here he thought so the operation's buggered now anyway.

'They went in an hour or so ago with an older man. I thought at first it looked dodgy so I sent in one of the lads, he's an amateur actor, pretending to be a drunk. He had a look around but he reported nothing unusual. He saw Azziz and Mansoor, naturally they seemed a bit annoyed with him but no more than you'd expect with a drunk barging in.'

Barden had thought that if Azziz and Mansoor had been up to mischief they would surely have locked the door. 'The older guy left by the back door some forty minutes ago carrying a hold-all and a takeaway. He looked a harmless old lad limping along on a walking stick. We didn't stop him in case he rang the shop later and gave the game away. Friend of yours, is he?'

Khan's heart sank, he could hardly believe what he was hearing. How the hell could this be possible? How?

'OK, Dave thank you my friend, I am deeply in your debt.'

Barden felt nervous, his copper's instinct told him something was very wrong and he wanted to play no further part in Khan's affairs. 'Look Khan, this can't go on' he said 'I know you helped me out in the past, even pointed to where we might make an arrest or two when it suited your plans but it's over, you got that? Lose my number from your phone. If you ring again I won't answer. The debts are settled, OK?'

Khan just grunted and hung up. He started his engine and drove to the shop. He had to find out what was wrong and put it right or he was a dead man.

*****

Jack got home shortly after leaving Khan's shop his head buzzing with what ifs. First things first he thought and went to his bathroom to get his first aid kit. His skinned hand hurt like hell and was still oozing blood. After he washed and dried it he carefully covered it in antiseptic ointment then bandaged it as best he could. Next, he went downstairs and picked up the body of Mischief and went into his garden shed. It took only a few minutes to bury her. He put her under her favourite magnolia tree where she had spent a lot of time dozing in its branches or pretending she was a big-time hunting cat. He heaved a sigh 'poor creature' he said aloud 'what the hell wrong did you ever do?'

Going back inside, he put the curry into the microwave and set it for four minutes then switched the kettle on for some much needed coffee.

His thoughts buzzed. Who could he trust? The police leaked like a sieve and now it seemed there was a traitor at MI5 and, worst of all, someone in very high Government office with access to ministerial level security. God, it was a headache. He sat with his coffee for five minutes trying to clear his head and decide on a course of action.

There was to be a jihadist strike somewhere in London imminently, but where? What was the target? London was full of potential targets. He had nothing that could be considered hard evidence. He'd been and seen yes, but he had no video or photographic evidence, just his word against so-called pillars of society with influence where it counted. Even if he was taken seriously and someone were to go to the madrassah and check out the bunker the terrorists would get prior warning. It would take them only minutes to empty it of weapons replacing the contents with motor cycles, generator fuel, gas bottles or other innocent stores. It was a mess, one hell of a mess.

He found and studied the detailed drawing he'd done whilst in his hide. An idea began to form in Jack's mind. It was a plan born of desperation but with a bit of luck he might stop these people himself. It would be dangerous in the extreme but he had to try. He quickly finished his coffee then thrust some survival gear into his rucksack and changed his clothes. He considered taking the gun with him but dismissed the idea, believing it may be more of a liability than a help.

Jack went to his cellar, first he booted up the captured laptop but found nothing of interest. It was used purely for the running of the shop. Next he went to the wall where a cupboard full of tools hung. He emptied it quickly then unscrewed it from the wall. Behind, the wall looked and felt like an ordinary brick wall. He climbed on the bench and reached over to the topmost left brick and pressed. There was a click and a section of the wall where the cupboard had been jumped out. It wasn't square cut but followed the normal brick pattern. Pushing it downwards revealing a shelved space into which he placed the money and the gun from the shop.

He collected his hunting knife, crossbow and a handful of bolts. Jack didn't know how much time he had before someone would come calling. Khan would soon find the bodies of his men and send someone after him. He left the house directly into the garage and started his car. Pressing the remote, the garage door swung upwards and he was off on the long drive to Northumberland.

Forty five miles from his destination Jack felt himself losing concentration at the wheel, fatigue was rapidly setting in making it unsafe to continue. Pulling off onto a side road he continued for half a mile then pulled in to a deserted lay-by. He couldn't afford the time to sleep but he knew his meditation technique of deep rest would help enormously.

Loosening his belt, he reclined his seat slightly and closed his eyes. His mantra and breathing rhythm came automatically and he told himself that in twenty minutes he'd feel fresh and awake. And so it was twenty minutes later Jack was able to continue his journey feeling as if he'd had four hours sleep.

Arriving at the madrasah with the same degree of stealth as before Jack ignored his old hide giving it a wide berth. He would never use the same place twice in case it had been compromised and booby trapped. This time he found a spot at the same elevation as his old hide at the end of the compound. It was at the opposite end to the entrance gate and the track with the stream directly below him on his right.

There was a lot of activity with the students coming and going loading motorcycles into four by four pickup trucks and securing them. It looks like things are getting under way he thought, hopefully I'm in time.

After a while a voice called out from the door of the madrasah and the jihadists made their way to the weapon store. Each man drew an AK47 and several magazines of ammunition plus what looked like a a suicide vest. As Jack watched through his binoculars he saw the unidentified boxes being opened. He gasped as he recognized the contents.

Oh Christ, he thought, rocket propelled grenades. His dismay was compounded when he saw that the mortars and their bombs were no longer there. They must have sent them ahead he realised, peparing a pit would take extra time. So, even if I succeeded in stopping these people here their brethren in London still have a load of highly dangerous weapons.

Jack's heart sank, he dug in his pocket and drew out the phones of Azziz and Mansoor, switching them on he covered them tightly with his hands to suppress the start up tones. He saw neither of them had a signal in this isolated location. He cursed softly to himself, feeling sick and bitterly disappointed.

Being unfamiliar with the dead men's phones he dared not risk using them for photos in case the flash went off under the dark shade of the trees and give him away. He cursed himself for a damned old fool, for not being more familiar with modern gadgets; his determination to carry out his plan hardened.

The smell of food drifted on the light breeze and triggered Jack's appetite. It had been over seven hours since he'd eaten the curry and he dug into his pack extracting a bar of Kendal Mint Cake. Not much of a meal but it would have to do.

In the madrasah Hassid ate with his protégés enjoying a splendid meal. He was pleased with the chosen men and was confident they would carry out the strike with great efficiency. The time was approaching now to reveal the more detailed plan of the attack. It was simple, uncomplicated and easy to remember.

After the meal, he called his followers into the classroom and, whilst they sat on their cushions giving him their rapt attention, he started to explain the detailed role of each of the motorcycle pairs using a flip chart to illustrate his plan. At the end he cautioned them 'remember, there will be police and army sniper teams on the rooftops use the RPG's on them exclusively, do not be tempted by any other target. They must be taken out first.'

After a brief question and answer session he instructed them all to retire and rest. 'Be calm and sleep well my brothers for it is your duty to be fresh when we leave one hour before dawn.'

Jack waited until the lights had been out for almost two hours before he slipped out of his hide and made his way to where the stream ran under the fence. Slipping on a pair of gardening gloves he had no difficulty removing the razor wire. Sliding under the fence, though, there was no way of staying out of the water. The cold bit into him as his feet and back took a soaking. He drew a sharp breath then slid clear.

At the back of the kitchen Jack tried the door, it opened silently. Slipping inside, he stood motionless against the wall for a minute allowing his eyes became accustomed to the deeper gloom. He then made his way slowly, quietly through the kitchen and dining area into the classroom taking great care where he put his feet.

From above he could hear men snoring. Looking around he saw the flip chart board. It was too dark to read anything but he saw the first two pages had been used. Slicing them off he folded them and put them inside his coat.

On a small table was a laptop and a satellite phone. He picked them up and crept back to the kitchen.

Outside again Jack put the computer and phone into his haversack and laid it near the door along with his crossbow.

Next he dug out the spanner he'd brought and uncoupled the three large gas bottles supplying the kitchen. Wedging the kitchen door open with his rucksack, Jack carried the large bottles one at a time into the building. It was difficult but he had to do it. He staggered to the classroom with the first one. The next he put in the dining area and the last one in the kitchen.

He then returned to the classroom and collected three cushions. Placing one over the nozzle of the first bottle he was about to turn it on when he suddenly froze. Someone was coming downstairs. He ducked quickly under the table and crouched ready to spring into action if need be, his knife held lightly in his right hand. The man was shining a small flashlight in front of him. He swung it briefly around the classroom walls, missing Jack by inches. Opening the front door, he stepped outside and lit a cigarette.

Jack felt his throat tighten, he couldn't wait for this guy to finish his leisurely smoke. What would he do after that go for a stroll around the compound? He had no option but to deal with him.

Holding his knife at waist level he tiptoed his way to the door. He remembered his old knife training well enough but had never had to use it before now.

Jack stood to one side of a small glass panel looking obliquely through it. Every nerve in his body tingled and he had a slight sickly feeling in his stomach. He hoped the man would have his back to him so it would be a simple hand over mouth, knee in the back, arch him over and shove the knife into his right kidney, twist and withdraw.

He was disappointed to see the fellow was standing sideways on, looking down the compound. He would see Jack the instant he opened the door, giving him enough time to shout. He was pondering his next action when the man suddenly threw down his cigarette and turning, pulled the door open. He almost walked into Jack in the gloom. He stepped backwards drawing a startled breath.

'Asalaamu Alaikum' Jack said calmly.

The confused man saw only a dark silhouette and automatically started to return the greeting as Jack leapt forward clamping his hand over the man's mouth and simultaneously plunging his knife under the man's ribs and into his heart. The fellow went rigid, eyeballs staring in shock. He shook for a second then died without a sound, sagging into Jack's arms. He lowered him gently to the floor. Time was pressing now and he had to move quickly and quietly.

He turned on the gas bottle and heard it start to hiss the heavier than air gas oozing out along the floor. He placed a cushion over the valve to deaden the sound, repeating his actions with the other two bottles. Jack retreated as fast as caution would permit and retrieved his crossbow and rucksack.

There was no sentry on the gate and the guardhouse was in darkness so Jack ran across the compound down the path towards the armoury. He selected a thick pine tree about seventy five metres from the madrasah where he had a good view of the windows and door. He prepared his bow.

Jack had several hunting bolts but only one incendiary bolt; one chance to get it right. He took out his wire cutters and went to work on the chain link fence cutting a hole about two and a half feet square. He couldn't risk his shot being deflected by the fence. As he completed this task he heard a shout of alarm from the dormitory.

The gas had risen to a level where someone had smelled it. A man ran out of the building clutching an AK47. He'd obviously found the body of Jack's smoker and now started firing wildly about him. One of the bullets struck the tree five feet over Jack's head. He lifted his crossbow and leaned through the hole. The man must have caught sight of the movement and turned his weapon on him.

Bullets cracked past Jack's head. He remembered all too clearly the handclap-slap sound that passing high velocity bullets made. The louder the 'clap' the closer they were. These were very loud. He took aim carefully and controlled his breathing; this was no time to rush his shot.

The gunman fired again and Jack was looking almost straight into the muzzle flash, the bullets passing even closer, forcing him to throw himself flat in the nick of time as a hail of bullets passed through the hole where he'd been standing less than a second ago. More shouts went up as people spilled outside clutching weapons spreading out along the madrassa walls, taking up defensive positions.

The firing stopped abruptly and Jack sensed the man was changing his magazine, it was now or never. Jumping up and leaning through the hole he steadied himself, lining up on the window three away from the door where there were no people to block the shot. He heard the generator start up as he began squeezing the trigger.

Instantly the compound was flooded with dazzling light as the football pitch was illuminated, blinding him. Instinctively he turned his head and closed his eyes against the glare. His bolt went low, shooting into the football pitch and exploding harmlessly ten metres from its target. He had failed.

His next priority was staying alive. Jack dived behind his tree as more firing broke out, though most of it was wild and unaimed.

The man who had fired first had reloaded and was running towards him. Jack cocked his bow and rapidly placed a bolt then waited. The man was at the fence now but he too had been dazzled by the floodlights and failed to see Jack crouching behind the tree. He started squeezing himself through the hole Jack had cut. It was an easy shot and he put his bolt through the top of the man's skull leaving him wedged halfway through the fence.

Over at the main building people were milling around shouting and shooting in confusion. Inside the madrassah someone made the fatal mistake of switching on the light. The spark made by the light switch contacts was tiny but it was all that was needed.

The whole world seemed to light up with an almighty roar turning night into day. A powerful shock wave of hot air blasted past Jack on either side of his tree as he threw himself against its rough bark. Branches were crashing down all around him. He pushed against the mighty tree as if trying to become part of it. He felt his clothing being tugged by the blast that tried to tear him from his sanctuary and hurl him into the woods.

After a few seconds, he stepped out to look at the building but quickly retreated again as stones and debris started raining back to earth. The body of the man who had been climbing though the fence was nowhere to be seen.

After what seemed an age, debris stopped falling and Jack looked out to see the remnants of the building. It was burning furiously. The upper storey was completely missing A great loom reflected light back from the clouds a thousand feet above. Someone somewhere would have heard and seen the explosion, even if they were miles away.

There was no need for caution now, he reloaded the bow and jogged around the fire lit compound past the blazing pick-ups lying on their sides. The twisted shapes of what once had been motorcycles were strewn about all but unrecognisable. Stepping over the charred remains of a headless limbless torso he searched for a weapon to use as evidence. A man fifty metres away, badly wounded, started firing at him, the shots were too close for comfort. Jack fired his bow in the man's direction and fled. He jogged down the track, his leg was hurting like hell, but it would just have to hurt.

Reaching his car, Jack sagged in the driving seat breathless and sweating profusely. The effects of the adrenaline had worn off on his forced march back. He could ill afford to wait around though, he had to get back to London. Somewhere, someone had sixteen mortars to aim at a vulnerable target. He had to make someone in authority listen.

After he had driven twenty miles or so he found an all night café, inside were a few truckers who looked as tired as himself. They took scant notice of him as he ordered the all day breakfast and a large mug of coffee then went and sat in a quiet alcove. The fact that he'd just killed around thirty men didn't bother him in the least. They'd said in the Army that if executing this type of bastard bothered you then get out, you're in the wrong job.

They'd deserved it each and every one of them. They had made their choice to become mass murderers, their motivation was not his concern. They had now paid the price. Tough. His problem was who to report to, who to trust?

There were sixteen deadly sixty six millimetre mortars in the capital and they were to be used soon, but against what target? A sports ground? A shopping centre? God knows there were hundreds of targets thronged with vulnerable people.

Jack mulled the situation over. The terrorists were clearly about to leave on their mission so the strike must be imminent. He glanced at his watch. The strike must later today. It was Saturday already.

How was he or anyone else going to locate the mortars before they were put to use? He knew the mortars had been cut down so that they could be buried without digging a massively deep pit. It was an old terrorist trick then they could be fired by remote control or by a timer buried with them. Maybe the computer held the secret? God, he thought, I hope so.

After he'd eaten Jack felt better, calmer, more able to think rationally. He studied the flip chart papers he'd taken. It looked like the heading was scrawled at the top of the first sheet in English. It resembled H of P but why would anyone want to mortar the Houses of Parliament on a weekend when there were no politicians there?

There were drawings of what appeared to be a rectangle with two straight lines running from it, a street perhaps? In the rectangle was written a time with a thick circle drawn around it,11 a.m. The rough red felt tip pen used had covered the rectangle with crude oblongs along the edges and arrows pointing in many directions. There were big blocks on a couple of sides. He could make no sense of it.

The second sheet contained a drawing of two straight lines with a large circle with a smaller circle within it and arrows pointing into it from all angles. There was Urdu writing here and there but very little.

He had to get these documents to MI5 regardless of risk as soon as possible. He had to make someone listen and take action.

Returning to his car he sat upright in the front passenger seat and meditated for twenty minutes after which he reclined the seat fully, allowing himself the luxury of a one hour's much needed sleep.

On awakening, he started the car immediately and started the long drive back. He could afford to waste no more time.

Jack was about five miles from the end of the M1 when he saw three police cars behind him, lights flashing, travelling fast. He pulled into the inside lane to allow them to pass. The first one did and cut in front of him the second drew alongside him and the third closed up right behind him in a smoothly performed classic forced stop routine. He was guided onto the hard shoulder.

'Armed police'. 'Get out of the car slowly. Keep your hands in sight. Do it now.'

Jack's heart sank he didn't need this right now so close to his destination but he knew better than to disobey. Slowly he got out of the car and raised his hands

'I'm not armed,' he shouted then knelt on the ground placing his hands behind his head. They handcuffed him and led him to the back of a police car. 'I've got stuff in the car that I need to get to MI5' he told them 'There is to be a terrorist strike in the capital later today. I have evidence in the car.'

'Save it for the interviewing officers mate.' Was all that sergeant in charge said, then they all fell silent, refusing to respond to his pleas.

In the interview room, he sat opposite Detective Sergeant Barden having given a complete account of his actions. 'I know it sounds far-fetched Sergeant but it's all true and I need to make an urgent phone call.'

'All in good time sir, all in good time.'

'No' Jack snapped, feeling exasperated now. He feared Barden was the type of plodding copper who only worked at one speed slowly ticking the boxes as he went. 'I waived my right to a lawyer because I know every second counts; can you not understand? This is an urgent matter of national security'

Barden eyed him suspiciously. 'As far as I'm concerned Mr. Ellis, you are the one most likely to be the terrorist here. We have three dead men, two of whom you were seen entering premises with. You were later observed leaving those premises alone. We've searched your house and have recovered a number of very suspicious items from your cellar, not least of which was a quantity of gunpowder.' Barden's eyes narrowed 'When you were arrested you were in possession of a crossbow and blood stained hunting knife' he paused 'you have also confessed to two acts of arson and the killing of yet another man' He shook his head in disbelief 'interview terminated at 0855. I suggest it's in your best interest that you consult a solicitor Mr Ellis. We've already sent for the duty solicitor so you don't need to phone anyone just yet.' Barden's fear was that Jack was in league with others and would get a warning to them.

'Right, that's it for now sir, let's go.' The Detective stood up and indicated the door.

Jack looked around the interview room. Barden had been sat opposite him next to an intelligent looking woman Detective Constable whose name he couldn't remember. She had taken down his statement but had not said a word. There was a bored looking Constable standing by the door who turned to open it at the same time as the female detective turned to switch off the tape machine. Jack struck then.

He leapt at Barden spinning him around and throwing his right arm over the top of his head to get a firm grip under the man's chin whilst his left arm grabbed him around his chest. Pushing his left knee hard into the small of Barden's back he forced him to arch backwards then dragged the helpless man into the far corner of the room.

The policeman at the door recovered from his shock first and started to move towards Jack.

'STAND STILL!' Jack roared, his voice cracked like a whip in the small interview room. 'One more move towards us and I'll break his neck.' The constable halted, uncertainty on his face 'look' he started 'we can sort this out Jack…'

'SHUT UP! You, behind that mirror, get in here with a phone NOW!' He jerked Barden's neck to emphasize his point.

The door opened and Beaker-Rosen hurried in. She signalled the female Detective ,who was standing with her mouth agape, to move towards the door.

'I want everyone to keep calm' she said in a hushed tone. Then she produced a phone from her pocket and spoke to Jack. 'Here' she said 'take my phone, I'll let you use it, just let the Detective go.'

Jack jerked Barden's neck again. The man's mouth was locked shut but he still managed a stifled cry of pain. 'Stay where you are and dial this number.'

She took a step towards him. 'I can't do that Mr Ellis' she said with a calmness she wasn't feeling 'until you let my colleague go...'

'I've killed over thirty people in the last forty eight hours lady' Jack interrupted 'I have no qualms about one more.' His voice sounded authoritative, without the slightest trace of indecision.

'Now, there'll be no delaying tactics, none of your negotiating bullshit. I'll count from five, you'll either do as I say or I'll snap his neck.' Jack's heart was pounding and sweat was running down his back, he knew he couldn't kill Bardon but if he betrayed even the tiniest sign that he was bluffing it would be all over. Five, four, three..'

Beaker-Rosen could see the sinews stretched to breaking point in Barden's neck. Looking into the unblinking cold Grey eyes of his captor gave her no reason to doubt that he would carry out his threat. She also knew she could never cross the two metres between them in time.

'Two, One...'

'OK, OK, give me the number' she held the phone in her left hand her right poised to dial.

'Put the phone on speaker' Jack said, his voice returning to the cold calm quietness of a man who knew he'd won. 'When you dial this number it will be answered within two rings. I will then take over.'

From the recesses of his memory he dictated his emergency contact number, hoping that the duty officer and Ahmed's handler were not one and the same person. He hoped whoever answered was on the ball and would act immediately.

Beaker-Rosen quickly did as instructed, she could hear Bardon's breath rasping in his nostrils his chest heaving with the effort of breathing, he was becoming very distressed.

'Yes?'

'Duty officer please.' Jack said

'Code name?'

'Blocat.'

'Number?'

'24702582'

'One moment please.'

The sound of a computer keyboard being rattled could be heard then the voice returned 'What is the nature of your emergency Blocat?'

'There is a jihadist strike about to take place today in London, I believe at 11 a.m. I don't know where. I have intelligence in the form of a laptop, locked of course, a satellite phone and two mobile phones. I also have some papers from a terrorist briefing written in Urdu. There are sixteen sixty six millimetre mortars ready to be fired at a target somewhere.'

'I see, so why don't you bring in what you have and we'll get right on it?'

'I'm under arrest at the moment on suspicion of murder.'

There was a brief pause 'ah, rather awkward then. Where are you?'

Jack told him.

The duty officer paused for a few more seconds evaluating this information, then he came to a decision 'I'll see what I can do but, by God Blocat, you'd better be telling the truth.'

'I wish I weren't' Jack said tiredly.

The phone went dead. 'Right' said Jack 'I'm all yours.'

He released Barden who collapsed on the floor moaning and holding his neck. 'Sorry about that old son.'

Everyone in the room seemed to rush at Jack at once then. He was seized by the large Constable. 'Right you bastard' he growled pushing Jack's arm up his back until he thought it would break.

Beaker-Rosen intervened swiftly 'None of that Hollister. Take him to a cell, and Hollister,' she paused.

'Yes ma'am?'

'Be very gentle.'

Beaker-Rosen had watched the interview closely and had a gut feeling that this was much bigger than three dead men in a takeaway.

Ellis's body language had been congruent throughout, there had been no hyperbole or no liars prefix 'tells' like "to be completely honest with you." Career enhancing opportunities may be had in extraordinary circumstances for sharp people and this had all the hallmarks of being very extraordinary.

Her instinct told her that despite the far-fetched nature of his story, there was something about this man Ellis that rang true. Not checking all possibilities and/or roughing up a prisoner on the other hand could lead to career threatening complications and she was a dedicated careerist.

All attention was now turned to Barden who was sitting up moaning and holding his neck in obvious pain.

Beaker-Rosen helped him up and sat him in a chair. 'I'll send for an ambulance Dave, just hold on' she said, deeply concerned for her colleague.

'I'll be OK in a minute or two ma'am' he croaked unconvincingly. 'The bastard would have done for me I'm sure. Christ, I was one small tug from being dead!'

Barden was very badly shaken and his neck hurt like hell but his greatest worry now was what may subsequently come out regarding his relationship with Khan.

Five minutes later Beaker-Rosen was talking to Oliphant who was duty custody Sergeant about speeding up the arrival of the duty solicitor when her phone rang: 'Who? Oh, good morning sir. Yes?

Oh yes, I see. Really? In that case I'll need an official order in writing from your department sir, or an email at least... very well sir, I'll see to it at once.'

She turned to Oliphant 'OK Bob, have Ellis brought out, we are to take him to MI5 without delay.' Her voice was urgent 'then have a Range Rover and a couple of motorcycles out back as quickly as possible, apparently there's no time to Lose.'

Oliphant looked dubious 'are you sure ma'am?'

'Yes, Sergeant she barked impatiently so crack on with it OK? And get all his stuff out of the evidence room, we have a laptop, phones and some papers?'

Oliphant instructed Constable Hollister to handcuff Jack and bring him to the desk. He was now in a quandary. The evidence Beaker- Rosen was talking of was not in the evidence room but in his car, about to disappear as per Khan's instructions. The end of his shift was just half an hour away and he'd been unable to ignore the offer of a cool quarter of a million pounds for their delivery. It was a risk worth taking.

Oliphant visited the evidence room and made a pretence of searching. He then returned looking nervous to report that all of the prisoner's possessions had been misplaced.

Beaker-Rosen glowered at him 'Then they'd better get un-misplaced Sergeant, and damn quick.'

Oliphant flushed and started to bluster but Beaker-Rosen cut him short. She had for some time been suspicious of one or two of her staff but she had, as yet, no hard evidence against anyone. Oliphant had been arousing her suspicions of late. Even for a single man on good pay he'd taken one too many expensive holidays and bought a brand new car on the limit of the means of the average police Sergeant. She had put some arrangements in place to test her theory. Turning now to the probationer on the computer behind the desk she asked. 'Well Sally?'

'He took the prisoner's possessions to the evidence room personally ma'am then went to the toilet. Just after that, he went outside for a quick smoke. I think they're in his car ma'am.' She said, blushing at the thought that her boss now knew she'd been spying on him.

Oliphant's face paled 'look at the CCTV then, I wasn't carrying anything. I went to my car because I'd left my cigarettes in it.'

Oliphant was a large man and Beaker-Rosen knew the laptop and papers could easily have been concealed up his tunic, the phones in his pockets. She decided to cut through his lies. 'So, if we searched your car Sergeant Oliphant, we'd find nothing incriminating?' She held out her hand 'keys please.'

Oliphant knew the game was up 'You bloody little bitch...' he started to curse his junior colleague who turned away in tears.

Beaker-Rosen's face set like granite. 'Robert James Oliphant, I'm arresting you on suspicion of misconduct in public office...' she went on to read him his rights whilst Oliphant collapsed onto his chair looking pale and broken.

Millbank

On the trip to the Millbank headquarters of MI5, Jack travelled in handcuffs at the insistence of Bardon who, though still shaken and with his neck aching like hell, had insisted on coming. It was a fast journey until they approached central London there, it seemed, everywhere they turned there was a traffic diversion. Even though they were allowed through, it still cost them time whilst barriers were hurriedly moved.

Inside, they were introduced to Andrew Porter, the Director of Operations for London. He ordered that the cuffs be removed from Jack immediately. They quickly gathered around the table in the ops room. Several other staff joined them and were quickly introduced. Shazmina Begum, Chief Interpreter Asian Languages, John Skinner, Head of Communications and Brian West I.T specialist. The laptop, satellite phone, Azziz's and Mansoor's mobile phones and the briefing papers were quickly made available.

Porter ordered the laptop connected to the secure line and linked to GCHQ in Cheltenham on the basis that many hands make light work. The SIM cards too were copied to them.

The Laptop was password protected but it was by no means a difficult one and Cheltenham cracked it in five minutes.

EidMurbarak a pretty obvious choice. The owner of the laptop must have seen very little possibility of it ever being captured.

Jack looked at the scrawl heading the Nobo paper he'd cut from the briefing board. It had been scribbled and drawn on as the briefing progressed until it looked like a piece of modern art. On top of the first page Jack thought he'd recognised some English letters 'That looks like H of P or some such but why would they target the Houses of Parliament in the summer on a Saturday when no one's present?'

West had been accessing the computer throwing its contents onto the large wall screen so all could see. 'Oh my God' he exclaimed as if he were not able to comprehend fully what he saw. There on the wall screen was a map they all recognised at once. 'It's the bloody Mall and Horse Guards' Parade.

Jack remembered the traffic diversion signs on his trip down now they made sense. Today was the Queen's official birthday parade, she always arrived at the dais at 11 a.m. sharp.

Porter looked at Jack, weighing up this older man who looked at first glance like any harmless pensioner you'd see on the street until you studied his eyes. They were quick, intelligent and hard as rivets. 'Right, over to you Mr. Ellis, tell us what you know.'

Jack looked around him, gathering the attention of all present to the import of what he was about to impart. His briefing was professional, rapid and always to the point as he told them about the madrasah and what he'd discovered of its true purpose.

'And you're saying you killed around thirty people up there?' Porter sounded incredulous but he'd heard early reports of what appeared to be a massive gas explosion somewhere in the Kielder Forest with an unknown number of fatalities just an hour ago.

'Correct' Jack confirmed, 'and if you want to pass it off as an accident you'd better get some folks up there sharpish to remove the weapons.' he was about to say something else when he was interrupted by West.

'It's a damn good job you did Jack. I've sorted this plan while you've been talking and it's bloody terrifying. Look.'

He pressed a few buttons and the wall map came alive with arrows and directions and crude drawings of motorcycles with the pillion passenger spraying bullets.

Shazmina let out a cry of horror, her hand shooting to her mouth in shock. Then she quickly recovered her composure and read the plan of attack to the others. 'They were going to fire hidden mortars timed to land on Horse Guards' Parade at precisely eleven o'clock as the Queen's carriage arrives at the rostrum for her official birthday parade. The motorcyclists, armed with RPG's were to take out the sniper positions then all were then to split into pairs and ride across onto the parade ground.

One of the pairs was to ride straight to where the rest of the Royal Family would be watching from the Duke of Wellington's office and kill them as they tried to escape. Another pair would help kill the Royal protection squad and then all would turn their attention onto the VIP enclosure. Their main targets then were to be the highest ranking officers and politicians, especially the foreign ones.'

She paused for breath hardly able to comprehend what she was reading. 'The rest of them were to ride around shooting the soldiers then down the Mall spraying the public and soldiers alike with automatic fire, herding them down to the gates of the palace.'

Beaker Rosen was aghast 'How the hell did they expect to get away with that?' she said.

Shazmina fixed her with a stare 'They weren't trying to get away with it' she said coldly 'they would all have been wearing suicide vests. Their instructions were to drive into the densest parts of the crowd then blow themselves up.'

Shazmina changed the subject 'there's a lot of technical stuff here about the mortars that I don't understand' she said puzzled 'but it also says that all police and military frequencies were to be blocked and internet communications cut. It even mentions the satellite system.'

Jack who had been listening intently to Shazmina now broke in 'not *were* to be blocked Shazmina, *are* to be blocked. As I said, the mortars were missing from the compound. We can only assume they're here in London pointing directly at the Horse Guards and due to hit at eleven a.m.' He glanced at his watch it was eight minutes to eleven.

Porter lifted the phone then dropped it again 'Shit, it's already happened' he snapped. He picked up the line to GCHQ that didn't use any junction boxes and was a direct connection 'Hi Remington, get onto the SAS and have as many as possible lifted by helicopter to St James's Park. I'll explain later but terrorist are about to hit the Royal birthday parade.' He pressed an intercom button and a man entered the room almost immediately. 'Jackson, get downstairs, grab those two motorcycle policemen and get them over to the palace immediately. The Royal party are on no account to leave.'

Jackson looked at his watch 'There'll all be there by now sir, the Queen and the Duke will be on their way already.'

'Right then, tell one of the policemen to ride for The Mall to intercept them' Porter said 'and the other to go after the Royal party at Horse Guards right now. He's to tell the protection squad to get them to hell out of it then tell the Guards' officers to get their men off the square at the double. He's to use whatever time is left to clear the VIP compound and get himself out of it before eleven. Is that clear?'

Jackson gave a curt nod and was gone.

Turning to West he was about to instruct him to search the files for the location of the mortars but he and Shazmina were already onto it. The trouble was there were pages and pages of stuff interspersed with sermons that had been delivered and press releases to be issued after the attack. It was all disorganised with nothing in files.

'My God, there are six men with the jamming equipment in three locations, they've sabotaged all the vital junction boxes. All military and police frequencies, even channel sixteen.' He continued to search with expert speed 'Ah, I've got the jammers' location,s there's three of them triangulating the area but they're too far away.'

After a couple more pages Shazmina said 'There's some guy called the Mullah, no name I'm afraid, videoing the attack too, it says here.' She frowned 'I don't know why he wants to do that when the whole thing will be in front of the world's T.V. cameras.'

West was running desperately through documents as fast as he could whilst Shazmina scoured them looking for clues as the clock ticked down.

On Horseguards' parade a thousand soldiers were formed up in rigid ranks along its edges, their medals shining brightly, reflecting a perfect summer's day. The massed bands of the Brigade of Guards played and the great and good looked on from their privileged positions in the VIP stand. Along the Mall a great crush of spectators watched in eager anticipation from behind double crush barriers.

Suddenly Shazmina gave a cry 'Oh God, I think I know where they are' she shouted. Every eye turned to her 'I jog to work through Hyde Park very early most mornings. Today I saw six gardeners all young Asian men, all dressed in park uniform but with a white pick-up truck, not a park liveried one. They were digging in a flower bed not far from the entrance. Would they bury the mortars in the ground?'

'That's exactly what they'd do' said Jack 'the barrels were shortened so they wouldn't have to dig a very deep pit.'

'Come on Shazmina show us where they are' said Porter, already striding urgently for the exit.

Jack followed hard on their heels with Barden and Beaker-Rosen clomping behind. Outside the Detective Inspector ordered the driver out and got behind the wheel of the Range Rover. With Porter beside her and Jack, Barden and Shazmina jammed in the back they took off.

'Shout the lefts and rights' Beaker-Rosen barked at Porter. Jack looked anxiously at his watch four minutes to go. Things were beginning to look bleak.

Jane Beaker-Rosen had started her career as a traffic officer and handled the big vehicle expertly with the blues and twos clearing the way they at last shot through the park gates scattering startled tourist left and right. Thrusting her hand into the front, Shazmina pointed 'over there, over there!'

They pulled up twenty metres from two flowerbeds 'Which one?' said porter

Shazmina looked stricken 'Oh' she gasped, trying to remember the brief incident of the morning. ' I'm not sure.That one I think' she said pointing to the far one. Everyone except Barden and

Shazmina ran towards it. Barden turned to the passers-by who had stopped to watch the unusual sight. 'Police officer' he bawled waving his warrant card 'clear the area now. There's a bomb.' People needed no second bidding and scurried fearfully away.

The tubes were well hidden among the vegetation and took precious moments to locate. Jack and Porter tried to grab them and drag them out but to no avail they were well buried with barely an inch protruding above the ground which had been firmly tamped down to ensure they stayed on bearing and elevation when fired.

Jack looked around desperately hoping to find a command wire. There wasn't one so the mortars were to be fired electronically by a timing device buried deep with them.

Jack, Beaker-Rosen and Porter started scratching at the hardened earth, scooping it with their bare hands and pouring it down the barrels with the hope of causing a premature detonation when the mortars fired. With sixteen barrels to deal with and the precious seconds ticking away it was a forlorn hope.

'Porter looked anxiously at his watch 'due to fire at eleven you say?'

'Minus time of flight, eleven's the time on target'' Jack snapped.

'Sweet Jesus! Clear the area, clear the area now.' Porter yelled.

Shazmina had stood by the Range Rover whilst all the others worked on the mortars, an idea forming in her head. Now she jumped behind the wheel and started the engine. It fired instantly with a throaty roar. She slipped into first gear and locked the doors.

Beaker-Rosen looked horrified as she ran for her life, guessing her intention she screamed 'No Shazmina, no!' She grabbed at the door handle but it was too late. Shazmina let up the clutch and pushed hard on the accelerator.

As she sped past the sprinting group tears were streaming down her young face. She drove straight over the mortars, slamming the brakes on when she was certain she had covered them all.

She made no effort to dismount and run, knowing it was already far too late. She had time for a quick glance in the rear view mirror and gave a smile of satisfaction as she saw that her companions were a good eighty yards away. She watched them throwing themselves down a bank where the ground fell away from the path affording them some shelter from the impending blast. She spread her hands palm uppermost and started a last prayer 'Allah' she whispered, then the mortars fired.

Sixteen 66 millimetre high explosive mortar bombs slammed simultaneously into the Range Rover's underside. The explosion sent pieces of metal screaming high into the air as the vehicle was torn into thousands of pieces whilst mortar shrapnel hissed viciously. The engine block flew over the cowering group, landing not ten feet behind them sinking deep into the grass sending a shock wave through them.

In the Mall, the motorcycle police officer stood beside the stationary Royal carriage. The Queen and Prince Philip had refused point blank to turn around and head for the safety of the palace. 'I have shared many dangers with my subjects' she had said with quiet dignity 'this will merely be one more.'

The crowd of onlookers had stopped cheering now they were looking bewildered and nervous. Soldiers who had been lining the route now sprinted down the mall and formed a protective cordon around the Royal coach. They looked formidable facing outwards weapons pointing to the fore, the full lethal purpose of their bayonets now revealed. An armoured car appeared it's hatches battened down and parked near the coach it's turret swinging three sixty looking for threats.

Then the explosion caused an outbreak of hysterical screaming, some people panicked, turned and fled. Others stood bemused and afraid. Women screamed and babies bawled. Then after a few seconds, when no immediate threat was apparent, they had started talking again. Most were anxiously pointing to where a pall of dirty orange and grey smoke was billowing above the London skyline. But the Royal carriage had not moved so things must be under control they thought so most people stayed where they were confused but calm.

In the Royal carriage, the Duke of Edinburgh fidgeted looking at his watch as the seconds slipped by. After a few seconds more the sound of the clock on Horse Guards Parade striking eleven came faintly on the breeze. The Duke looked irritated 'well we're bloody well late now, officer' he swore at the Motorcycle cop 'and we're never bloody well late.' He nodded in the direction of the smoke 'seems whatever it was has been dealt with, what?' Without waiting for a reply he shouted 'drive on, drive on!'

As the carriage began to move the policeman heard the Queen say 'Be calm Philip my dear, please be calm.'

Aftermath

With the world's media present in such numbers so close to the attack it had been flashed around the world as it happened.

The Guards had marched off Horse Guards Parade in double time but in good order. In the VIP enclosure, an undignified scramble to escape disintegrated into wild-arsed panic. Women and children were pushed aside by some to be first to the exit. Many of the foreign dignitaries did themselves no favours in the eyes of their watching citizens and the rest of the world

In the aftermath of the attack many heads of state were now redoubling their security measures and cutting all but essential public appearances. Media speculation, of course, was rife with the more sensationalist foreign press printing wild stories about an armed Islamic uprising and fighting on the streets of London.

A damage limitation programme was rapidly put into operation. One important facet that had helped to restore calm more than any other was that an incredibly brave young Muslim woman had selflessly sacrificed her own life to save thousands from disaster.

This disarmed to a large extent the ranting right wing organisations who wanted to hijack this thwarted attack to vilify all Muslims everywhere. Shazmina's bravery had stymied them.

At a COBRA meeting in Downing Street, Porter had briefed government ministers and then other Heads of Departments. It was essential that they all sang from the same hymn sheet. No statements by anyone unless with prior approval and then a strict script had to be adhered to. It was made clear that off-the-cuff remarks to the media would be career ending.

They destruction of the Flame of Truth madrasah hundreds of miles away was put down to a gas leak, a tragic accident in which twenty eight devout young men and three teachers had all perished. Any attempt by the media to connect it with the London incident was ridiculed as irresponsible speculation and an insult to Islam, the victims, and their law abiding families.

The media that had tried to make a connection had backed off. Sure, the six people who had blown themselves up rather than surrender to police in London had all attended the madrasah at one time or another, but so had many hundreds of others over the last two years. These other people were clearly innocent and were horrified by the attack.

The Palace gave a press conference wherein it was announced that the Queen would shortly be visiting Shazmina's London mosque. This was termed as a show of 'accord' by the palace and its aim was to express respect for Shazmina and sympathy for the madrasah disaster. It was also made public that the Queen and Duke had met Shazmina's family in a private meeting at the palace too offer their condolences and thank them personally for their brave daughter's sacrifice.

Jack was debriefed the very next day. Porter told him that, in order to expedite things, two American Secret Service personnel were to be present. As the Americans had become inadvertently involved it would save time and effort. Jack had readily agreed.

The two agents came into the room and eyed Jack with some surprise. 'So this is the old boy who killed all those people?' said Greenwood, the senior of the two, effecting surprise. He emphasised slightly the words 'old boy' addressing Porter not Jack. He didn't take Jack's outstretched hand. Jack was instantly wary of him.

The other man was one John Westaway, he looked embarrassed at Greenwood's blatant rudeness. Westaway's attitude couldn't have been more different. He shook Jack's hand warmly and said 'Pleased to meet you Mr. Ellis.' Jack felt he might have said more were it not for the malignant presence of Greenwood.

They listened in silence at first then Greenwood breached protocol butting in with several aggressive questions. One such question was 'And at what point did you decide to assassinate these people without authority?'

Jack, a veteran of many debriefings, looked to Porter to say something but the man simply glanced down at his desk and stayed silent.

Deeply incensed by Greenwood's attitude, Jack eyed him coldly, feeling his anger rising almost beyond control. 'Listen, Greenwood, *old boy*, please remember you're a guest here and save any *pertinent* questions, should you be capable of thinking of any, to the end. I'm sure Mr Porter will afford you the opportunity.'

The Jack's icy voice cracked like a whip and shocked Greenwood, the cold killer stare chilling his soul. For a few seconds there was a stunned silence then Porter, belatedly, responded. 'Gentlemen please. We're all on the same side here so let us conduct this meeting as professionals.'

It had the desired effect and the debrief continued with Greenwood silenced, but Jack knew he had made an enemy. Why Greenwood had taken such a dislike to him he could only wonder. Westaway had smiled weakly throughout the exchange, his embarrassment obvious.

Later, when Westaway had a chance to speak to Jack alone, he tried to explain Greenwood's attitude.' Greenwood's an excellent administrator but he's never worked in the field Jack.'

'That much is obvious for sure.' He was glad to note that Westaway made no attempt to justify his boss's rudeness.

'You see Jack, he's by-the-book man. He hates mavericks and people working on their own initiative.'

Greenwood. had risen rapidly in his career by ensuring his good work got noticed and anything bad landed on the toes of those beneath him. This, coupled with some judicious creeping, not to mention back stabbing, had ensured this plumb position.

Greenwood went away in a foul mood not waiting for his colleague. He had a problem dealing with the Westaway's and Ellis's, he came across occasionally. Experienced, clear headed and said what they thought.

He had no hold over Westaway except rank. He'd have to work on that. Compromise him in some way then move to protect him. That would give him an edge, keep him on his leash. It had worked before with other subordinates, it would work again. All he needed was time and opportunity.

Greenwood had an envy complex when dealing with people like John Westaway and Jack Ellis. They were the kind of men he himself would like to have been. But he never had the courage to 'go field.' Nor would he go out on a limb in his own job without his arse being covered one hundred percent.

When he saw Jack he had been completely taken aback. He had been expecting to meet some sort of James Bond character. Or at least someone much younger, tall and athletic like Westaway. When he saw Jack's age and apparent ordinariness he was shocked and irritated beyond measure.

On the following Monday morning Beaker-Rosen sat at Porter's desk being debriefed. She had brought a file with her that lay on the desk between them. 'I've prepared a draft file on Ellis for the Director of Public Prosecutions Mr. Porter' she announced before Porter could even offer her a coffee. 'The law will require him to answer at very least for the murders in the warehouse and the takeaway, also for the assault on my colleague with threats to kill.'

Porter looked aghast 'Are you mad, woman? Have you not spoken to your Chief Constable?' Porter asked. His usual politeness banished by what he regarded as crass stupidity. 'To put him on trial or even mention him in connection with this incident would be to invite utter disaster.'

'Those takeaway killings, including the fellow at Khan's warehouse, are to be put down to rival gangs, squabbling over drugs. The two arsons and the warehouse killing were a warning to Khan, when he ignored them the other killings followed.'

Porter looked at her with disdain, he recognised naked ambition when he saw it. Beaker-Rosen had been given the weekend off to recover from her shock and distress. She had used the time to prepare this file. By rushing out her report without consulting her superiors she was trying to steal a march, gain kudos.

'I thought you had a first from Oxford' Porter said sarcastically his mouth twisting to a sneer.

'Double first, as it happens' Beaker-Rosen replied snottily 'and I don't need you, Mr Porter,or anyone else to tell me my duty. This man has killed God knows how many people. He manufactures explosives and incendiary material. He also carries all sorts of offensive weapons and acts as a vigilante. Even if all the killings were justified, he still has to answer to the law.'

Porter shook his head in disbelief. He took on the air of a patient parent explaining some of life's murkier quirks to an adolescent. He realised that because of her education, Beaker-Rosen's promotion had been fast tracked, missing out on years of vital experience.

'Look, Inspector, The Palace wants this playing down as far as it is humanly possible. They don't want to give the impression they are scared, that royalty worldwide is a vulnerable or even a viable target.' He eyed her coldly. To her credit she didn't react but stared into his face like a woman trying to make a new assessment.

'The Kielder incident was a tragic accident, totally unrelated to Saturday's events. The whole site has been forensically sanitised. The Khan connection with the attack doesn't exist. The six remaining jihadi's who planted the mortars and sabotaged the lines of communication were the only ones involved in this plot. They chose to die rather than be arrested. The chief orchestrator of this little shindig, one Imam Bhakti is already being dealt with on a diplomatic level. Jack Ellis and his lady friend are in one of our safe houses until we can arrange new identities and relocate them. Officially they do not exist.'

'So' Beaker-Rosen said, understanding the situation at last, 'one bloody great cover up that leaves all the glory to our noble MI5 who had no bloody idea what the hell was going on until Ellis placed it all neatly in their lap. She glared at him, seeing her chance of glory slipping away.

'You lot will get all the credit for discovering and stopping this attack.' She looked at Porter sourly. 'And you'll get a sodding knighthood for this I shouldn't wonder.'

Porter flinched, clearly stung by her remarks. 'If I'm ever offered an honour for this, which I doubt,' he said crisply trying to disguise the anger he felt, 'I'll certainly refuse it. The main focus will be, quite properly, on our dear departed and much respected colleague Shazmina Begum. We'll be recommending her for a posthumous George Medal, which she richly deserves.'

He picked up the file she'd prepared and scanned it briefly before pressing his intercom. 'Would you come in Johnson, please?' He handed the file to the man whilst staring at Beaker-Rosen with dislike. 'Shred this immediately Johnson, please, the remains to be incinerated.'

'Yes sir' said Johnson. He took the file and disappeared.

'I really must protest Mr Porter' Beaker-Rosen said indignantly 'this is all highly irregular. What you are suggesting is that I should conspire to pervert the course of justice.'

Porter interrupted her 'you're very naive for an ambitious young copper' he said 'I blame the system of rapid promotion of graduates for this.' He sighed looking tired 'During our investigations into the activities of this Khan fellow we made certain discoveries.' He leaned back in his chair wondering how much he should tell her. He decided that she should know about her Detective Sergeant Bardon. 'Your man Bardon, for instance, is not as squeaky clean as you might imagine' he said.

Beaker-Rosen looked at him quizzically.

'Now, I'm not suggesting he ever took money from Khan but he did benefit from the man's connections to various charities when his daughter was ill.'

'You can hardly blame him for that' Beaker-Rosen protested 'I'm sure any one of us would have done the same.'

'Yes, but things went further than that. He accepted a hugely discounted holiday for instance that was indirectly linked to Khan. We think he also gave him hints about planned drug raids though we can't prove it.'

Anticipating her next question, he went on 'we know this because we uncovered one of our own in Khan's pay. We had a source close to Khan, a chef in a takeaway. His handler was close to retirement and saw an opportunity to line his pockets for a very comfortable old age.'

Beaker-Rosen looked shocked at this revelation 'David Bardon's a damn good police officer' she said 'frankly, I find what you're saying hard to believe, may I personally interview this officer of yours?'

It was Porter's turn to look uncomfortable 'Sadly not' he said 'the fellow knew the game was up. He jumped from a car park roof just yesterday.'

'How very convenient.'

Porter flushed angrily 'damned inconvenient you mean. He must have had all sorts of information he never put on file, a veritable goldmine and now we'll never know. Of course, his suicide will be put down to the stress of overwork.'

'I see, and where does all this leave me a mere police Inspector?'

'You're covered by the Official Secrets Act Inspector. Should you breathe a word to anyone you would be prosecuted. I wanted an informal chat to make absolutely sure you understand the gravity of all this and why it must be as I've laid it out.'

Porter could see the dissatisfaction etched on her face. His face hardened 'let me make it crystal clear, Inspector: To have one bent copper on your watch is unfortunate. To have two would reflect badly on you personally. The rapid promotion could slow down somewhat. Also there's your partner.'

'Mary? What's she got to do with anything?'

'She's a mid-ranking civil servant is she not? She, too, is very ambitious from reports I've had.'

'You blackmailing bastard!'

Porter smiled, genuinely amused 'yes, I am Inspector; it's a necessary trait in my profession. I want to impress upon you that no one, not even the Prime Minister, will be authorised to talk to you about this, either now or at any time in the future.'

Beaker-Rosen looked incredulous 'Well who the hell is higher than the Prime Minister?'

'The Head of State, of course.'

'You mean Her Maj....'

He broke in 'It will all be placed under a one hundred year embargo. That's all you need to know.' His air became impatient 'look, I could have just called you in here and ordered you not to speak of this under the OSA. You're a highly intelligent person bound for very high office that one day you will doubtless achieve. I thought you deserved better than mere orders. Now, if you've no further questions I think we've finished here.'

She half rose as if to go 'just one more thing Mr Porter, what about Bardon and Khan?'

'Khan has disappeared for the moment; we're looking for him as we speak. You may be interested to know that during our search for him we've had to lean on one or two people rather hard.'

'Nothing new there, then' she said sarcastically.

Porter ignored her 'we uncovered a certain guest house run by an ex prostitute called Elizabeth Grayson. She was calling herself Mrs, Grey and providing very young children to wealthy clients.' Beaker-Rosen raised a quizzically eyebrow but remained silent.

'Our friend Khan was one of her regular customers.'

Beaker-Rosen felt nausea hit her stomach. So the rumours were true. 'The bastard' she said and sat back down.

'This Grey woman is, at this moment, at Battersea police station coughing her guts up for all she's worth. She's desperate to do any deal to reduce what she knows will be a long sentence.'

'At least that's something positive to come out of all this crap' Beaker-Rosen said weakly 'but what about my detective?'

'Bardon? He had no way of knowing about Khan's dirty habits, besides, we've no proof he's done anything wrong. He's a damned good officer in all other respects. I should let sleeping dogs lie, Inspector.'

*****

After his debriefing Jack had put his house on the market, it simply wouldn't be safe to live there anymore. Khan had not been seen at any of his known haunts since just before the London attack. It was believed he had gone abroad using a false passport. This theory was enhanced by the fact that his wife, son and daughter had disappeared from their house in Lahore at around the same time as he went missing.

Jack knew it wasn't over until Khan had been located and either arrested or eliminated. He was still with Indira but their relationship was showing signs of strain. She was a gentle person who deplored all forms of violence and this incident had shaken her to the core.

Indira had translated Jack's recordings from the takeaway and knew the madrasah that had recently been in the news was the one Jack had visited. Shortly afterwards it had blown up killing everyone there. On the following day she had been watching the Queen's birthday parade on T.V. when there was a huge explosion and chaotic scenes. The drama was played out before the world's media and all sorts of questions were raised. Wild theories were put forward and all sorts of bizarre speculation advanced.

At the Queen's insistence, a foreshortened version of the parade had gone ahead amid greatly heightened security. In spite of this, most VIPs' had melted away.

Two hours later, Indira had been called on by agents from MI5 who moved her into a safe house far away from her home, job and friends. She was scared stiff and very confused.

Telling lies used to be his stock in trade in the old days but lying to Indira sat ill with him. Jack elected to tell her the truth about his campaign and how it had led to this. He left out his killings whilst in the Army as she didn't need to know. She couldn't accidentally let something slip if she didn't know about it in the first place.

Jack knew she would recoil at the violence, he feared losing her more than anything. Indira sat quietly sniffling through Jack's explanation, a crumpled handkerchief in hand. When he had finished she looked at him with tear filled eyes unable to speak for a long period. When she finally spoke, her voice was trembling with emotion.

'Oh Jack, I feel as though I've been in love with a total stranger. I simply don't know you, do I?' She reached out and rested her hand on his. 'I'm sorry my dear but I'm not prepared to change my entire life for this. I would have to give up my family in India, my friends, my job here; all that has been, and still is, my life. And all because this Bhakti person might want revenge. Tears brimmed in her eyes and smudged her kohl eye-liner 'you ask too much of me.'

Jack squeezed her hand 'But Indira your life may well be in danger because of your association with me. Khan has disappeared. He is known to be a very resourceful and vengeful man it's not just Bhakti. If either thought they could get to me through you they would be capable of anything.'

'That's a risk I'll have to take, Jack. I'll go to my family in India for a while and hope things go back to normal whilst I'm gone.' She gave him a wan smile. 'I'll always love you Jack for the kindness and gentleness you've shown me but it's over.'

'Then why?' he started to ask but she held her hand up to silence him.

''Please, Jack, this is very hard for me. How can I explain?' she paused, her luminous brown eyes full of sadness. 'You know I'm vegetarian, that I follow a Hindu philosophy. I have never harmed a living creature in my life. I could never live with someone who has killed his fellow man for no matter what reason. I'm sorry Jack, I know you think it isn't logical but it's the way I feel and that is final.'

'I read a quote somewhere once' said jack quietly It went something like this: "We only walk in peace and freedom because rough men are willing to do dark deeds on our behalf." He felt his sadness as a physical pain in his chest. 'I was one of those rough men Indira, everything I've ever done has been from necessity. I am not a person who uses violence for any other reason. I, too, hate violence, but sometimes it's the only way.' He paused choking back his emotions 'I know I love you, I believe you love me, but I cannot change who I am inside Indira, I'd be lying if I said I could.'

'For someone who hates violence Jack, you're awfully good at it.'

'That's not fair Indira and you know it.'

Yes Jack, I'm sorry, but I also can't change who I am inside.'

They sat in silence holding hands, each with an aching heart. At last Jack spoke 'Porter and company will not be pleased with your decision, Indira. You know too much.'

'Do you think they'll harm me Jack?'

'No, it's not the way we do things in this country despite what a lot of people think. They will try hard to persuade you to change your mind and they will insist you sign the Official Secrets Act that's all.'

'Well, I'll sign of course, but I won't change my mind' she said with an air of finality 'and I'll tell them so, too.'

'You already did' Jack said 'this is a safe house so it's bound to be wired.'

Indira looked horrified 'do you mean to say they're listening to us Jack?'

'Watching as well, I shouldn't wonder.

Skulduggery

Porter had done his best to persuade Indira to change her mind but she stubbornly refused all offers of help. She had told them she just wanted to get away to her family in India and recuperate. She had willingly signed the Official Secrets Act then left.

Jack sat across the table from Porter on his last debriefing. Westaway was also present but Greenwood was otherwise engaged. When it was over Porter poured them all a large scotch and eased himself back in his chair his dark eyes brooding. 'That bastard Bhakti will get away with this you know' he said a tone of resignation in his voice 'the man's got more strings to his bow than Robin bloody Hood and all his men.'

'I've seen him on TV' said Jack 'he's a cool sod and no mistake. Talk about a polished performance, there's more than a few politicians wish they had his skill' he took a sip of his whiskey 'very convincing performance he put on.'

Westaway looked glum 'There's not much we can do either but monitor him. If he ever comes Stateside it will be different.'

Porter nodded 'that's not likely, he knows where he's well off. He founded The Flame of Truth as he freely admits but left Hassid to run it on a day to day basis not knowing the depths of the man's fanaticism, allegedly. He blames the late Mullah for hijacking his project then humbly claims he's partly responsible for being too trusting. Phone records show very little contact between the two of them, they never worshipped at the same mosque and never met much socially either as far as we know.' he winced after taking too large a gulp of his drink 'He's a clever bastard all right and obviously made contingency plans in case the job went bad.' He continued 'The slimy bugger's even got the minister for security on his side. The fact that the minister's secretary was killed in a botched mugging two days after 'accidentally' accessing your records, Jack, seems to be being glossed over. I don't believe in coincidence.'

Jack emptied his glass and Porter promptly refilled it with his fine single malt, offering one to a grateful Westaway. who nodded his thanks then said 'that speech he gave on TV calling for unity and understanding between all faiths and the need for vigilance in the face of terrorism was a stroke of genius; so well delivered, too.'

Porter swirled his drink thoughtfully. 'God Jack, I wish you were younger, I could really use an agent with your nous.'

'I'm flattered' said Jack 'but your guys are the cream of the crop, are they not?'

Porter let out a long sigh 'well, yes and no Jack. I mean they're all Oxbridge types, terribly bright and well trained boys and girls. They're all dedicated, too, but that stroke you pulled up in Kielder, blowing those buggers up with their own gas and suicide vests, my guys would never have done that.'

'Really' Jack said genuinely surprised 'why ever not?'

'Please don't take this the wrong way Jack, but unlike you, they're too civilised, too influenced by the rules of polite society. Play the game and so on. They've not got your low cunning.'

'And you can't imbue a guy with low cunning' said Westaway sincerely 'he's either got it or he ain't.'

Porter placed his drink on the desk and scratched his ear absently. 'In your position my people would have sent for the nearest military unit, probably at Catterick or even called for a Squadron of the SAS with the ensuing massive fire fight, death and destruction. And then we would have had endless official inquiries. The radicals would have had a field day pointing to how Muslims were being persecuted. There would have been snivelling bloody human rights lawyers crawling out of the woodwork' he sounded bitter. 'Then the liberal judges, who know three fifths of fuck-all about the real world, would do their utmost to come down on the side of the terrorists, the whole sodding circus.'

Porter looked him admiringly 'good lads and lasses my people are Jack, but they simply lack your nous.'

Westaway could see Jack's embarrassment and changed the subject 'So, this Bhakti guy, can't you do anything? Introduce what Jack here calls the 'buggeration factor' into his life perhaps?'

'Covertly you mean?'

'Yes'

'Not a chance. We've been told hands off in no uncertain terms. Should anything untoward happen to our friend the Muslim community could be very adversely affected. The top politico's are shitting bricks, believing his arrest would cause riots.'

Porter finished his drink and poured himself another 'The Home Secretary is in a flat spin of petrified panic. I guess the slippery bastard gets to slide off the hook this time.'

'Maybe' said Jack thoughtfully.

Porter sat bolt upright, at once alert 'if you're thinking of a hit Jack, forget it.' His face clouded 'the days of "thuggery, buggery and general skulduggery" are long gone. This isn't the seventies anymore. If anything happens to Bhakti and I think you are responsible I'll fry your arse. Is that clear?'

'Whoa mate' said Jack raising his free hand defensively 'what I meant was that he's failed his ISIS masters, they are not rational men and could take a very dim view of that failure.'

'I see' said Porter relaxing again, though not sounding convinced 'but I don't think there's a realistic prospect of that, Jack, he's too valuable to them, too highly placed.'

'Greenwood won't be happy when I brief him' Westaway said 'so the Imam will be left free to plot God alone knows what other atrocities.'

'Barring a miracle, John, yes.'

After Indira's departure from the safe house Jack didn't want to stay there either. Despite the protests of Porter, Jack moved out and into a hotel. He needed to be free of bodyguards and surveillance cameras and all the restrictions of movement. He needed to be able to think. A few days after he'd moved Westaway rang with a request to meet for a drink.

Westaway looked worried when they met, he told Jack that Bhakti had recently been activating contacts in the USA.

'The Whitehouse is deeply concerned, Jack, that you British are simply letting him off Scot free' he said.

'So, what's this got to do with me, John?'

Jack looked Westaway in the eye, he liked the big friendly Americanm, sensing in him a kindred spirit. He, too, was less than pleased that the main orchestrator of the thwarted attack was walking away to fight another day.

When Westaway hesitated Jack said 'I take it this is not a social call.'

'Yeah, you're right Jack, I have a proposition to put to you and don't really know where to start.'

'Try at the beginning, John.' Jack said stifling a yawn in order to feign disinterest. He already had an inkling of what the proposition would be.

Westaway took a gulp of his drink then launched into business. Jack sat and listened intently without offering comment or asking questions. When he had finished he looked quizzically at Jack.

'Well? What do you think?'

'Is piss off a plain enough answer, John?'

'Yeah, I thought you'd say that' said Westaway looking a little sheepish. He got up to leave.

'Where are you going John?'

'I thought this meeting was over.'

Jack gave him a wry grin, waving his empty glass 'but it's your shout mate.'

Whilst Westaway dealt with the drinks order Jack had time to gather his thoughts. When once more they were settled Jack said 'OK let me take it from here John.'

Westaway raised a quizzical eyebrow but said nothing. 'You, that is the CIA, want Bhakti eliminated. You don't want to do it yourselves in case you get caught out and are seen to be interfering with the internal affairs of a foreign sovereign power. Right so far?'

Westaway nodded 'something like that.'

'OK, the whole thing is a political hot potato so if Bhakti were to have an unfortunate accident any time soon the world and his wife would smell a large rodent.' Jack took a swig of his scotch savouring it's rich smooth flavour before continuing 'however, if a deeply aggrieved civilian was to eliminate him, that would let everyone, the CIA and MI5, off the hook. But why would I do that? I've got nothing to do with this case, remember?'

Westaway smiled, he'd liked this older man ever since he'd first set eyes on him and the more he got to know him, the more he liked what he saw. He was as shrewd as he was clever. Jack had guessed what the agenda was. It was Greenwood's plan and Westaway wasn't at all comfortable with it.

Jack continued 'I suppose if it went according to your script I'd get busted straight after the hit and evidence would come to light that I had believed Bhakti was responsible for the death of my goddaughter or maybe that I'd mistaken him for Khan?'

'I think you're jumping to conclusions my friend' Westaway said hotly 'we CIA people don't go around framing innocent citizens of a friendly power. We just don't do shit like that, honestly Jack.'

Westaway's use of the word 'honestly' confirmed it for Jack. The biggest lies he'd ever heard were usually prefixed with terms like honestly or: 'to be completely honest with you.' They were what he called liars tells. He would not let him down lightly.

'And beware of Cassius he protesteth too much.' Jack quoted.

Wha''?

'Look, John, I know this was not your plan' he said lightening up a little 'it was probably Greenwood or even someone above him.'

Westaway's eyes never gave away a thing so Jack went on 'I've worked with duplicitous bastards like the Greenwood's of this world in the past. He's working to a secret agenda. This offer of a million dollars and a new ID in the USA is total bullshit.'

'Come on Jack, you're not being fair, he's a good....'

Jack laughed out loud 'he really must think I'm stupid John. Even if he could authorise that kind of money, which he can't, I'd never live to spend it.'

'Look Jack, I've discussed it with him, he swears it's a straight deal.'

'Oh please, spare me the bullshit John. I thought I saw something in you, obviously I was wrong.'

Westaway was stung and snapped angrily 'That's not fair Jack, you're shooting the messenger.'

'I don't give a shit about what's fair John, if I hit Bhakti I'd be a liability, a witness. I wouldn't survive a week.' Jack was flushed and felt angry now 'what was the plan? I find out I'd hit the wrong man and kill myself out of remorse?'

'No one talked about killing you Jack, believe me.'

'I do believe you, John. I also believe that Greenwood wouldn't tell you that part, suspecting you wouldn't go along with it.'

Westaway was at first shocked by Jack's aggressive attitude then it dawned on him the man was probably right. Greenwood, he suspected, had been angling for a hold of some sort over him. He had been keen to get him to organise this coupe. What then? A quiet leak to MI5? Greenwood would then step in and save his arse. He's be in the bastard's pocket then, obliged to him. He decided to wind the meeting up. He needed thinking time 'I take it we won't get any help from you in this matter then.'

'Correct, and you can tell that cynical bastard Greenwood he can shove his fictitious money right up where the sun don't shine.' Westaway again got up to go 'Where are you going John?'

'I thought we were through here.'

'Not quite, and it's my turn to buy. Please, sit down.'

Westaway felt puzzled, Jack had seen though Greenwood's plan before he'd even got through proposing it. He sat down again wondering what else was to come.

'I'm going to look at this Bhakti fellow in more detail John' Jack said as he placed a triple scotch before Westaway 'I decided that long before this meeting.' Westaway went to speak but Jack shook his head. 'If I take him down it will be in my way, in my time.'

'What do you have in mind?'

'Nothing yet, but I will be looking. I'm telling you this because I don't want any CIA tramping all over my operation, that understood? Westaway nodded. 'If I see anyone following me or anything even slightly suspicious from a cat to a candy bar where it shouldn't be, then the operation is off. Is that clear?'

'Perfectly.'

'If, after two weeks, Bhakti is still around you may take it that I have failed so you can take whatever action you deem fit.'

Westaway reported to Greenwood. 'Who does that cocky bastard think he is? He raged' I'll...'

'You'll do nothing if you're smart Nathan' Westaway's eyes glowed with defiance 'The guy's a lot smarter than you gave him credit for and you're pissed with him. Don't let your ego balls this up.'

Greenwood's eyes filled with shock, he was not accustomed to subordinates talking back to him 'Who the hell do you think you're talking to Westaway? That's insubordination in my book.'

'Westaway spoke his next words quietly and calmly. 'Mr Greenwood sir, part of my job description says I am to assist, help and advise you in all operational matters. This is what I am doing. You are an excellent administrator, sir, but you lack field experience.'

'Well, I don't like your attitude Westaway, goddamn it.'

'Well now Nathan, I don't know what sort of sycophants you've had working for you in the past, but I'm no ass licker. If you do go ahead and have him watched and he calls it off then I may well be talking to my ex-boss.'

Greenwood was pompous and egotistical but he recognised plain truth when he saw it, even if he hated the way it was delivered.

'OK' he conceded 'we'll give him a week, no surveillance. If he comes up empty we'll have to think again.'

Westaway felt he'd pushed his luck as far as he could for the moment 'OK Nathan' said Westaway, his smile restored 'I really think that's best.' He turned to leave feeling far from convinced that Greenwood would keep his word.

'Oh, by the way John, this conversation never took place, OK?'

Westaway paused in the doorway knowing he'd have to butt heads with Greenwood yet again. 'I'm afraid I've diarised all of our conversations on this matter Nathan. Official procedures, remember them?'

Greenwood's face flushed 'So, all this is on your laptop, is it?'

'Mine and about four thousand others in and around D C Nathan. Oh don't worry, the files are carefully hidden and encrypted, too.'

'Why the hell did you do that you conniving bastard?' Greenwood shouted.

'Because if you renege on your word not to interfere and cause this op to go bad Mr Greenwood, sir, then you're going to have to eat your share of the shit for once.'

Jack watched the big house which overlooked Hampstead Heath. He took several photos from the front and from and the back using a telephoto lens. It wouldn't be easy to get in and out unseen. A surveillance camera covered the front including the drive with its high wall and eclectic gates.

At the back were two cameras high on the corner of the building. One could see down the side of the house the second covered the back garden. There were also a PIR floodlights. After careful study Jack saw a route he could take through the next door property through the panel fence to a French window on the rear elevation of Bhakti's property. He had not formulated a plan at this stage but as he was about to leave he saw something that gave him an idea.

A car pulled up outside the house and the driver got out, rummaged in the back for a moment then took a parcel and a clip board and pressed the bell on the gatepost. After a brief conversation, the gates slid back and the man went up the drive.

Jack saw a well dressed woman he assumed was the Imam's wife at the door sign for the parcel and close the door. The delivery man returned to his car and drove off. Jack followed him.

After no more than a few hundred yards the man stopped again and repeated the process but this time walked up a long ungated drive. Jack quickly left his car and looked into the delivery vehicle. It was full of parcels from an expensive mail order catalogue. Jack remembered his late wife Joan was always buying stuff this way and they were not always delivered by a parcel carrier company but often by private individuals with a contract to deliver.

Hurrying back to his car again Jack followed the man, this time closing up to his car at the next drop off. As the man was about to walk up the drive Jack asked pleasantly 'Oh, that parcel for here?' 'Yup, you Mr. Holroyd?'

'I'm going up there' Jack said and took the proffered clip board signing in an unreadable scrawl.

The man tore off a copy of the delivery note and handed it and the parcel to Jack grateful for the time and legwork he'd saved.

Jack took the parcel and started to amble up the long drive. When he heard the delivery man's car pull away he turned around and left.

Back at home Jack got to work. He carefully steamed the label off the parcel and scanned it into his computer. Next, he removed the name and address on the label image before printing a new one.

Googling Bhakti he discovered the name of his wife, this he printed on the forged label and stuck it on the parcel in place of the now defunct original. He then repeated the process with the copy of the delivery document. On a clipboard, similar to the delivery man's, he placed a sheet of foolscap paper with his hands in surgical gloves so leaving no prints or DNA. On top of this paper he placed the altered delivery note so that an inch and a half of blank paper protruded below. It wasn't perfect but with luck it would work.

Jack was up early next morning, he bathed and shaved and dressed casually in jeans and a lightweight black leather bomber jacket over a grey tee shirt. He ate a hearty breakfast then made up some sandwiches and a flask. It could turn out to be a long day.

About ten thirty, Jack saw what he'd been hoping to see. The electric gates slid open and Mrs. Bhakti drove out in a white Toyota four by four. She turned in the direction of Central London and accelerated away. Jack waited five minutes then went to the gates and pressed the bell. 'Yes?' said the disembodied voice of Bhakti.

'Parcel delivery' said Jack. He heard Bhakti muttering impatiently and the gate started to slide open. Jack walked briskly up the drive with the parcel and clipboard and waited in front of the door.

The door opened, Bhakti stood with a phone wedged between his ear and shoulder. He took the parcel barely glancing at Jack who proffered the clip board, tipping it slightly, letting up his thumb sending the pen sliding gently down the paperwork.

Instinctively Bhakti grabbed the sliding pen. 'There please, sir' said Jack pointing to the bottom of the sheet.

'Yes, that's right minister' Bhakti said into the phone as he hurriedly signed where Jack had indicated then thrust the pen back.

'Thank you, sir' said Jack handing him the delivery note. Bhakti snatched it and hurriedly turned away, closing the door. Jack noted that Bhakti was left handed.

Returning after dark, Jack sat on the heath watching as the lights went out downstairs and came on upstairs at Bhakti's house. After the place had been dark for over an hour he made his move. He slipped around the back of the neighbouring property the old sense of operational excitement tingling his every nerve.

He approached the six foot panel fence that separated the gardens. No way could he climb it without creating an almighty din. He pushed up the panel closest to the house but it didn't budge. The next one he tried slid upwards quickly and quietly in the concrete grooved fence posts. Ducking underneath he lowered it gently. Jack flattened himself against the house and listened intently for a full minute. A dog fox barked in the distance then all was quiet.

Reaching the French windows he took out his lock picks. The door was an old one, the lock's tumblers worn from years of use so that he had little difficulty unlocking it.

Pushing it open an inch he knelt and felt the bottom rail. There was no magnetic contact. He repeated this at the top then opened it wide. No alarm went off. A passive infrared detector's red light came on across the room as he entered but no alarm sounded. Jack knew from his years of experience in the security business that most people don't set the zone alarm when at home. They feared an accidental triggering would annoy their neighbours. It was a gamble he had taken being reasonably confident he would win.

Jack found himself in a dining room at the left hand end was an open plan kitchen. Turning to his right he found what he was looking for, Bhakti's study.

Switching on a small torch Jack looked around finding a two desk top computers. They were both on stand-by. He double clicked the mouse on the first and it sprang to life with a quiet buzz. To his chagrin he found the keyboard in script he could make neither head nor tail of.

To his immense relief the second computer proved to have an ordinary QWERTY keyboard. Opening the Word programme Jack typed for a couple of minutes then printed his work out on the sheet of foolscap paper he'd brought with him. He then closed the file without saving it. so the machine's owner wouldn't come across it should he open the programme. He knew his note would probably be traceable by a forensic I T analyst.

A noise from upstairs caused Jack to freeze. Heavy footsteps thudded briefly then silence. He waited in the study, should he make for the door? If he made the slightest sound the game could be up. He was still pondering when from upstairs came the sound of a toilet being flushed; a further thudding of the heavy footsteps then all was silent once again. With a sigh of relief Jack headed for the French door. It took him only moments to relock it he then carefully retraced his route. Part one of his plan had gone well.

The next day, Jack knew Bhakti would be conducting Friday prayers at his local mosque. He went into the cellar of his old house and retrieved the Walther P38 cleaning it meticulously, his hands in latex gloves. Next he donned his old man disguise once more. He drove a few miles then parked on a quiet side street with no cameras. He walked half a mile before buying a local paper.

Turning to the classified adverts he found what he was looking for. He bought a battered old Ford Fiesta privately for four hundred pounds cash giving the owner a false name and address. There was no way he could use his own vehicle for what he had planned.

Bhakti climbed into his car for the journey back to his home from the mosque. Turning into a road near his home he saw in the rear view mirror an old car driven by an elderly looking man. It looked out of place in this prosperous neighbourhood. As he slowed to a stop at the next junction the car behind ran none to gently into his back end. Bhakti was furious and leapt out of his car. Why was an old fool like him still driving? The elderly man looked confused as he climbed out of his car and tottered to meet him.

'What do you think you're playing at?' Bhakti began angrily then broke off as the Walther was jammed into his ribs.

'Do exactly as I say or I'll drop you right here' Jack hissed prodding the barrel hard into his man's well padded ribs to emphasize his point. 'Move, move, move Jack said aggressively and with each command prodded the barrel hard into him. It had the intended effect of disorienting and confusing his prisoner. He backed towards his car. Bhakti sat behind the wheel looking pale

'Who are you? Who sent you? What do you want? Money?'

'Shut up and drive' Jack ordered prodding the gun barrel hard into the back of Bhakti's neck.

Bhakti started the car.

'OK, we're going to have a little talk on the heath, I'll direct you'. Bhakti was bewildered, this man didn't look like a secret serviceman he was far too old and anyway he had the minister's personal assurance he'd not be targeted. Then realisation dawned as his panic began to subside a little. 'You're Ellis, right?'

'Correct Bhakti, now shut up until I tell you to speak.' Jack again prodded him viciously. He had to keep the man off balance, intimidated. He guided him to a quiet spot away from dog walkers, joggers and perverts.

'This'll do. Move your mirror so you can see me.'

Bhakti looked into the cold grey eyes, the gun still pressing into the back of his head. The Imam was regaining some composure now 'what do you want Ellis, money? A confession? If you hope to scare me with this theatrical performance, think again.' Jack had to admire the quick way his man was recovering from his initial shock. He could almost hear the cogs of his mind working out the angles.

'I already have a signed confession mate' said Jack transferring the pistol from his right hand to his left.

'That's just not possible and any forgery would be quickly detected you damned old fool.'

Jack grabbed the Imam's forehead jerking him back against the headrest 'It's not a forgery my friend I have your confession typed on your own PC. I was the delivery man who called yesterday to allow you to sign your own death warrant.'

Awful realisation dawned on Bhakti now. He remembered his wife had complained that the fools at the catalogue company had sent garments she hadn't ordered. Like most husbands Bhakti took scant notice of his wife's purchases, these petty domestic arrangements didn't interest him at all. She had stormed off into the study to ring the catalogue to arrange for them to be picked up.

Totally aghast Bhakti sat staring into the mirror. 'Look, Ellis, I have money, a great deal of money.....'

Jack curled his right arm around Bhakti's head and deftly pinched his man's nostrils closed. As his mouth open automatically to take breath. Jack shoved in the barrel of the Walther pushing it into the roof of his mouth. He ducked to avoid the blood splash as he squeezed the trigger. Bhakti died instantly, his brains splattered on the roof of his car. Jack let the pistol drop and noted where it landed by the gear shift.

Released, the dead man slumped forward blood still pumping from his mouth and the exit wound. Jack looked around him, the nearest person was a dog walker about three hundred metres away. Clearly the woman had heard nothing as she picked up a ball and threw it for her pet. Climbing out of the car he got in the front passenger seat. Picking up the gun in his gloved hand he pressed dead man's left hand onto the grip, trigger and barrel.He slipped out the magazine and made sure Bhakti's prints were on that, too.Rreplacing the gun exactly where it had fallen as if from the Imam's dead hand. He straightened the mirror again.

Taking out the signed suicide note he had written the night before Jack made sure the Imam's fingerprints were on it before he slid it into the corpse's pocket. 'And that, my dear Imam Bhakti' he told the corpse with cold satisfaction 'comes under the heading of thuggery, buggery and general skulduggery.'

Jack strolled across the Heath back to the old Fiesta feeling the adrenalin slowly draining from his system. After driving for several miles he stopped in a down beat area, dropping an incendiary device on the back seat. Three minutes later the vehicle went up in flames. Later that day Jack's phone rang 'I need a word with you Ellis.' snapped Porter 'Get in here now.'

Jack reacted with well practiced surprise 'What on earth are you talking about Andrew?'

Porter's voice seethed with barely concealed rage 'You know bloody well why I want to see you, just get in here.'

Jack affected annoyance, he knew the call was being recorded and would later be carefully analysed 'Look, Porter, I don't know what the hell your game is but no one speaks to me like that no matter how bloody important they think they are' he drew a deep breath as if finding it difficult to control himself; 'Obviously there's been some sort of development, a leak perhaps? Well it didn't come from me, Ok?'

Porter's hand gripped the phone hard his knuckles almost glowing white. Christ, this old bugger was so good he almost believed him. 'You know damn well what's happened because you caused it. Now, do you come in or do I send someone to bring you?'

Jack sat opposite Porter all trace of their former friendliness gone. 'I don't know how you pulled this off, Ellis, but it has Army Intelligence hit stamped all over it. If this got out it could ruin years of carefully built up relationships across the Middle East.'

Jack fixed him with an icy stare 'Then it better hadn't get out, had it? '

'So you admit you did it?'

'No way' said Jack his face an unreadable mask.

Porter tried to contain his annoyance 'Look, Jack, everyone knows Bhakti was not the suicidal type, there's not a shred of evidence to suppose he was. Already people are talking of a conspiracy. Do you not realise the implications of this act?'

Jack stayed impassive like he was briefing a client from his former security days. 'Then I suggest you use your remarkable resources to uncover some evidence suggesting that he was suicidal.'

'I can't...' Porter began.

'I would also suggest that a link be 'found' between our American friend Greenwood and Bhakti, just in case it's ever needed. It's common knowledge in your circles he bore the man a grudge.'

'Everyone loves to hate the Americans so it shouldn't be too hard to convince your Middle Eastern friends.' Jack paused before twisting the knife 'surely I don't have to advise a man of your experience of the value of disinformation?'

Porter's rage boiled over 'You facetious old bastard' he roared 'I could bloody well have you taken out, maybe that's the best solution all round. What do you think?'

Jack knew Porter was just blowing off steam. He smiled broadly 'Go ahead and see what happens.' he said feigning nonchalance 'I've taken precautions against that.'

'What?' Porter snorted 'don't tell me you've written anything down man? Surely not?'

'Better than that, I've made a video, chapter and verse. If anything should happen to me or mine then the International Press Corps will get a copy. Your "D" notices won't help you. The vidoeo is encrypted on thousands of government computers. My new best friend Westaway showed me how to do it. If nothing happens to me it will auto delete fifteen years from now.'

Porter was astounded 'What the fuck...?

Jack gave him the hard eye 'I know I'm OK for now Andrew, but what about the future? You leave office and I'm at the mercy of whoever takes over. Maybe at some point I'll become a loose end, an embarrassment and no one will look too deeply at a guy of my age suffering a heart attack or doddering in front of a speeding car.'

Porter looked pale 'what a cynical bastard you are.'

'Cynical bastards live longer Andrew.'

'But what if you should have a fatal heart attack? An accident?'

'You'd better make sure I don't Andrew, American and Middle Eastern accidents included.'

Of Condolence

Jack stared at the pile of money he'd taken from Khan's safe. He should by rights hand it in. He had no want to keep it for himself nor did he have any need. His attitude to money was philosophical. Enough was enough and he had enough and to spare. Enough was all anyone needed in his view. He found it difficult to understand why some people spent their every waking hour money grabbing. They seemed to believe that the more money they had the happier they would be. There was plenty of evidence in the newspapers almost every day that that simply wasn't true. After his daily meditation, he knew what he would do with the cash.

One of the secret service men who had looked after Jack at the safe house had been the great nephew of one of Jack's former military colleagues. They had got on very well, Jack phoned him and asked him to research an address and phone number. The man had willingly complied once Jack had assured him his reason for wanting it was innocent. 'She was a close friend of my late goddaughter' he'd lied 'I'd like to pay her a visit of condolence.'

Jack limped down the street once again dressed in his 'old man' disguise, leaning heavily on his bamboo stick. He was looking for the address he'd requested. It was cold in the pre-dawn light and he shivered slightly in spite of the thick overcoat. Some summer this is he thought.

At last he came to the right door. It was a dingy old Victorian house that had been split into bed sits. The lock was an ancient

Yale and no match for his skills. He climbed the stairs until he found the right door.

Marcia was laying in bed, her son next to her. The little boy stirred but didn't awake when her phone rang. Sleepily she looked at the clock it was three a.m. Who could be calling at this time? Her thoughts went to her parents, had anything happened to them? They may have disowned her in their self-righteous religious indignation, but she had not disowned them.

She answered quickly, not wanting Jackson to be woken up 'hello' she said anxiously.

The pleasant male voice said 'go to your front door Marcia, you'll find a hold-all containing the estate of the late Waldo Williams.' Jack thought the white lie the best explanation of the cash and make her feel better about accepting it 'as his next of kin, your son is the rightful heir.'

'Who is this?'

'My name isn't important Marcia, so hurry now before one of your neighbours wakes up and steals it.'

Marcia did as she was bid. Looking around the empty stairwell she hurriedly took the hold-all in. Putting the bag on her dining table she pulled the zip and almost fainted when she saw its contents.

There was a note on top which read: There is two hundred and sixty four thousand pounds here which rightfully belongs to you and your son. It won't last a lifetime but it will help you make a new start and bring up your son up in a decent environment where he won't be influenced by people like his father. Keep quiet about this Marcia and let no one know of your good fortune. Rent yourself a safe deposit box, don't try to bank it. Good luck.

It wasn't signed.

Marcia's emotions were all a whirl, who could have done this? None of Waldo's so-called friends that was for sure and the police would have confiscated it as the proceeds of crime if they'd found it.

She hadn't heard a car so whoever it was could still be close by. She slid up her sash window and stuck her head out into the chilly air.

Looking up and down the street for her mysterious benefactor she was puzzled. The only person in sight was a scruffy looking old man limping along, leaning heavily on a walking stick.

Khan's Revenge

On the Saturday morning, when Khan heard the news about the terror attack in London going wrong his blood ran cold. He knew who had thwarted it and he knew that Jack Ellis had got his initial information from him. So did Bhakti. Now there would be a fatwa out on him.

The police would probably be calling at his house anytime soon, too, as Oliphant blabbed to save his arse. He had to get out. Scurrying around he threw a few clothes into a hold-all. He grabbed some of the false passports he held just in case of such an emergency as this. He had only a few thousand pounds in cash so he'd have to be careful how he used it. Credit cards would be out of the question.

Where could he go? Who could he trust? What should he do for the best? His heart raced and his head spun. He felt panic rising in him. All his efforts had gone for nothing, his legitimate business and his drugs business, too. The Columbians were pissed off with him for not following through on the deal to buy fresh drug supplies. They were not the kind of people you let down. He felt trapped.

He took his car to the nearest underground station and dumped it then took a bus in the opposite direction. For the first time in years he had donned traditional Asian dress in the hope of disguising himself. No one he knew had ever seen him in it so it might work.

One of Bhakti's associates rang 'Khan, give yourself up to me and I will plead your case with the brothers. I'm sure a sincere apology and a large enough financial penalty will appease them' he said sounding conciliatory. 'They are short of funds at the moment so they will listen.'

'Like hell they will. They'll take my money and kill me. I'll take my chances on my own.'

'In that case I will put a fatwa on you with fifty thousand pounds reward for anyone not just our own.'

Khan cut the call. 'Cheeky bastard' he muttered to himself but he felt worried and his spirits sank. A fifty grand reward could start a lot of people actively seeking him out. All his old haunts were now off limits.

The fatwa meant any Moslem could kill him on sight, not that many would. If the Columbians caught him they would torture him then sell him to the brothers for the reward. Plenty of people knew and hated him, anyone would shop him with that incentive. He was now being hunted by just about everybody. 'That old bastard' he said through gritted teeth, the blood rush swelling the arteries of his neck as his fury rose, 'that interfering, geriatric old bastard Ellis. 'He'll pay for this.'

Khan never considered for one moment walking into a police station and giving himself up. It was a matter of using a new identity and disappearing with his millions. There would be an all ports watch for him so it was best to wait a week or so until the authorities believed he'd slipped the net before attempting to flee. This, he believed, was his best hope of escape., Where to hide in the meantime he had yet to consider.

Jonny Burke's phone rang 'Hi Jonny it's me.'

'Christ boss, where are you? Everyone is saying you've skipped the country.'

Khan was not about to tell him. Not with a fifty thousand pound reward on his head, that kind of news travelled fast. He needed to be sure of his man first.

'That doesn't matter at the moment Jonny my friend' he said sounding a lot calmer that he felt 'how would you like to become very rich?'

'Providing I don't have to risk my neck, the question is how rich?' 'A million to start with and, if you do well in what I tell you, you'll be my future partner, fifty-fifty.'

Burke thought for a moment, the partnership offer was bullshit, of course. Khan would never share with anyone but, with a million pounds, he could start a sizable operation of his own.'

'OK, sounds cool, what do you want me to do?'

'You have a gun don't you?'

Burke sounded embarrassed 'Yeah, sort of, an old Smith & Wesson .38 why?'

'You will need it, I have an escape idea but first I need to eliminate a certain man.'

'But Mr Khan, I've only got one bullet for my gun.'

Khan was shocked 'Only one? Then get some more you damn fool.'

Burke didn't really like guns, he much preferred the knife. He'd grown up with knives. Close up and personal was what he enjoyed, he liked to see his victim's shocked eyes, feel their blood run.

He kept the revolver under the floorboards of the derelict house next door to his place, seldom getting it out. 'Everybody on my crew uses 9 mm these days boss .38 ammo is like rocking horse shit down my ends. I can...'

'It doesn't matter' Khan interrupted him 'you only have to scare the bastard anyway. If it comes to a fight pop him in the arm or leg. I must be the one to kill him, you understand?

'Fine by me, now what about my million?'

'You get that after the job, when I'm safe.'

'Are you having a laugh Khan? Who the fuck do you think you're dealing with?' Burke snapped, deeply irritated at being taken for a fool.

Khan felt a surge of anger, his ego was pricked, just a couple of days ago Burke would not have dared to speak to him that way.

With an effort he controlled his tongue, he needed this man if he was to escape and have his revenge.

'OK, what about ten percent now and the rest afterwards?'

'Bollocks. Fifty percent now and cast iron arrangements for the rest afterwards or no deal' Burke's voice was hard and uncompromising. 'Take it or leave it Khan, one more attempt at haggling and I put the phone down.' He had no love for Khan or anyone else for that matter save for himself, his mother and his kid sister.

Khan knew he had no bargaining power 'OK, OK, it's a deal. One more thing, I need a place to stay Jonny, just for a few days, can you help?'

There was a pause whilst Burke considered this. Sheltering Khan could be dangerous. On the other hand he thought it would be better to know where I can get my hands on the slippery bastard.

'Yeah, my uncle left me a farm last year, you know, where they took Waldo; the guy who rents it from me grows cannabis there so he can't afford to get tricky.'

Khan gave Burke his location and he came and collected him, driving him to the farm. On arrival Burke produced a laptop. 'Those are my bank details in the Bahamas, you need to transfer the money now' he told him bluntly.

Khan scowled sourly, feeling bitter at having to part with such a large sum. For a moment he looked like he was about to say something but held his peace. He had no alternative other than to do as bid.

'Right, what's next Mr. Khan? You mentioned vengeance on the way down here?'

Khan told him of Jack Ellis, his eyes blazing and his stomach churning 'I have to kill the bastard personally' he hissed he produced a wicked looking flick knife and shot the blade open 'I want to cut the bastard's heart out, but I need to locate him first.'

Four days later Burke had arranged with a people smuggler to get Khan out on a luxury sailing yacht the following weekend. He also made sure the yacht could connect to the Internet. Until he got the balance of his cash, Khan was going nowhere.

'What have you found out Jonny?' Khan's dark eyes flashed 'have you located him?'

'We think he must be in an MI5 safe house because there have been no sightings, nothing. We found out his girlfriend's address though, she lives in London.'

Khan's eyes lit up in surprise, this news caused great excitement in him 'Girlfriend? I didn't know he had a girlfriend, I thought he lived alone?'

'He does. They haven't been going out all that long, months only.' Khan smiled for the first time in days, his heart sang with joy.

'Great, that makes things so much easier Jonny, well done.'

He was happy now but he needed to plan this carefully. He sent Burke to look Indira's house over but, he warned him, on no account approach or be seen observing by anyone.

That night Burke came back to report what he'd found out and show Khan Photo's he'd taken on his phone. Khan studied these carefully for a few minutes then he thought for a while in silence. Suddenly he snapped his fingers and then ran through the numbers in his phone.

'Ah yes! I thought I did.'

'Did what?'

'Azziz told me he rang in once to order a takeaway and I thought it might be useful to acquire his number as a precaution. He's not the only clever kid on the block, as he'll soon find out.'

'So, what do you want me to do boss?'

Khan thought for a moment. Ellis would have warned her about him even if he believed he'd fled the country. He would have cautioned her about opening her door to strangers and of being careful not to walk in lonely places.

'Get me a couple of balloons, those long thin ones, some string and some Cellotape. You'll need a hard hat, a day glow jacket and a photograph of yourself, plus an ID card holder.' Burke looked puzzled 'er... right' he said but knew Khan well enough not to ask why.

That evening the items had been acquired and Khan explained his plan.

'Christ Mr Khan, that's bloody clever, but also dangerous for you. Why don't you keep your head down here until it's time to go? You can always put out a contract on him later.'

Khan was in no mood for reasoned argument 'I need to do this myself Jonny, it is a matter of honour. Revenge must be mine and now, with the help of this woman, it will be.'

*****

Indira was heartbroken. The hopes and dreams she'd had for a future with Jack were shattered. She had booked a flight to India that was due to leave next morning. A couple of months with her beloved elderly parents and her siblings living the simple village life would help her heal.

She sat on the edge of the bed her head in her hands. In the middle of packing she had suddenly become overwhelmed by it all. How could he? she thought, how could this gentle, witty man whose quiet humour had made her giggle like a school girl, whose love making had sent her to the heights of ecstasy, be an accomplished killer? It didn't make sense to her, she who had been brought up to respect all living things. She who trapped spiders in a glass and put them outside even though they terrified her. Indira sobbed quietly, her tears washed her cheeks and hands spilling copiously into her lap.

Jonny Burke walked boldly up Indira's path and looked around him. The road was quiet. From under his coat he took the long balloons that Khan had put domestic gas into. He checked the Cellotape was still stuck firmly to them then and pushed the ends into the letterbox. He hoped Khan was right and that when he pricked the balloon through the tape they would deflate slowly and not pop loudly. They did, and he squeezed the gas into the house. He then pocketed the deflated balloons, rang the doorbell and began knocking urgently.

Upstairs Indira heard the din and came cautiously down into the hall without switching on the light. She went to the door and peered through the viewfinder.

A young man in a hard hat and a day-glow jacket was banging and he looked worried. Indira got a strong whiff gas.

The letter box opened and the young man called through 'Anyone home? Emergency. Is anyone there?'

'Who is it?' she inquired.

'Gas engineer madam, this is an emergency' the young man held his ID card forward' there's been a major leak and we need to vacate all these premises now.'

Jack had told her not to open the door to strangers under any circumstances and not even to talk through the door. Don't accept parcel deliveries for yourself or your neighbours he'd instructed. These warnings were now uppermost in her mind. Ordinarily she would have stuck rigidly to Jack's advice but the smell of gas was strong and the man seemed genuine and most anxious. She opened the door.

Burke stepped in quickly. Grabbing Indira, he covered her mouth and pushed her hard against the wall, kicking the door shut behind him.

'Keep quiet bitch if you know what's good for you' he snarled. Indira whimpered in terror, her eyes wide with fright, her mind unable to grasp what was happening.

Burke slapped her hard across her head 'do you understand me bitch?' 'Do you?'

Indira at last was able to nod and Burke eased his grip. Reaching for his phone he pressed a quick dial number 'I'm in' was all he said and stuffed it back into his pocket.

Khan left the car and walked around the corner looking neither left nor right he went up the drive and into the house.

Ushered into her living room Indira was forced into an armchair feeling utterly terrified and bemused. Khan slapped her hard across the face then gripped her chin forcing her to look into his face. 'You're going to ring your boyfriend and invite him round woman. Where's your phone?'

Indira was beginning to gather her wits and refused to answer. Khan struck her again.

'It's here in her hand bag.' Burke said, a note of triumph in his voice.

Khan held it out to her 'ring him'

'He won't come around we've ended our relationship' she said defiantly 'I think he's gone abroad.'

'Liar' screamed Khan and struck her hard across the face. 'Ring him.' Indira looked at him her face dignified and composed 'No matter what you do to me I will not betray him' she said quietly.

Khan sneered and drew his knife. Indira drew a sharp breath as she saw the blade flash and heard the vicious click. She, believing she was going to die, lowered her head in resignation of her fate. Khan drew her to her feet and started cutting her clothes away.

'You fancy a fuck Jonny?' he asked.

Indira knew that they intended to kill her or this man she now realised was Khan wouldn't have named his accomplice. She stood naked and trembling before them making no attempt to hide herself, managing to glare defiantly at them in spite of her fear.

'I could manage one I suppose to teach this bitch a lesson.'

Khan leaned into her face 'I prefer anal myself, has Ellis ever done that to you?' He squeezed her breast hard and laughed.

He held out the phone to her 'last chance. Ring and an invite him or I'll cut your face.' He waved the knife threateningly.

Jack answered sounding pleasantly surprised 'Hi Indira, I thought you'd gone to India?'

Her voice was controlled with no hint of distress 'Khan's here' she said.

Khan's face suffused with rage he snatched the phone from her. 'That's right Ellis, I'm here and if you want this woman to live you'll come here alone right now.'

'If you hurt her Khan I promise you a very slow, painful death.'

'Shut up and listen you bastard' Khan screamed 'I've an ISIS fatwa on me thanks to you, everybody is after me. I've nothing to lose. I need hostages to get out of the country and you and her are it' he took a deep ragged breath 'I have some of my people watching the house. Any sign of police or anyone else and she's dead you got that? Dead!

He screamed the last word and Jack knew he wasn't dealing with a rational man. His heart sank. 'I'll be there in half an hour and, Khan' he paused for a second 'if she's hurt in any way I'll kill you no matter what it takes. Know that you will not survive, you lowlife bastard.'

Jack hung up, he knew the hostage talk was a lie Khan wanted to kill him. He'd kill Indira first in front of him and in some horrible way then he'd kill him, too. At least Jack figured that was his plan.

Did Khan have people watching? Probably not, rats don't stay on sinking ships. However Jack couldn't he afford to take that chance. Khan could probably bribe one or two of his old gang if the money was right and he wasn't short of money. Should he walk into Khan's trap? He had no weapons and his house was too far from his hotel to get there and to Indira's house within the half hour. He thought of ringing the police but with Khan in god alone knew what state of mind he would almost certainly be condemning Indira to death. No, he wouldn't phone the police. He did however make one brief phone call, then he left.

On arrival, Jack drove slowly around the adjacent streets looking for anyone who might be hidden, watching. It was an impossible task, the area was overflowing with parked cars and vans and there were dozens of alleyways. To be sure he would have to scour the area on foot and he didn't have time for that.

Indira's door was ajar, the hall was in darkness except for anaemic light that filtered in from the street. Jack pushed the door and it swung back with a slight creak. The hall was empty.

His thoughts raced. Was he going to get it as soon as he walked in? No, Khan wanted vengeance, to make him suffer, to humiliate him to the maximum. He hesitated, trying to think where Khan would be holding her. He could see the living room door to his left was open, the room unlit. Then it hit him, he'd be in the main bedroom in the back of the house. Feeling his guts trembling and cold sweat running down his back Jack stepped in.

He was passing the living room door when he sensed a movement and in a flash a gun was pushed into the side of his head.

'Evening Ellis' the voice was one he didn't recognize, so Khan wasn't alone after all. Jack risked moving his head a fraction to see a large bloke in his mid twenties with glinting blue eyes and a confident sneer on his face. The way he was holding the revolver told Jack the guy knew nothing much about firearms. He was holding it in what Jack called the Hollywood gangster grip. The gun was high above his shoulder so he could point the barrel downwards, the weapon turned on its side. It looked good in the movies but the only way you'd hit an oil drum shooting like that would be to sit inside it. From this range that was a moot point but it gave him a tiny glimmer of hope.

Jonny Burke felt good, in total control, he eyed Jack and saw nothing special about him. Just some old fart.

'Up there Ellis.'

Jack played dumb 'where?'

Burke sneered waving the gun like a Hollywood 'baddie.' He flicked his gun towards the far end of the hall 'stairs, idiot.'

Jack's hand moved like a flash the instant the barrel pointed away from him. He knocked the gun sideways and down. Burke made the mistake of wasting time trying to re-point the gun instead of punching Jack in the face, knocking him backwards to gain time.

Jacks saw his man's chin was down looking towards the gun, partially obscuring his throat. His left hand shot out, fingers stiff and splayed as he rammed them hard into Burke's eyes.

Burke screamed in agony as his eyeballs were gouged. His hands flew to his face, the weapon falling to the carpet. As he reeled back Jack kicked hard through his legs crushing his testicles on his shin. Burke groaned and sank to the carpet and Jack followed through, stamping hard on his opponent's neck. He heard and felt the vertebrae snap.

Jonny Burke rolled on his back, eyes staring lifelessly at the ceiling. Jack couldn't afford to leave him alive and injured behind him in case he recovered and came after him. He picked up the gun and checked it over.

Hell, he thought feeling disappointed, it's older than god's granny and not been cleaned since the old king died. Only one bullet, too. One lousy round. It would have to do, maybe Khan didn't know.

Upstairs Khan had heard Burke scream and knew things had gone wrong. He grabbed Indira off the bed where she had rolled herself in the duvet. 'Up whore' he said pulling her up by her hair and dragging her in front of him. He turned to face the door his knife at her throat. The room was lit only by the bedside light.

Jack entered, gun in hand.

'Drop the gun Ellis.'

'No.'

Jack aimed at what he could see of Khan's head. The drug dealer was crouched behind Indira his head behind hers with just his left eye and about a third of his face showing.

'Drop the gun or I'll slice her.'

'No' Jack said again in a flat calm voice. He pulled the hammer back slowly and deliberately and drew a bead on Khan's eye 'if I see one drop of her blood you're dead.'

Khan had not expected this response and it shook him; he had to think fast 'That's an old gun Ellis, a piece of shit from world war two and only one bullet. If you miss I'll kill her then you.

Jack's aim never wavered though inside he knew the gun was indeed an ancient unreliable piece that had been poorly maintained. 'If I put this down Khan me and her are both dead and you know it.'

'If you put the gun down I'll let her walk Ellis, it's you I want. You and me what do you say eh?' He pricked Indira though not enough to draw blood. If he had expected her to scream he was disappointed.

'Please, Jack' she said calmly as if resigned to death 'don't worry about me darling, save yourself.'

Jack ignored her 'I'm going to count three Khan, if your still holding the knife you're dead one.... two..'

Khan started throwing Indira about stepping left and right in quick succession. Jack now had no alternative. He fired.

The bullet went slightly right clipping Khan's ear. He spun away screaming clutching his ear as Indira dropped to the floor but he retained his grip on the knife. Jack turned the pistol to use as a club and ran at Khan. The man's reflexes were cobra quick and he side stepped thrusting at Jack with his blade. The blow struck Jack in his rapidly descending arm going through his triceps. He cried out in shock and pain but managed to aim his left fist at Khan's throat. The blow made only slight contact as Khan swung backwards with the awareness of a street fighter.

Jack saw the knife flash again and managed to block it with his left arm. His right shot across and gripped the knife hand twisting it but his arm was weakening from the wound and he couldn't wrest the weapon away.

Khan twisted to the side protecting his balls so Jack kicked him in the shin and the man screamed in rage and pain. He still held the knife but his grip had slackened and as Jack twisted desperately as hard as he could and the knife flew away across the room.

'Get out Indira' Jack yelled 'go and get help.' But shock was now paralysing her she stood naked and trembling her eyes wide with horror, no longer capable of thinking or acting.

Khan punched Jack hard in the guts and drove the wind out of his lungs then he hit him on the wounded arm sending pain flooding through him. A vicious right sent Jack to the floor, his head swimming. Khan dived on him and straddled his chest his hands going to his throat.

'Got you, you bastard.'

Jack managed to wrench his head aside before Khan had a full grip. 'The knife Indira, the knife' he shouted.

Indira looked around dazed but stood rooted to the spot. Khan hit Jack again and this time got his thumbs into Jack's windpipe. Jack couldn't reach Khan's throat or eyes his wounded arm was all but useless now and Khan was kneeling on both. He felt the agony in his throat and fought desperately for air. He saw Indira at last start to move in the direction of the knife.

Picking up the knife Indira screamed at Khan 'let him go, let him go' but a lifetime's conditioning of none-violence stopped her stabbing Khan. She simply could not make herself to do it. She screamed, high long and terrified.

Jack's senses were fading fast under the vice-like grip around his throat his heart pounded, blood roared in his ears and his vision blurred. He knew he was beaten now, he was going to die. His one regret was his failure to save Indira.

Indira screamed again as the bedroom door flew pen and a big man ran in, kicking Khan in the head. Khan's grip loosened on Jack's throat but he still hung on eyes bulging with insane hatred.

The man's arm went around Khan's neck and dragged him backwards off Jack throwing him to the floor before kicking him again. Khan sank down with a groan.

Westaway bent over Jack and started massaging his neck. To his immense relief he saw Jack draw a great rasping breath. 'Take it easy Jack, I'll call an ambulance.'

Jack tried to speak but found it impossible to manage anything but a croak. John Westaway was helping Jack to his feet when he heard a scuffling noise behind him. Khan had recovered and had shot out of the room and down the stairs. He was going to ignore him but Jack gesticulated urgently and Westaway went after him with Jack staggering behind.

Out in the street Khan desperately turned right running in the direction of the Underground. As he was passing a parked car the doors flew open and two men dressed in a black shalwar kameeze and pakols jumped out and grabbed him.

Khan screamed and started pulling frantically at the men trying to free himself. He managed to turn towards Westaway and Jack 'These men are ISIS. They will kill me. I surrender. Arrest me, please arrest me, I'll confess.'

Westaway looked at Jack who shook his head in the negative 'Sorry Khan' he yelled 'I'm an American citizen. I have no powers of arrest here.'

Khan was dragged screaming into the vehicle and it took off at speed.

'What made you ring me Jack, why not your own people?'

'They'd have turned up gang handed' Jack croaked every word hurting him 'it would have buggered the whole operation' he looked Westaway in the eye 'you and me are birds of a feather John, I sensed it the minute I saw you.' He took a few more rasping breaths before being able to continue 'I know that had Khan got me you'd have killed the bastard.'

Westaway gave a wry grin 'Maybe I would have at that.'

Ten minutes later an ambulance turned up to take Jack and Indira to hospital.

Two days later Jack and Indira left the hospital together Jack's wound had been treated and his arm was in a sling. Indira had been treated for severe shock and now was well on the way to full recovery. Sitting in the back of the taxi she leaned her head on Jack's shoulder. 'I don't want to be without you Jack Ellis, not now, not ever.'

Jack's heart sang with joy 'I'm glad you changed your mind Indira, so glad.' He kissed her softly on the mouth. Not daring to ask why, just accepting that she had changed her mind.

'I don't care what you've done in the past Jack I want us to be together always. Will you come to India with me?'

Jack's eyes had tears in them 'Yes, yes of course I will.'

'I couldn't stab Khan Jack no matter how I tried, I just couldn't bring myself to do it.' She looked pale and apologetic 'now I understand the full meaning of what you told me in the safe house.'

Seeing the puzzled look on his face she smiled "We only walk in peace and freedom because rough men are willing to do dark deeds on our behalf."

The End

Please feel free to send your comments to the author.

blocat582@gmail.com

Printed in Great Britain
by Amazon